All Eyes on Me
(A Miranda and Parker Mystery)
Book 1

Linsey Lanier

Edited by

Editing for You

Donna Rich

Gilly Wright
www.gillywright.com

ISBN: 1941191088
ISBN-13: 978-1-941191-08-8

ALL EYES ON ME

The popular Miranda Steele stories from Linsey Lanier continue in a new series!

A woman determined to fight for justice.
A man determined to keep her alive.

Nobody deserves to die that way.

In the Las Vegas desert a once famous pop singer lies dead, the only clue to her murder a bizarre disfigurement.
To avoid the hassle of a media frenzy, the local police sergeant calls in his old mentor Wade Parker to consult on the case.
After nearly dying eight months ago, Miranda Steele can't wait to get back to real detective work. But Parker harbors secret reservations about their new venture together.
Especially when he suspects there might be more to this murder than meets the...eye.

Fulfilling your destiny…one killer at a time

THE MIRANDA'S RIGHTS MYSTERY SERIES

THE MIRANDA AND PARKER MYSTERY SERIES

OTHER BOOKS BY LINSEY LANIER

THE PRASALA ROMANCES

For more information visit www.FelicityBooks.com

"Even the best things are not equal to their fame."
Henry David Thoreau

WHO IS MIRANDA STEELE?

He told her she was stupid. He called her a whore. He said she was ruined. He told her he'd given away her three-week old baby to strangers.

"I got rid of her," he said. "You'll never find her again."

And then he beat her and threw her out into the snow.

But Miranda Steele wasn't defeated yet.

Yes, she suffered a mental breakdown. Who wouldn't? But after a time, somehow she pulled herself together and made herself strong. Inside and out. And then she went on a thirteen-year search for her daughter. A search the led her to Atlanta, Georgia and to Wade Parker the Third, the gorgeous rich CEO of the top private investigation agency in the southeast.

Little did she know when she walked into his office, her life would change forever and she would find her ultimate destiny.

Now, after solving half a dozen murders and facing the worst Fate could throw at her, PI Miranda Steele is ready to take on more.

CHAPTER ONE

To me the desert has always represented death.

With its murderous heat and air so dry it sucks the moisture out of you, its spiky needle grass and cacti, its scorpions and vultures, its occasional cattle skull. All around you is death.

No more so than tonight, with the big star-filled sky above me, the dark craggy mountains ahead of me, and the city with its lights and glamour behind me.

I can just make out the flashing glow of the last casino in my rearview mirror.

The city. Sin City some call it. A bastion of revelry surrounded by miles and miles of desert. A place where no one thinks of anything but entertainment and lust and carousing—and winning. The most important thing of all. Perhaps because I've lived in it so long, I've become numb to it all—except the winning. How else could I do what I was about to?

Here, I think, looking off to the shoulder of the road. Right here.

I slow the car and pull to the side. Again I check my mirror. No one coming. No one traveling this way at this time of night. I turn off the engine and get out of the car.

The silence of the desert is all around me, the dry sand in the wind caresses my face. How did Shakespeare put it? The road to dusty death? Something like that.

At any rate, it was the perfect place to dump the body.

I go to the hatch and open it. There she is, wrapped in plastic like a mannequin. And under that, her bathrobe. The frozen expression on her lifeless face still stuns me. I can't believe it. My heart races, and I feel nauseated and sick as I pull the wheelbarrow out and tug on her until she tumbles into the tray. Who knew a body could be so heavy? Dead weight, I suppose.

Laughing at my own morbid joke, I close the hatch.

Under the moon and the stars, I roll the barrow out onto the sandy dirt. It sways from the rocks and the uneven ground beneath the tire. I struggle to cross the patches of desert weed and shrubbery. But the slope of the ground here is perfect. Though I'll have to cover up these tracks. And my footprints. Any trace of the car, too.

This was going to be more work than I'd bargained for.

About twenty feet from the road, I stop and turn the wheelbarrow over. The body, still wrapped in the plastic sheet I put her in, tumbles onto the sand. I bend down to arrange it, the gloves I pulled on hours ago still on my hands. I stop and stare down at her. Even in the middle of the night, the wind is hot. Once more it blows the dry dust against my face.

"This is your own fault, you know," I tell her. "If you hadn't been so worried about your looks, about what everyone thought of you, about being a has-been—"

I stop. It's too late for words. She wouldn't listen, anyway. She never listened to me.

I gaze back at the road. Yes, this is just the right spot. Far enough to look like someone meant to hide the body. Close enough for it to be found, anyway.

Just one more thing I need to complete the job.

I kneel down and take the tool from my pocket. The utensil I took from the kitchen. I've used it before, but never for a task like this. As I hold her head steady with my other hand, for a moment I stare down at that gorgeous face. The perfect features, the high cheek bones, the almost wanton mouth. The face so many have adored for so long. What a shame to disfigure it like this.

But it has to be done. It has to.

Bracing myself for the nausea I'm sure will come, I raise the tool and get to work.

CHAPTER TWO

Feeling his miserable self, Sergeant Sid O'Toole of Homicide, sat at the bar in the dark casino off Flamingo and nursed a cheap beer while he inhaled the smoky air and stared blankly at one of the big screens overhead.

The low lights, the salsa music, the wall of TVs, the never-ending dinging and ringing of the slot machines drifting in from the floor—it all was part of the twenty-four-seven party that was Las Vegas. His town, you could say. But he wasn't here for the party. No, his job was to take care of the grimy underbelly tourists never saw.

Criminals and corpses, that was his lot. And as usual, after a too long shift with too much paperwork, he'd just about had *his* belly full of it.

He took a swig of beer and curled a lip at the bartender. "Five bucks for this piss water?"

The guy just shrugged at him. "I don't set the prices."

"Yeah, yeah." O'Toole dug in his pocket for his last fiver. "Like they say, the more bread you have, the less shit you have to drink."

He slapped it down on the bar, picked up the bottle and wandered over to a small table for some privacy.

What was he doing, spending the last five dollars in his pocket on crappy beer? He could have bought a six-pack and gone home. But he didn't want to go home. Not just yet. The house was too empty.

He settled into a chair and eyed the sparse crowd of three a.m. gamblers. A redhead with a flirtatious smile sat on the other side of the room sipping a daiquiri. She wasn't looking his way, but she reminded him of Ginger.

She always called him a tightwad when he complained about the price of this or that. Maybe he was one, but he'd been trying to save for their future. Only Ginger hadn't seen much of a future with him.

She'd wanted more. More than a homicide cop who'd been passed over for promotion three times in the last five years could give her. And because he'd been passed over, who could blame him if he cut a few corners now and then, fudged his time, goofed off a little? What the Lieutenant didn't see, the Lieutenant didn't need to know. Right?

He'd thought Ginger had been happy with her dancing job at the Last Chance. He'd thought she'd been happy with him. He'd thought she'd quit her job someday and they'd have a kid or two. He'd always wanted a kid. But no. None of that was enough for her. She wanted more than being a showgirl. She wanted to be a star. So six months ago she told him she wasn't getting any younger and took off for LA.

Just like that. Just the way his mother had left him when he was six.

Feeling more miserable than ever, he took another pull of his beer and gazed up at one of the big screens. Ah, now *there* was a sight.

Waves and waves of long blond hair and deep blue chiffon. A commercial for the show at the Dame Destinado. That was right. Ambrosia Dawn was in town.

A line from one of her old songs floated to his ears. "All Eyes on Me." He loved that song. It had been number one on the charts about fifteen years ago. What a voice. She had a way of making you feel like she was singing just to you.

He watched her image. Those legs. Long and shapely. He'd always had a thing for legs. Ginger had had great legs.

He looked down at his empty bottle. He didn't want to face his empty house yet. Why not have another? He'd have to hit the ATM. Or use his credit card, which he didn't like to do. Just as he was getting up to head for the machine, his cell rang.

He sat back down and set the bottle on the table with a slap. Only one reason he'd get a phone call at this time of night.

"O'Toole," he said as he answered, trying not to sound irritated.

He listened to the dispatcher describe yet another incident. This time it was a body along I-15.

Aw, Jeez. Why tonight? Why him?

But he had no choice if he wanted to keep paying his bills. Okay, okay. No rest for the weary.

"I'm on my way."

He hung up and let out a long groan as he got to his feet and headed out to the desert.

4

CHAPTER THREE

It took Sid about twenty minutes to reach the spot on I-15 the dispatcher had given him. He pulled up behind one of the three squad cars already parked alongside the road and got out. Using their flashing lights to navigate, he made his way over the dark patch of desert trying not to trip over the Mojave sage and Creosote bush.

Too many feet on the ground, he thought. They'd never get footprints. Then he spotted his detective, Kim Ralston, standing over the body. How'd she get here so fast?

"What do we have?" he asked as he reached her.

"Female Caucasian, sir." Her tone was as dry as the sand they stood on.

He eyed her makeup-less features, the dirty blond hair she kept pulled back in a ponytail, her plain shirt and slacks, and wondered for the hundredth time how anyone so young and innocent looking had made it on the force.

"ID?"

"Just about to attempt that, sir."

He looked down at the amorphous lump on the ground. It was wrapped in a large sheet of plastic. The kind used during building projects. Not much of a clue. There was always construction going on in this town.

He slipped on a pair of gloves while he waited for the CSIs to finish snapping photos of the body the way they'd found it. Ralston already had her gloves on, of course.

"Ready, sir," one of the uniforms told him.

O'Toole bent down, carefully turned over the body and began peeling away the plastic near the legs. Ralston took the head.

A CSI took more shots as the body was revealed. At first look, O'Toole didn't see any defense wounds.

"No blood," Ralston commented.

She was right. That was kind of odd. O'Toole stared out at the highway beyond.

5

The lights of the Last Chance casino, the final one on the way out of town, flashed in the far distance. The place where Ginger used to work. Not much traffic on this road this time of night. But to dump a body here, the killer either had to be butt dumb or wanted it to be found pretty fast.

The plastic gave way, and the vic's bare, shapely legs appeared, sticking out from under a terrycloth robe. He lifted the hem. Not much under the robe. The head was wrapped in a towel, turban-like. Looked like she'd been getting ready for bed.

He tugged at the turban, trying to identify hair color and the head turned enough to reveal the side of the face.

He dropped the cloth again. "Aw, hell."

"What is it, sir?" Ralston asked.

O'Toole couldn't answer. His mind was reeling. Hadn't he seen that gorgeous face, that form, those shapely legs just a half hour ago? But that was a TV spot, probably recorded weeks ago.

He stared down at the unmistakable features. "This is Ambrosia Dawn."

"The singer?" A uniform bent down to get a better view of the face.

Ralston peered at it. "Are you sure?"

"Course, I'm sure. She's got a unique look." Or had one.

"It's Ambrosia Dawn, all right," the uniform agreed.

"Aw, hell," O'Toole repeated as his mind went in a different direction.

Once the news ferrets got wind of this, he'd have the whole department breathing down his neck every step of the way on this investigation. The last thing he needed.

Suddenly he remembered an email he'd received about a week ago.

His old mentor Wade Parker was looking for consulting work. Unsolved cases, cold cases, wherever extra manpower might be needed. What was the matter? O'Toole had thought at the time. Not enough rich clients in Atlanta?

But now, he liked the sound of that email.

There was enough money in the budget to spring for the fee. Which wasn't cheap. For a high profile case like this, he could get the expense approved. But first, there was the matter of notifying the deceased's family. He sure didn't want to deal with the distraught relatives of a star tonight.

He turned back to his detective. "Ralston, you'll pay the visit to the family."

"Me, sir?" She was still near him, kneeling over the body.

"You have a problem with that?"

"No, sir. It's just that—wait. What's this? The murder weapon?"

She pulled something shiny out from under the dead singer's shoulder. It was about six inches long and had a rounded end caked with a grimy substance.

"What the hell is that?"

"I think it's a—a miniature ice cream scoop? No, it's a melon baller." Ralston let out a startled gasp. "Wait." She gave the body another push. "Oh, my gosh."

It rolled over, revealing the entire face.

"Oh, Lord," one of the uniforms said.

O'Toole took in those unmistakable features. The high cheekbones, the full mouth. There was no doubt the dead woman was Ambrosia Dawn.

But one of her eyes was missing.

O'Toole wanted to gag. "Did the birds get to her? I didn't see a hole in the plastic."

"I think someone used this on her. Let's hope after she was dead. I think it's still got tissue on it. See?" His detective held the melon baller near his face.

"Aw, jeez, Ralston. Don't show me that."

"It's evidence, sir."

"Jiminy Cricket on a turd pile." O'Toole brushed off his pants and paced over the sand, away from the body and the disgusting melon baller.

Why would somebody scoop out Ambrosia Dawn's eye with a kitchen tool? For a souvenir? Was it a crazed fan who'd been stalking her? Someone keeping the eye for a ransom? How sick was that? Wait. A serial killer? Serial killer. He didn't want any part of that.

Again he thought of the email from Wade Parker. For years the investigator had been known as the best of the best in the southeast. The reputation of his Agency had only grown more sterling during that time. He was probably looking to enhance it even more. Adventure, the email had said. Something out of the norm.

If this case didn't fit the bill, he didn't know what did. He'd get the budget request pushed through as fast as he could and call Parker in the morning.

In the meantime, he turned to his rookie. "Ralston, are you going to let the family know tonight or are you going to wait a week or two?"

The young woman got to her feet, suppressing a glare. "Right away, sir."

CHAPTER FOUR

Miranda Steele stepped into her boss's brightly lit, blue-and-gray corner office on the fifteenth floor of the Imperial Building in Atlanta and exhaled her anxiety.

"You wanted to see me?"

Parker glanced up at her from the computer screen he was studying. "Yes. Have a seat."

He indicated the plush blue chair in front of his elegant glass desk.

Miranda settled herself into the seat without too much pain.

A little over six months ago she'd faced down her psychotic ex-husband—the man who'd regularly beaten her and who'd stolen her daughter from her when she was just a baby. The battle had taken its toll. She'd suffered a gunshot wound to the chest, a gash in the back of her head, and a bunch of bruises. She'd nearly died from the injuries. But after months of physical therapy and another five weeks of easing into workouts in the company gym, she was almost as good as new. Good enough for light duty at the Agency, anyway.

Parker continued to peer at the screen. She couldn't be in trouble. She hadn't done anything. Or at least she was pretty sure she hadn't. She hadn't jumped anyone while serving subpoenas. She hadn't cussed out any clients. Okay, she'd taken a few long lunches with her buddies Becker and Holloway, but Parker usually didn't mind that.

Waiting for him to start the scolding—or whatever he planned to do to her—she took in his good looks, his distinguished salt-and-pepper hair, his pricey suit, his delicious features. He was Old Southern wealth. Well-bred, classy, well-heeled, successful. The sexiest man she had ever laid eyes on.

After almost a year, it still took her breath that she was married to him.

At last, he finished whatever he'd been doing and turned to her with an expression in his gray eyes she couldn't read.

"Do you remember my proposal?" he said in his sensual, mint julep voice.

Her breath caught. "You mean the one about us going out as investigative consultants?"

"That's the one."

How could she forget it? Parker hadn't mentioned it since they got back to Atlanta, but she'd been counting the days until she'd recovered enough to get started. "What about it?"

Parker sat back in his chair and studied his wife. Her wild, dark hair. Her lean, muscular body he knew so well. Her crisp white shirt and black slacks that expressed her Spartan tastes. He loved her more than his own life. And he wanted more than anything to share the thrill of his profession with her in this new way. To feel the excitement that came with new cases and new challenges with Miranda at his side.

But she was just fully recovering from her injuries last fall. A bullet to the upper chest near the heart and a deep gash in the back of her head. She'd been unconscious over three days. He'd thought he'd lost her. If something were to happen on one of these new cases? If he lost her because of this new plan of his? He'd never forgive himself.

But he'd also never forgive himself if he didn't give Miranda the chance to be all she could be. She was a fine detective and he knew she'd been looking forward to this venture.

Besides, the case from the first client promised to be fairly innocuous. More publicity than danger. And he wanted to see his wife's reaction to it.

"I put out some feelers last week just to see what sort of response I could get," he said.

Miranda gripped the arms of her chair. "Did you get anything?"

"Only one."

She watched him inhale, as if he were struggling with something.

"I got a call from a former Agency employee this morning."

Her blood began to pump with excitement. She thought of the dream she'd had in the hospital all those months ago. A hazy vision of some sort of bright spirit telling her she had a gift and a destiny to fulfill.

Back in her hospital room, she'd told herself there would be no more nightmares. There hadn't been since that ordeal. Still, something lurked in the dark recesses of her subconscious, just beyond her grasp. Something she hadn't yet figured out. Something she hadn't yet faced.

She wasn't sure she wanted to.

All she knew was that she never felt more alive than when she was on a case.

"We're taking the job, aren't we?"

Parker raised a dark brow. "Don't you want to hear what it is first?"

Okay, maybe she was jumping the gun. She sat back, trying to look skeptical. "Sure."

"Do you remember Ambrosia Dawn?"

She frowned. "Who?"

"She was a popular singer about fifteen years ago."

Miranda only shrugged and lifted her palms.

"'The Love I Have for You?' 'All Eyes on Me?'"

She thought a moment. She wasn't a big music listener. Fifteen years ago she'd still been married to Leon. No wonder she couldn't remember any love songs from then.

"Coco sang some of her hits."

Now one of those titles came back to her. "All Eyes on Me." It was about a singer, duh. One who had enjoyed outrageous fame and fortune, but who was now down on her luck and had lost it all. And all she wanted was for her true love to look at her and really see her. It was touching when sung right.

"Oh, yeah."

She started to hum the tune she remembered her friend singing at the Gecko Club. Of course, Miranda sounded more like a frog.

Parker cleared his throat. "It went something like that."

"So what about her? Ambrosia Dawn, I mean."

Parker's face went grim. "She's dead."

"Oh, my God. That's awful." Miranda vaguely remembered seeing the singer on TV. "She wasn't that old was she?"

"Forty-one."

"I'd have thought she was younger. She had a variety show, didn't she?"

"A few years ago, yes."

Now the image of the singer came to her. Always in long, flowing gowns, with lots of background singers. She had a set of pipes, too. "What a classy lady."

"Indeed. And she was still popular. She's been performing in Las Vegas."

Miranda let out a sad smirk. "The place where all old singers go?"

"Perhaps." Parker inhaled. "Sergeant Sid O'Toole of the Las Vegas Metro Police has asked for our help."

Miranda sat up again. "That's our case? Wait. Ambrosia Dawn was murdered?"

Parker nodded. "Her body was found in the desert. One of her eyes had been gouged out with—a melon baller."

Miranda's lip curled. "With a what? That's disgusting."

"Yes."

Instantly her mind shot into work mode. Had the killer taken the eye for a token? Was he making a statement of some kind? "Does O'Toole think it's a serial killer? Wait a minute." She snapped her fingers. "'All Eyes on Me.' Wasn't that her signature song?"

"I believe so."

"That's got to have something to do with it." She got up and paced all the way to the far end of the huge office.

She felt hot and cold and antsy all at the same time. She couldn't wait to sink her teeth into this case. She'd find the person who murdered the famous singer. After all, hadn't one of her best friends sung her songs? Come to think of it, Coco reminded her a little of a modern version of Ambrosia Dawn.

"Miranda," Parker said, caution in his tone.

She stopped pacing. Uh oh. She knew there was a catch. "What?"

For a long moment he studied her, as if considering his next words carefully. At last he said, "Are you sure you want to take this case? We don't have to."

She thought about the cautiously gentle way he'd made love to her since she'd come home. Like she was some sort of fragile glass doll. Okay, maybe that was necessary the first few weeks, but lately she'd wanted to rip those expensive clothes right off his luscious body and get hot and sweaty with him.

Good grief. Hadn't she hauled bricks and pounded shingles alongside the burliest of men? Hadn't she beaten a co-worker in the ring with her martial art skills?

She scowled at her husband. "Don't baby me, Parker."

Parker rose, strolled to the window with that maddening patience of his, and folded his arms. "I wouldn't dream of it, my dear. I'm simply trying to ascertain your state of mind."

She wagged a finger at him. "Well, ascertain this. My state of mind is ready and raring to go."

"Are you sure you're ready? Are you sure you want to leave home?"

Her mouth opened then shut again at the tenderness in his voice.

Okay, it was a fair question after what she'd been through. After what Parker had been through because of it. She stepped toward him to the table along the wall where several new photos were on display and ran a finger over one of the silver frames.

She smiled down at Mackenzie's picture. The daughter she'd found after a thirteen-year search. Thanks to Parker.

And next to her was a photo of Wendy Van Aarle—the girl Miranda had once thought was her daughter—who was now Mackenzie's best friend.

When she came home from the hospital, the two girls had celebrated their fourteenth birthdays together with a big party given by their families. Then came the holidays with gifts and parties. Miranda never thought she could be so happy. But then the New Year came and went. The girls went back to school and became lost in their activities and the world of the young.

She loved both of them, but they had their lives. And so did she. She was well enough now to work a case.

She took his hand.

He squeezed it and put it to his lips. All her anxiety melted away.

"Of course, I'm ready, Parker," she said softly. "How could you think I'd want to turn this opportunity down?"

The wrinkles around Parker's sexy eyes creased into a grin. "Just what I thought you'd say."

"So we're going? We're taking the case?"

He turned back to his desk. "I'll notify our new client right away. I must warn you, though. O'Toole wasn't the best employee the Agency ever had."

That was odd. Parker didn't usually turn out duds. "What was his problem?"

"I felt he never really applied himself."

Lazy? Or more than that? Parker always loved to understate things. But who cared? They were going out on their first case as consultants together. She wanted to dance around the room.

Instead she folded her arms and gave Parker a cocky smile. "Well, that's why he needs us, isn't it?"

"I suppose so." He eyed her again and she could see the wheels in his head turning.

"What now?"

"I think it's best we keep our personal relationship undisclosed."

"Okay." Evidently O'Toole hadn't kept up with Parker since he left the Agency.

It sounded like a smart idea. A married couple might not command the same respect as two investigators. O'Toole could accuse Parker of favoritism, and she'd be relegated to Parker's wife, instead of the professional she'd become. She'd kept her maiden name for business purposes, so they could pull it off.

The corner of his lip turned up. "And as a matter of protocol, one of us should be in charge."

She put a hand on her hip. "Protocol, huh? On a police case?"

"On our part of the investigation. It will ensure things go smoothly."

"Uh huh. And I suppose that should be you?"

With a sly twinkle in his eye, Parker turned to his credenza, opened a drawer and took something out. "I thought we'd roll for it."

He opened his palm to reveal two red dice.

Miranda laughed out loud. "You're on."

"Brace yourself." Parker took the dice in one hand, shook and let them fall onto the shiny desktop. The cubes spun and settled.

A five and a one.

"Easy six." Could she beat it? "Okay, buster."

Miranda picked up the dice, blew on them, shook. Nerves of excitement coursing through her, she let them go.

They seemed to spin forever then finally came to rest in the middle of the desk.

Two sixes. Miranda let out a hoot.

"Boxcars. I win!" She gloated with a little dance and Parker couldn't hide his amusement.

She came around the desk and slid her arms around his neck. "Don't be a sore loser. I'll let you win next time. When do we leave?"

"I can get us on a flight this afternoon."

She couldn't wait to get there. "Hot dog. City of Lights, here we come!"

Then she grew somber as a zealous indignation rose up in her breast, fueled by the excitement. A woman was dead.

"Ambrosia Dawn's killer won't get away with this," she said darkly. "We'll make sure of that."

CHAPTER FIVE

The four-hour non-stop flight Parker managed to snag was uneventful and landed them in McCarran International Airport by late afternoon, Las Vegas time.

After fighting through the crazed passengers heading for the slot machines and the traffic on Paradise—which to Miranda seemed a tad too hot to really be paradise—they arrived at the Metro police station on Sierra Vista.

As Parker opened the glass double doors to the white building with the silver façade at the front, Miranda turned to gaze across the dusty yard to the street. Beyond the pavement lay the southern tip of the Las Vegas strip with its tall casinos and flashing lights.

"Doesn't look like it does on TV." She'd been all around the country but never this far west.

"It will when the sun goes down," Parker said wryly.

She'd wait and see.

Inside the building, they made their way to a glassed-in reception area and Parker stepped back to let her do the honors, thanks to the roll of the dice.

He was such a good loser, she thought, as she presented her Agency card to the officer at the desk. "We're here to see Sergeant Sid O'Toole," she told him.

He nodded and gestured toward a door. "He's expecting you. Go through there, down the hall. Third office on the right."

"Thanks."

Parker held the door for her again and in they went.

The LVMPD station was a lot like most of the police stations Miranda had been in. Garish fluorescent lights on the ceiling. Cheaply painted walls in a pale puke green. Equally cheap flooring in an unimaginative design. Benches along the walls where people sat with anxious or irritated faces. The muffled noise of heated discussions or long-winded instructions from this or that office. The smell of stale coffee.

Still, it felt good to be a real guest for a change instead of a guest of the state.

Before they had reached the end of the hall, a man appeared at the far corner. He was wearing a sour look and carrying a Styrofoam cup. The coffee in this place must really be bad.

The man stopped short and stared at them. "Parker? You here already?"

"Hello, Sid. I didn't see much point in wasting time."

"No, you were never one to do that."

Sid moved toward them and they met three-quarters of the way down the hall. Miranda watched the man transfer the coffee to his other hand and shake with Parker. "Thanks for coming."

"Happy to be of help." Parker gestured in her direction. "Sid, this is my associate, Miranda Steele."

"Glad to know you." The man extended his hand to her.

"Likewise." She shook the hand, eyeing the husky frame under his khaki slacks and short-sleeved checkered shirt.

His wavy, dark chestnut hair looked like it needed a cut. His fair, Irish-looking complexion, spattered with dark freckles seemed like it couldn't stand up under the Las Vegas sun. His bottle green eyes were bloodshot and sullen and seemed too wide apart. There was something in them she didn't like. But other than the vague remark Parker had made in his office about the man's performance at the Agency, she couldn't say what.

Sid grinned widely, revealing a crooked eyetooth and a less-than-Hollywood-white smile. Probably from too much coffee drinking. "Well, let's go to my office and I'll brief you."

They followed the man down the hall, around the corner, and into a small, windowless office with a metal desk and filing cabinet.

There were no pictures or photos or decorations of any sort except for a lone calendar on the wall behind the chair turned to last month. It must have come from one of the casinos because the picture on it was of several showgirls decked out in tiaras and shocking pink feathers and showing a lot of skin.

Miranda resisted the urge to grimace.

Sid set his coffee down on the desk and eyed the single guest chair. He scratched his head. "Sorry about that. We don't have a lot of perks around here. There's another chair in the next office." He gave Miranda a wink. "Why don't you get it for us, sweetie?"

Miranda's brows shot up. "Excuse me?"

"Sid—"

Sid stepped around the desk waving a dismissive hand at Parker. "What's a matter, honey? You don't have to be afraid of us police officers."

Miranda's brows shot up. "Afraid?"

"That's right, baby. We don't bite."

"Listen—" She stopped herself before she'd called their first client a jackass within ten minutes of meeting him.

Sid moved behind the extra chair. He lifted it an inch off the floor and set it down. "See? It's not heavy. You look like you're in good enough shape to handle it."

As Miranda wrestled down her tongue, she could feel Parker tense beside her

"Sid," Parker said, as smooth as silk, "I neglected to mention that Ms. Steele is one of the top graduates of the Agency's training program. And she'll be in charge on this case."

Sid blinked once, twice. He looked at Parker. Then at Miranda. Then back at Parker. Then he let out a high-pitched squeal of a laugh. "You've got to be joking, Parker. You put a *girl* in charge of murder investigation?"

For an instant, Leon's face flashed before her eyes. That did it.

"Hey!"

Miranda took one step toward the jerk, wrapped her foot around the back of his leg and pulled him off balance and onto the floor. With the speed of a comet, she rolled him over, grabbed his wrist and yanked his arm behind his back.

"What the fuck are you doing?"

"I'm wondering if you'll be able to carry that chair once I break your arm." She gave it another pull.

"Uncle! Okay! Get her off me, Parker."

What a baby. She leaned down and hissed in his ear. "The name's Steele. Miranda Steele. *Ms.* Steele to you."

"Okay, Ms. Steele. Can you ease up a little?"

"Apologize."

"What?"

"I said apologize."

Sid groaned like a whiny teenager. "Parker, help me out here."

Parker strolled around to get a full view of Sid's face. "I think you had better apologize to my associate, Sid, or we might be here all night."

"Okay, okay. I'm sorry. I didn't mean it."

Miranda glanced up at Parker and was relieved he seemed amused rather than angry. After all, she'd probably lost their first case. Okay, her reaction might have been overkill, but she couldn't help it. The combination of her former life with Leon and her days showing up men on construction crews could bring out her inner bitch at times.

Besides, she wasn't really going to break his arm.

She released his arm and let him up. "Apology accepted, Sergeant O'Toole."

Nursing his appendage, Sid turned over and sat up, whimpering like a puppy.

Parker exhaled. "Would you like us to leave now, Sid? All you would owe us is traveling expenses."

Sid's face turned the color of a three-alarm fire. "You can't leave, Parker. I need you."

"Are you sure, Sid? Ms. Steele and I are a package deal."

Miranda couldn't express how grateful she was Parker was standing up for her.

"Of course, I'm sure. I don't care who works with you."

Parker raised a brow. "Or who's in charge?"

Sid stared down at the floor a moment, as if weighing the options. Apparently he didn't have many. He struggled to his feet and brushed off his clothes looking sheepish and almost contrite.

He turned to Miranda. "Like I said, I apologize, Ms. Steele. I'll get the damn chair."

"Forget the chair," Miranda said, trying to sound good-natured. She didn't dare show how glad she was she and Parker didn't have to turn around and go home. "Has Ambrosia Dawn been examined by your ME?"

"Yeah. He's working on her now."

"Then you can bring us up to speed while you take us to see him."

Sid had a funny look on his face as he nodded. "As you wish."

CHAPTER SIX

"Call came in around three this morning," Sid said, pushing the elevator button in the hall. "Ambrosia Dawn's body was found on the west side of I-15 about twenty miles south of here."

"Just lying on the side of the road?" Miranda asked.

"Right there in the sand. About twenty feet from the pavement. She had a towel around her head and had on a robe. The body was wrapped in polyethylene."

"You mean the kind used as enclosures and protection on a construction site?" Miranda had experience with that.

"Exactly. Hey, you know your stuff."

"Yeah, I do."

Parker frowned as he followed Miranda into the small compartment. "I-15 goes straight through the desert on to California."

"Yep."

That was nice. The killer might have cruised on to Los Angeles, hopped a flight, and could be in Argentina by now.

Sid eyed Miranda cautiously as he stepped into the elevator and gave his arm another rub before he pressed Down.

"Who called it in?" Miranda wanted to know.

"Anonymous."

She pondered that as they rode one floor down.

"There couldn't have been much traffic that time of night," Parker murmured half to himself.

"Usually isn't," Sid said, keeping a steady gaze on the elevator's red numbers.

The bell pinged and they stepped out into a long, sterile-looking hallway that reminded Miranda way too much of a hospital.

Sid led them down the corridor and through a set of large double doors. He swiped an ID card and another door opened. He pressed a button on a box on the wall. "Sergeant Sid O'Toole requesting entrance."

17

"I've been expecting you, Sergeant," said a voice with a touch of a British accent.

Yet another door opened and Miranda followed Sid into a wide, brightly lit room lined with two long rows of stainless steel tables. The air was cool for preservation purposes, but it still had the wonderfully pleasant aroma of disinfectant thinly disguising decay.

A man in a face mask and blue scrubs stood at a table where a body lay.

She'd been in a morgue a few times during her training. She didn't care for them. Not many people did. She couldn't imagine working here day after day.

Sid ushered them over to the man and introduced him as Dr. Andrew Eaton, the medical examiner. "Mr. Parker and Ms. Steele will be helping me on this case."

"You'll excuse me if I don't shake hands?" The doctor was the one with the British accent. He raised his gloved appendages.

"We'd prefer it, Doctor." Parker said, acknowledging the dry coroner humor.

Miranda gave Eaton a nod as he removed his mask.

She took in the tall, thin frame under the scrubs, the glasses, the elongated face and nose, the head of thick blond curls. She'd put his age around forty. A very nerdy-looking forty. But he also looked like he'd been around the block. And his block had included a big dose of gore.

Sid jiggled a hand toward the body. "So are you done with my vic yet, Doc?"

Miranda saw Eaton's cheek twitch.

"About two hours ago. You didn't call me."

O'Toole gave the ME a surly look. "Been a little busy. What can you tell me?"

"The patient was female, Caucasian, age forty-one."

The sergeant made a rolling gesture with his finger, indicating the doctor should speed through the details they already knew. Miranda glanced at Parker and read his thoughts. This must be a delightful working relationship.

"She has had numerous reconstructive surgeries on her face, abdomen, buttocks and breasts."

No wonder she looked so young on TV.

"Time of death?" Miranda asked.

"Between eleven p.m. last night and one this morning. Given the liver temperature taken at the scene, I'd say closer to one."

"So she was dumped after a few hours of her demise."

"That would be my math." The ME lifted the sheet covering the body to reveal a placid face and the long, V-shaped incision on her chest.

"She was a good-looking woman," Parker said.

That was an understatement. The singer's bone structure was the kind a New York model would envy. Delicate arched brows, perfect nose, luscious mouth. Even after a long and waning career, even in death, she was still gorgeous. Just like Coco. Well, Coco was alive, thank goodness.

And then there was that eye. A dark hole where something beautiful had once been.

"Apart from some minor bruising," the doctor continued, "the body shows no signs of defense wounds or constraints. No knife marks or bullet wounds."

"What about the eye?" Sid said. "Was that melon baller the murder weapon?"

"I was getting to the eye. The only disfigurement."

Miranda didn't think it was likely the melon baller had been used to kill, and the look on Parker's face said he thought O'Toole was wasting time.

But the ME indulged the sergeant. He strolled over to one of the tables where instruments of his craft lay and picked up a silver object about six inches long. "Tissues on the bowl of this item tell you what you already suspect. This tool was used to gouge out the victim's left eye. The person used it to sever the optic nerve, the muscles, the blood vessels, and lift the globe out of its orbit."

Gruesome. "Was she—"

"No." The ME anticipated the question. "It was done postmortem."

Thank God. So it was some kind of statement. "Fingerprints?"

He shook his head. "Wiped clean."

"Where's the eye now?" Miranda asked, hoping its condition could tell them something.

Sid raised his palms. "Don't know. It wasn't at the crime scene. It appears the killer took it with him."

"Or her."

Sid gave her a cautious glance. "Normally, I'd say the body of a full grown female adult would be too heavy for a woman to carry. But the patterns in the sand indicate the body was rolled."

"Rolled?" Parker asked.

"In a wheelbarrow, we think. The ground was all rock and sand. Must have dumped her out and let the body roll some more on its own. Desert shrubbery stopped the corpse from going any farther."

Miranda's ears perked up. "Were there tracks? Footprints?"

Sid shook his head. "Whoever dumped her there was careful to cover up the evidence. The CSIs took photos, of course. They haven't found anything yet."

"I see." Miranda hoped the CSIs were more thorough than Sid. Maybe they'd find something he'd missed.

She looked back at the body, and that familiar anger at the sight of a murder victim began to creep over her. Kill her, wrap her up in plastic like leftovers from dinner, carry her out to the desert, and gouge out her eye. Who would do such a thing to a famous singer? She'd find out.

Parker beat her to the next question. "Dr. Eaton. Have you determined the cause of death?"

"I have. She was poisoned."

O'Toole's brows shot up. "Poisoned? Are you sure?"

"I am. A fatal amount of abrin was found in her blood stream."

Parker rubbed his chin. "Abrin. That's similar to ricin isn't it?"

Miranda had heard of ricin. Several decades ago in London a dude who was suspected of being involved in espionage had been injected with it. Death by ricin involved vomiting, hemorrhaging, and intense pain. Nasty way to go.

The ME nodded. "Yes, but abrin requires only one seventy-fifth of the dose of ricin to be fatal."

Miranda let out a low whistle. "How would someone get a hold of a substance like that?"

"It could be found in certain medical research facilities. It's been used as an experimental cancer treatment."

Miranda shot Parker a look and saw he was deep in thought.

"However, it would be more likely to come from a house plant."

"House plant?" she said.

The doctor nodded. "*Abrus precatorius*. Sometimes called the lucky bean plant. It produces pods that contain the toxic seeds.

"She wasn't so lucky this time."

"No."

"Are you saying it was an accident?"

"No. This was deliberate. She didn't have much left in her stomach. The poison could have taken effect within an hour of ingestion. She likely suffered respiratory distress, coughing, tightness in the chest, and severe nausea. The nausea would have escalated into vomiting, followed by seizures, internal hemorrhaging, and then unconsciousness."

"If her stomach was empty from barfing, can we determine how she swallowed the abrin?"

"I did find a small trace of herbal tea in the stomach contents. The tea contained mint, raspberry leaf, ginger, and a trace amount of abrin."

Sounded like she had a bath and a relaxing drink before bed. "Someone slipped the poison into her tea?"

"So it appears."

They stood silently staring at the motionless body of the lovely performer who would never sing again. Miranda's mind spun with the details.

At last, Parker broke the silence. "Is there anything else you can tell us, Doctor?"

The ME scowled and spoke the most un-objective words he'd said yet. "Just that I hope you find the bastard who did this. Ambrosia Dawn was one of my favorite singers."

CHAPTER SEVEN

Back in O'Toole's office, Miranda paced back and forth in the small space—which still only had one chair—her mind buzzing with what the ME had told them. "This could be an organized crime hit," she said. "The eye thing could have been a message. Ambrosia Dawn saw too much."

With a smirk, O'Toole sank into his chair and put his feet up on his desk. "Ambrosia Dawn involved in organized crime?"

"Some stars are into drugs. Maybe she pissed off her supplier. Or maybe she just stumbled onto something innocently. A robbery or something."

Parker rubbed his chin. Miranda noticed he was getting a five o'clock shadow. It was three hours later back home.

"Abrin poisoning isn't the usual method of organized crime," he said.

She marched over to the filing cabinet in the corner, drummed her fingers on it. "Yeah, you've got a point." And by now the killer had probably gotten rid of all the evidence. "Next question. Where did the plastic sheeting come from?"

"Could have come from any place. There's always construction going on in this town." O'Toole let out a yawn.

Miranda curled a lip at him. "Are we boring you?"

O'Toole narrowed his bloodshot, bottle green eyes at her. "I didn't get much sleep last night, as you might deduce. And I'm hungry. Why don't we get some food."

"Sounds reasonable," Parker said, giving Miranda a let's-keep-things-civil look. "I can drive. We have a rental."

"That's fine, but I'll take my car." As the sergeant stood and tucked the case file under his arm, he eyed Miranda as if he were sizing her up. "You like Mexican food, Ms. Steele?"

She met his gaze. "My favorite."

"I know a great place. You can follow me there."

"Sounds terrific."

Wondering what he was up to, with Parker at her side she trailed O'Toole out the door and down the hall.

CHAPTER EIGHT

Miranda bit into her fajita quesadilla and savored the fiery flavors of grilled meat, veggies, cheese and guacamole. "Hmm, this is really good." She swiped the juices running down her chin with her napkin.

From behind a plate of chicken taquitos, Parker eyed her lovingly. "You are hungry."

"Guess so."

The sergeant grinned at her with an expectant expression. "Pretty spicy. Huh, Ms. Steele?"

Miranda cocked her head as if she were thinking about it. "No, it's just about right." She took another bite.

O'Toole had taken them to a lively place on the strip called Don Chachi's Cantina where the music was peppy, the décor colorful and festive, and the staff eager to please.

A smiling waitress in a red-and-yellow costume dress appeared at their table to refill their drinks. "How is everything?"

He winked at her. "Good, honey. Do you have those *chile de arbol* peppers I ordered?"

"They're right here." Another grinning waitress in green and yellow set a plate down in the center of the table. "Be careful with those, sir. *Caliente*."

"That means hot," O'Toole said to Miranda.

Miranda looked at Parker and they exchanged a meaningful glance. He was struggling not to grin. They'd played this game the first time he'd taken her to a Mexican restaurant back in Atlanta.

Wide-eyed, Miranda turned to their host. "Oh? Does it? Better be careful then."

"Can I get anything else for you?" the waitress asked.

O'Toole chuckled. "I think we'll need some more water in a minute, but we're fine for now."

"Just let us know." And the server moved on to another table.

Miranda eyed the plate of long red dried peppers. "*Caliente*, huh?"

"Actually, they're not so bad." O'Toole pushed the plate toward her, smiling. "Try one."

She smiled back. "You first."

She watched his lip twitch.

Then he shrugged. "Sure, why not?" He reached for a small one, held it by the stem and bit off the tiniest piece of the end. Miranda watched him cough and struggle to control the look of pain on his face. What a wimp. "Pretty good," he said. "Try one."

"Don't mind if I do." She reached for a mid-size pepper, saving the big one for her "manly" opponent. She bit off half an inch and chewed.

The skin of the pepper crunched in her mouth and the seeds burned against her tongue, but the flavor was good. Her eyes didn't even water. "They have a smoky flavor. I like it."

O'Toole looked at her as if she'd just performed some kind of magic trick. "Yeah, I do, too." He put the small pepper on the side of his plate and picked up another medium sized one. This time, he took half of it.

"Aren't those similar to chipotle peppers?" Parker asked as if he were talking about the weather.

The sergeant coughed and reached for his water glass. "Yeah, they are," he sputtered after a minute.

"Now you've got me hooked." Miranda put the rest of her first pepper in her mouth and bit it down to the stem.

Fire seared her taste buds and her eyes threatened to water, but she forced herself not to even glance at the ice water beside her plate. "Mmm," she managed.

O'Toole just stared at her.

"*Chile de arbol.* Also called 'Bird's Beak Chile,' I believe. About twenty thousand heat units." Parker pressed his lips together and pretended to study a hacienda painting on the wall.

Miranda hoped he wouldn't burst out laughing anytime soon. This was too much fun.

"I don't want to hog these, O'Toole. Here. Have some more." She picked up the plate and pushed three of them right on top of the sergeant's chalupa.

O'Toole's face went from shock to anger to defiance. He wasn't about to be one-upped by a *girl.* "Sure, sure. The more the better." He snatched up the biggest pepper, put the whole thing in his mouth and chomped down.

Miranda stared at him. "Isn't that overdoing it a little, Sergeant?" She hadn't meant for the guy to kill himself.

"Not for me—" his face turned red. Then white. He started to cough and choke. He reached for his water.

"Use a tortilla. Or a chip. They'll soak up the heat." Miranda handed him one.

O'Toole shook his head, giving her a murderous look. He picked up his napkin and spat out what was left of the poor chipotle. Then he grabbed his glass with both hands and started to gulp.

Bad idea. It only made it worse.

He wasn't going to listen to her advice. All she could do was sit there and watch the poor guy choke and sputter and cough, his face turning colors that went really well with the décor.

"Would you like us to take you to the hospital?" she asked innocently.

"Grrr!" was all O'Toole could get out. And with his napkin against his mouth, still coughing like a bad engine, he got to his feet and scurried off to the men's room.

Miranda turned to Parker with a shrug. "More for us. You want one?"

His sexy gray eyes twinkled with an I'm-no-fool expression. "No, thank you. I learned my lesson a long time ago."

She gave him a smile. "You did, didn't you?"

He leaned in and she drank in a whiff of his expensive cologne. "You really shouldn't toy with the client."

"It was his idea."

"You didn't have to go along."

She pursed her lips, satisfied with her performance. Parker knew she could never resist putting someone like that in his place. "You told me the guy was a dud at the Agency. You didn't mention he was a chauvinist."

"He didn't display such behavior when he was with us."

"When was he there?"

"He joined us not long after I started the business. Judd was my only employee at the time."

No women on board yet. No opportunity to put them down, though she'd love to see O'Toole try to take on Detective Tan.

"You've come a long way since then," she told him.

"Yes. And with you, I hope to go farther."

A nice thought, but at the moment, she had her doubts. She reached for a chip and just for good measure, dunked it in the spicy salsa. "Want to bet on how long before the sergeant sends us packing?"

"Save your money, Miranda. I think O'Toole's desperate for help on this case."

She chewed thoughtfully on the chip. Maybe Parker was right. She hoped so.

CHAPTER NINE

After about twenty minutes, O'Toole came back to the table and finished what he could of the meal. He was still nursing his sore tongue when they reached the vehicles outside.

Miranda's mind was back on the case and she was downright frustrated. "So we're looking for someone with access to a medical research facility or a lucky bean houseplant and who knew how to use a melon baller. Doesn't make much sense at all. We've just started and we're already stuck."

"And when you're stuck—?" Parker prompted.

O'Toole didn't say anything, but he was still having trouble getting out anything but grunts and coughs.

Miranda decided to answer. "When you're stuck, you follow procedure. So that means we start by questioning the immediate family and close acquaintances."

Seeming pleased with her response, Parker nodded. "With someone like Ambrosia Dawn, that will be a long list."

O'Toole made an unintelligible sound and turned to his car. He opened the door and reached for something on the seat. When he straightened, he had the case file in his hand.

He passed it to Parker. "Efferything's in zere."

Parker's brow rose. "You're giving me the police file?"

The sergeant patted it. "Copy."

"You're giving us authorization to act on behalf of the police department?"

O'Toole nodded. "Theck in tomorrow. Thalk to you then." And with that, he got in his car and drove off.

Miranda put a hand on her hip and stared at the car as it turned onto Las Vegas Boulevard. "Guess he had to go home and lick his wounds. Except his tongue isn't working so well."

"Perhaps we should call it a night as well."

She spun around to him. "Why?"

Parker looked at his watch. "It's past midnight back home. Ambrosia Dawn's family hasn't had even twenty-four hours since the news of her death."

It sounded reasonable. If one of them wasn't involved and destroying what might be left of the evidence as they stood there. But Parker was right. They'd both be sharper if they got some rest.

"Okay. Where are we staying?"

"Right up the street."

CHAPTER TEN

Parker drove around a side street and made his way south down the crowded Strip, giving her the view she'd wanted of the city at night.

There were palm trees and marquees and too many huge flashing billboards to count, each one beckoning tourists to this show or that. One side of the road looked like a solid wall of neon, as if a giant Christmas tree had been decorated by a psychedelic artist from the sixties. On the other side were tons of shops. Gucci and Prada and McDonalds, and the Hard Rock Cafe with its giant guitar.

They rolled past sidewalks crammed with visitors making their way to the restaurants, bars, and wedding chapels. Then came shooting fountains afire with a rainbow of light. Pirates in pirate ships putting on a mock battle. A building fashioned after the Eiffel Tower. Another one that looked like the Statue of Liberty. It was as if you had traveled around the world in the space of half an hour. Were they in New York or Paris or Hollywood?

At this point, Miranda wasn't sure.

They were staying at the Dame Destinado—the hotel where Ambrosia Dawn's show had been booked. It was across from the place that looked like a castle and down the street from the one that looked like a pyramid.

Miranda was still glassy-eyed from the glitter as Parker valeted the car and they were ushered inside into even more opulence.

Just the casino lobby was beyond classy. And immense.

On one side, sheets of sparkling water trickled over shimmering light and down an artistic arrangement of walls that seemed to stretch to the sky. On the other side guests traversed tall golden stairways and brass escalators that lead to huge rainbow-colored globes serving as bars and meeting areas on an elevated floor. The perimeter of the space was carved into huge modern art shapes revealing shops and restaurants and spas.

As she rode the glass elevator up to their suite with Parker, Miranda felt as if her heart would stop from glitz-overload.

They reached their room, and after the bellhop had left them alone, she took in the muted gray velveteen of sofas, the gilded silver pattern of chairs, the flower arrangements on tables. This wasn't just a room.

Stealing a peek at the huge, pillow-laden bed in the next room, she gave a low whistle. This was nicer than the honeymoon suite they'd had in Maui.

She turned to Parker. "Pretty fancy accommodations for someone on an expense account."

He picked up a remote control and pressed a button. The curtains opened revealing a stunning view of the colorful lights below while soft, seductive music began to play.

He raised a questioning brow at her. "I decided against the champagne massage tub and the private pool and the basketball court."

She laughed. "They really have rooms like that here?"

"For a price." He began to loosen his tie.

"I'll bet. Still, we have a whole suite."

"We need a place to work." He moved into the bedroom and hung up his coat. "And these rooms don't even come with the golf simulator or the stripper pole."

She took a step toward him with a sensual grin. "Stripper pole? Now that could be interesting."

"Perhaps I should have stretched the budget a bit." He drank her in for a long moment, then took her in his strong arms and pulled her to him. With a heavy breath, he kissed her hard.

She kissed him back, relishing the feel of his lips against hers, the smell of him, the heady taste of his mouth.

But just as she was really getting into the kiss, he pulled away.

She blinked at him, stinging with disappointment. "I won't break, you know."

As Parker watched the wounded expression appear on Miranda's face, his heart broke. He loved her to distraction. She was strong and vigilant and passionate and more beautiful than she knew. But her doctors insisted it would be another month or two until she fully healed and he wouldn't do anything, no matter how tempting, to jeopardize that. The kind of unbridled sex they'd enjoyed before her injuries would have to wait until then.

"I'll let you shower first," he said firmly and stepped away from her to unbutton his shirt.

After he removed it, Miranda stood there, eyeing the delicious shape of his muscled arms and torso.

They hadn't bathed together since her hospital stay. Maybe the sight of her injuries under lights and water was too much for him. The bullet wound, the knife slashes her ex had put across her chest. But he should talk. Parker had a few slashes of his own.

She was tired of the gentle treatment. She stepped over to him and ran her hands over the hard contour of his chest. She traced a finger along the scar on his abdomen. "You know, I think you've been babying me too long."

He regarded her with longing and caution. "Have I?"

"Yep. Tonight I'm feeling a little risky. And frisky." She opened her mouth and ran her tongue along the side of his neck.

Inhaling with desire, he caught her wrist to stop her movement on his torso. "Don't, Miranda. It's too soon."

"No, I think it's been too long. Way too long." She began nibbling the other side of his neck, knowing that was a weak spot.

"I don't want to risk hurting you."

"I'll take the risk."

"I won't let you."

"Nothing will happen." She reached for his belt buckle, began to loosen it.

Once more his breath grew ragged against her ear. "You don't know that."

"I think I do."

"You don't."

"I'm pretty sure I do."

She felt him inhale, drawing in a new reserve of resistance. "How can you be sure, Miranda? Your physical condition—"

With a swift move, she let his pants drop, kicked one of his legs out from under him and had him on the floor beneath her. "See? I'm just fine. You, on the other hand, seem a little vulnerable." From her straddling position, she started to make lazy circles over his chest with her fingers.

His eyes grew hot and smoky as he watched her. "Are you sure you can handle it?"

She stopped and captured his gaze for a long moment. He loved her. He wouldn't do anything to hurt her, even if things got a little rough. And she meant it that she wouldn't let him go too far.

Slowly she nodded. "Very sure."

"Very well, then." And with one lightning move, he grabbed her and spun her over.

He plastered her to the floor with a kiss as hot as the peppers she'd eaten tonight. Laughing with delight, she kissed him back and drank in all she could of him.

This was going to be a fiery night.

CHAPTER ELEVEN

The next morning, Miranda opened her eyes to the smell of hot coffee and a delicious sense of satisfaction. They'd made it to the bathtub last night—after about an hour on the floor. Parker had been like his old self, doing things to her she had fantasized about for months.

And she hadn't broken.

In fact, right now she felt better than ever. She stretched and yawned and looked over at the clock. It was past nine already. She got up and after finding a pair of jeans and a T-shirt to throw on, plodded into the suite's living area to find Parker had already ordered breakfast—of course.

"How are you?" he asked with a scrutinizing eye after he'd handed her a cup of coffee and seated her at the small portable table near the window.

She smiled up at him. "Just fine."

"Not too...sore?"

"Nope. How about you?"

"Never been better."

She could tell he didn't really believe her, but that only made her want to prove it to him. No time for that now. They had work to do.

She eyed the case file he'd laid on the table. "Have you had a chance to go through that?"

"I thought we'd do that during breakfast."

"Sounds good."

Over poached eggs, gourmet bagels, and exotic fruit cups, she studied the file's contents. There wasn't much information. Besides background details on the victim you could get off the Internet, O'Toole had only spoken to the hiring manager at the casino by phone.

Though a regular at the Dame Destinado, Ambrosia Dawn had just come off a mini-tour about three weeks ago. While in town, she resided at her home in Costa Rica Hills, a country club about six miles west of the Strip.

Traveling with her was her usual entourage. Her husband and personal manager, forty-year-old Cameron Forrest, a former Elvis impersonator. Her sister Blythe Star, two years her junior, who helped coordinate the music. Assorted friends and staff who took care of everything from her hair to her shoes to making sure she arrived at rehearsals on time and cooking all her meals just so.

There must have been fifty names on the list.

"Not much specific information, but a lot to work with." Miranda handed the file to Parker.

Parker took his time reading over it, absorbing the data. "It's obvious Sid wants as little to do with this case as possible."

"Too hot for him, I guess. I suppose the media is involved by now."

"Let's see." Parker picked up the remote and switched on the huge plasma TV over the fireplace.

A news lady was talking about Ambrosia Dawn. "The tragic death of the popular singer has the entire town in shock."

The picture switched to a crowd on the street carrying flowers and signs.

"We love you, Ambrosia," one of them said tearfully into the camera. "We're all going to miss you so much."

"Her songs will live on forever in our hearts," another said.

"Las Vegas Metro has declined a statement pending further investigation into the matter."

Parker turned the TV off. "Avoidance," he grunted under his breath.

Regarding the blank screen, Miranda finished off her coffee. "Sounds like at least O'Toole had enough sense not to leak the bit about the melon baller and the eye."

"He has ability. He chooses to use it in a passive fashion rather than active." Which was a fancy way of saying he was lazy.

"Yeah. Well, it's all us now."

As she set down her cup, her phone buzzed in her pocket. She pulled it out and looked at the text message. It was from her friend Coco back home.

OMG, Miranda. I just heard the news about Ambrosia Dawn on the TV. I can't stop crying. They told me at the office you and Parker have taken her case. You have to find the person who did this. You just have to. I know you and Parker can.

It was all up to them, all right. She shoved the phone back in her pocket. She'd answer Coco later when she could figure out what to say to her.

"Okay. Where do we start? We have a boatload of possible suspects."

"You're the lead. What do you suggest?"

Oh, yeah. She was the lead. A thrill rippled through her at the idea.

She thought a minute. Her usual first inclination in a case like this was to think the husband did it. It would be law enforcement's too. But for her, it was her violent past with a psychotic ex-husband talking. Still, might as well get the nagging doubts out of the way first.

She got to her feet. "Let's go talk to the immediate family."

CHAPTER TWELVE

The six-mile trip to Costa Rica Hills took them forty-five minutes in the mid-morning traffic. When they arrived, they found a throng of mourners huddled around the gated community's entrance in the baking sun. Two security guards stood alongside the salmon-colored stone wall on either side of a tall iron gate looking very uncomfortable.

The grieving were mostly middle-aged women, though there were some men and teens. Many had armfuls of gifts. Candles, flowers, stuffed animals, homemade placards expressing their devotion. They began laying them along the wall.

"We love you, Ambrosia Dawn," someone shouted.

Someone else started singing "All Eyes on Me" and others joined in, filling the air with a sad lament and making Miranda wish she could find the killer in the next five minutes and deliver him—or her—to this crowd. On the other hand, one of them could be the killer.

Parker eased the rental car through the group and up to the gate. He pressed a button and explained to a third guard inside a little hut that they were investigators here on police business on behalf of Sergeant Sid O'Toole of the LVMPD.

The booth guard couldn't very well refuse that. But the guards out front had to hold back the mourners when he opened the tall gate.

Parker rolled inside without incident.

"I don't think I'd care much for being a celebrity," Miranda said watching the gate close behind them, shutting out the adoring fans. "Kind of stifling."

"I don't imagine you would."

As they found their way along the curving roads, the desert sun beat down on the sprawling stucco and stone palaces surrounding them. Most of the roofs were red clay, but the rambling buildings were all shapes and sizes.

Squares and rectangles and triangles and circles, mostly done in desert colors of sandstone and cream and coral and burnt sienna. Yards were masterpieces of decorative rock and pebble and cactus arrangements. Here and

33

there was a landscape of grass and small trees, and beyond the homes, the golf course. Given the climate, all the green had to be kept alive by a multi-million dollar underground watering system.

Megabuck city.

At last they came to the estate where Ambrosia Dawn had lived.

A huge collection of tall arched windows and apricot-colored stucco blocks that rose to three stories, it made Parker's family mansion back home look like a garage.

Parker brought the car to a stop along the large circular drive and they traded the cool of the rental for the hot, dry desert air as they got out and made their way toward the big glass-and-iron archway that was the front door.

Parker was in his usual dark suit and Miranda was in a lightweight seersucker suit of black. They should have worn white for comfort, but they were okay as far as appearance went. They looked like they could be from the FBI.

Parker's sharp gaze took in the estate. "No doubt there will be staff to interview," he said.

Miranda thought about that. "Can you get started with them? I want to talk to the husband first."

For a moment he looked like he might question that decision, as if he didn't want her to suffer the ordeal of handling a grieving husband. But he must have thought better of it.

He simply nodded. "As you wish."

"And we both need to be on the lookout for a lucky bean plant."

"I was just about to mention that."

She'd looked it up on the way over. It was a plant with dark shiny leaves with large red beans that could fit into a medium size pot.

They stepped onto the portico and Parker rang the bell. The first bar of "All Eyes on Me" rang out in chimes. Not too self-absorbed, was she?

After about five minutes, a man in a black suit appeared behind the glass, making his way toward the door. Must take a while to get around this museum.

Another thirty seconds passed before he reached the front and opened the door. "I'm sorry. The family isn't taking any visitors right now." His look was stern.

Miranda eyed his black tie, crisp white shirt, polished dress shoes. His sandy hair was perfectly styled and his tan, good-looking features made her put him at no older than late twenties. She wondered if Hollywood was his ultimate career destination.

"We're from the Parker Agency." She handed him her card. "We're assisting Metro in the investigation of Ambrosia Dawn's demise."

He stared down at the card, flustered. "The police?"

"Sergeant Sid O'Toole, specifically. Feel free to call him to verify." Though Miranda hoped he would at least invite them in first and out of the baking sun before he did that.

Bewildered, he glanced over his shoulder as if hoping someone would come and give him directions. Then he pulled the door open. "Of course, please come in. We're in such a state, as you can imagine."

"Yes, I understand."

"We're very sorry for your loss," Parker added as they stepped into a large, square foyer that was all off-gray stone and drenched in light both from the windows and from a glimmering chandelier high overhead.

No need to worry about the light bill when you're this loaded, she supposed.

The young man extended a hand to Miranda then to Parker. "I'm Derrick Dane, the family's house manager. What can I do to help you?"

"We'd like to speak to some of the staff, if we may," Parker said.

Derrick Dane's fair brows knit together as if the request was difficult to comprehend. At last he put his hands behind his back, military fashion, and nodded. "Certainly, sir."

"How big a staff is there?" Miranda asked.

"You mean the household staff?"

"Anyone who works in the estate."

He blew out a breath. "Well, let's see. There are the housekeepers, the caretakers for the yard, the chauffeurs, Miss Ambrosia's personal assistant, her personal trainer, her personal chef, her hair dresser, and her wardrobe assistant."

While he listed a few more, Miranda slipped a pad out of her pocket and took a few notes. A lot to narrow down and that was just the start. No wonder O'Toole didn't want this case.

"Is there somewhere we can go? For privacy?" Parker said as casually as if he were asking for a glass of ice tea.

The house manager blinked at him. "Why, yes. One of the sitting rooms, I suppose."

"That will be good. If you'll bring them to me one at a time?"

"Certainly, sir." He gestured toward a room.

Miranda raised a finger. "Before you disappear, is Mr. Forest at home?"

Again, the young man looked confused. "Yes, of course. He's in the viewing room. He's given strict orders not to be disturbed. He's very upset, of course."

"I understand. But while Mr. Parker speaks to the staff, I need to ask him a few routine questions."

Derrick Dane's pale green eyes went wide with shock for a moment as he took in the implication that his employer, that anyone on the staff, and that even himself, could be a suspect in a murder investigation.

"I—" he glanced up at the fancy filigree banister on the second story overhead. "I'll see if he'll speak to you."

Miranda listened to the clicking heels of his polished dress shoes as the house manager crossed the tile floor to a small room. There must have been an intercom of some sort in there because he returned a moment later.

"Very well. Mr. Forest will see you, Ms.—is it Steele?"
"Yes, it is. Thank you, Mr. Dane."

CHAPTER THIRTEEN

After showing Parker to the sitting room, and notifying the first staff member to be interviewed, the house manager led Miranda up the wide white staircase and down a long passageway. At the end of it, they turned a corner and headed down another corridor.

Here, posters of Ambrosia Dawn's world tours were plastered all over the walls. Her image was everywhere, in various poses from her performances, foreign language text exclaiming her presence. France and England. Australia and New Zealand. Thailand and Beijing. Walking past the images of the woman she'd seen in the morgue last night gave Miranda a creepy feeling, but she ignored it and focused on the job at hand.

So far, she hadn't seen any clues or any houseplants.

At last they reached a pair of red tufted vinyl doors with two round windows. Viewing room. Now she got it. Movies.

Derrick Dane reached for one of the golden handles and held the door open for her. "Mr. Forest is inside."

She was on her own. "Thank you," she told the man and stepped inside the darkened room.

It was a viewing room, all right. Movie theater seats padded with thick red velvet cushions, ultra-low movie theater lights peeking out from symmetrically placed walls, and up front, a movie theater screen.

Band music played, and Ambrosia Dawn's distinctive voice rang into the empty air while, dressed all in silver, with out-stretched arms her larger-than-life celluloid figure shimmied to the beat across the screen. A pattern of colored lights flooded the stage while a chorus of dancers sang and bobbed around her, building to a dramatic crescendo. All the thrill and glitz of a big Las Vegas show.

As Miranda's eyes grew used to the dark, she could just make out the figure of a man in a middle row. She felt her way down the aisle toward him. As she approached she could hear he was sobbing.

This wasn't going to be easy. "Excuse me. Mr. Forest?"

She watched his shoulders shudder as he stared up at the screen.

"She was so beautiful. She lit up the world with her songs. How can it all be over?" He seemed to be talking to himself.

Miranda's heart went out to him, but in the back of her mind she knew this could be an Academy Award winning performance. She'd been announced, after all. Tread lightly, she thought. She usually didn't have a lot of tact when she questioned people, but being around Parker and his subtle style had been rubbing off on her.

"Mr. Forest, I hate to bother you at this time," she said. "But I need to ask you some questions on behalf of the police."

Slowly he turned his head and stared at her, as if coming out of a trance. He must have held her gaze for a full minute. Then he shook himself. "Oh, yes. Derrick mentioned that." He lifted a hand and with a remote control froze the performance on the screen.

The room went silent.

Ambrosia Dawn's face loomed before them, large and still. Even without sound or movement, she was mesmerizing. She had the kind of charismatic sensuality only top celebrities possessed.

Forest pressed another button and low lights came up.

He kept his gaze on Ambrosia Dawn's image.

"May I sit down?"

He turned to her again as if to ask, *Are you still here?* Then again he shook himself. "Yes, of course. I apologize for my—condition."

"Perfectly understandable. I'm so sorry for your loss." Miranda eased into a seat two away from him. It was so cushy and comfortable she thought they might both fall asleep after a minute or two.

Elvis Cameron Forest was looking up at the screen again, as if willing the frozen figure to come to life and step down out of it.

Miranda took in his features. He was a large man, in pretty good shape. Broad shoulders, muscular torso, long legs stretching out into the isle. He had on white designer jeans and a tank top under an open, patterned shirt. Several thick gold chains hung around his neck, embellishing his chest hair and several golden rings adorned his fingers. On his feet he wore sandals. He had hair of pure pitch-black, probably dyed that uncommon color, and styled in an old-fashioned pompadour, albeit a modified one. It was complete with sideburns, but it had a rumpled look, and his clothes looked like he had slept in them.

Miranda slipped her notepad out of her pocket. "Mr. Forest, when was the last time you saw your wife?"

"Saw her?"

"Yes."

"They said I could come and identify the body today. I haven't gone yet."

"I meant the last time you saw her alive."

"Oh." He turned to Miranda now, as if waking up from a dream. "Um, let me think. Tuesday, that would have been. Tuesday night. We've been in town a few weeks and Abbey's been rehearsing her new show at the casino in the evenings."

"Abbey?"

"That's what I call her. Her real name is Abigail." His voice was low and resonant, with a touch of a Southern accent. Just the right timbre for bellowing out "Blue Suede Shoes" or "Hound Dog."

"I see. So you saw her at the rehearsal, then?"

"Yes. We wrapped up earlier than usual. Around eleven, I think. I had an errand to run, so I told Abbey to have the driver take her home."

An errand to run at eleven at night? Possible in a twenty-four-seven town. Still, she tucked that little detail away in the back of her mind. "That was the last time you saw her? When she left?"

"Yes." He touched his cheek. "She kissed me and told me to take care of myself. It was sort of our ritual." He leaned his forehead in his hand and stared blankly at the floor.

He was getting to her.

As gently as she could, she asked, "So she was in a good frame of mind?"

"Frame of mind?" He stared at the walls as if the question had been in Martian. "Why, yes. She was in a good mood. Happy about the show. Rehearsals were going well. We had the possibility of long-term contract with the casino."

Ambrosia Dawn sounded ambitious. Or maybe Elvis was the ambitious one. Had he pushed her harder than she wanted? And when she balked—?

She was getting ahead of herself. "What time did you get home?"

"Home? Um—" He rubbed his face. "I think it was about one. Or two. I'd had a few drinks."

"At a bar?"

"Yes, I stopped in to see a friend at the Blue Palm Lounge. It's just down the street, right off the Strip."

"Must have been a good friend to keep you out so late."

"Reedy Max. Used to be my manager."

"When you were an Elvis impersonator?"

"Yes. But I quit that when I met Abbey and became her business manager. Sort of ironic. She's a singer. An artist. She doesn't have much of a head for contracts and negotiations and such."

Miranda noted he referred to Ambrosia Dawn in present tense. He was still in shock. It would be a long while before he was normal again. If ever.

She pressed on. "So you got home at one or two and your wife wasn't here? Even though she came home in the limo?"

"I thought she might have gone to her sister's. She was nervous about one of the numbers and wanted to go over it again with her."

"Would that be Blythe Star?"

"Yes. She arranges Abbey's music."

Consistent with O'Toole's notes, at least. "What did you do when you got home?"

"Do? I went to bed."

"You didn't see or hear anything unusual?"

He pursed his lips and suddenly looked ashamed. "Sometimes I have trouble sleeping. I took a pill."

"Was anyone else in the house who might have heard anything?"

"Brandon was in his room, but that's on the far west end of the third floor."

"Brandon?"

"My son."

That detail wasn't in O'Toole's report. "You and Ambrosia Dawn had a son?"

"No, we've only been married seven years. He's sixteen. From a previous marriage."

"Where's your ex-wife?"

"Julia?" He laughed. "God only knows. She took off with a rich Australian and said they were sailing around the world when we broke up. I heard she's had several husbands since."

A jealous ex-wife? Could be another lead, but things were too wide open. She had to start narrowing it down. "So only you and Brandon were in the house?"

"The only servants who reside with us are two of the housemaids. Oh, and Suzie."

"Suzie?"

"Suzie Chan. She doesn't reside here, but she works all hours. She's Abbey's personal chef. She's a real wonder. She ran a five-star restaurant in Santa Monica. We were so lucky to get her. Her dishes are beyond amazing. At least Abbey always thinks—I mean—thought so."

Personal chef. Miranda turned the moniker over in her mind. Just the sort of person who could wield a melon baller. Miranda wondered if Parker had gotten to her yet. "I'd like to speak to Ms. Chan."

"Certainly. Oh, wait. That's right. She's not here. She went to visit her sister. She runs the restaurant in Santa Monica now. Abbey was worried Suzie might leave us and go back into business with her."

"Did Ms. Chan and your wife have a problem?"

"Problem? No. They got along just fine as far as I know." He gave a little laugh. "I stay out of the kitchen."

"When did Ms. Chan leave?"

"For her sister's? Let's see. Sometime Tuesday? Yes, I remember now. One of the housemaids had to bring the food."

"Food?"

"To the party. Abbey likes to throw backstage parties after a long rehearsal. Just some drinks and finger food. You know, sandwiches, canapés. Oh, and those melon balls. Abbey was very particular about the melon balls."

Miranda dropped her notepad onto her lap. "Melon balls?"

40

He gestured with his hands. "A whole tableful of them. Melon balls on toothpicks with turkey slices, in frozen cocktails, with sherbet, a huge melon ball centerpiece. Oh, Suzie can carve the most intricate designs in the rind."

Miranda drew in a slow, measured breath. Then she forced herself to speak slowly and calmly. "Mr. Forest, did Sergeant O'Toole give you details about your wife's condition?"

His thick black brows drew together and a deep crease formed over the bridge of his longish nose. "I—do you mean the officer who came here to tell me—? That's when I knew Abbey wasn't home. That she wasn't coming home." He forced down another sob. "No, that wasn't a man. It was a woman. Wait. She gave me a card."

A woman?

He dug in his pocket and pulled out a wrinkled business card. He had slept in his clothes.

He handed her the card and Miranda read it. *Detective Kim Ralston. LVMPD.* O'Toole had even sent someone else—a female—to do the dirty work of informing the family. Miranda was developing a real fondness for that guy.

She revised her question. "Did Detective Ralston explain to you how Ambrosia was found?"

Elvis Cameron Forest's face went pale. He glanced up at the screen, then down at the floor, then over to the corner where there was nothing. He was in serious denial.

After what seemed like a half hour, he closed his eyes and put a hand over his face. He nodded. "Yes. She said—she said someone had taken one of Abbey's—*eyes*." He let out something between a howl and a whimper. "Why would anyone do that to her? Why?"

"I don't know. But I promise you I'll find out." She got to her feet. "You've been very helpful. Thank you. One last thing. Do you have a way to contact Suzie Chan?"

He looked up at her with glazed eyes as if he didn't want to think about the implication of her words. As if all he really wanted was to crawl into a hole somewhere and die himself.

But he answered in a half whisper. "Derrick would have that."

CHAPTER FOURTEEN

Miranda left Elvis Cameron Forest to his films and his grief, and zigzagged her way back down the corridor, peeking into rooms as she went. All were empty. None contained any houseplants.

As she reached the stairs and began to descend into the entrance hall, she spotted Parker coming out of a side room and caught his gaze. He had something.

She met him at the foot of the stairs, excitement coursing through her veins. "Are you finished?"

He nodded. "You?"

"Yes."

Parker turned to Derrick Dane, who had shadowed him as soon as he left the room. "Thank you for your time."

"As I said, all of us are willing to do anything to help find Ms. Ambrosia's killer." Though he seemed relieved they were on their way out, Miranda noticed.

"We'll keep you posted on our progress," she assured him. "Oh, I'll need Suzie Chan's contact information from you."

Parker patted his breast pocket. "Mr. Dane had already provided that."

So Parker had uncovered the same lead she had.

Okay then. Miranda headed for the door. "We'll be in touch, Mr. Dane."

Without a word, she and Parker crossed the walkway and headed for the car, neither of them wanting to reveal their findings until they were well away.

When the car rolled out the country club's iron gate and past the lingering mourners, Miranda turned to Parker. "Spill."

He smiled for a second then got that intense look he always wore when he was onto something.

"I took a short tour of the grounds and spoke to one of the gardeners."

"And?"

"No *abrus precatorius* growing outside."

Darn. "Okay. What else?"

"The house manager showed me the first floor. There's an indoor garden."

She held her breath. "With a lucky bean plant?"

"Mostly palms and ferns along a rock bed waterfall. Nicely designed."

So he was going to make her pry it out of him. "Keep going."

"The housemaids gave me the details of their daily routines. Nothing much unusual. Shall I go over them?"

Miranda narrowed her eyes. "Just cut to the chase."

He glanced at her, anticipation in his eyes. "The personal chef, Suzie Chan, is an expert at making melon balls."

Now they were getting somewhere. "That's what the husband said. She made a whole variety of them for after rehearsals. For all the cast and crew."

Parker nodded. "According to the downstairs maid, Suzie hated making the melon balls all the time. She claimed it was stifling her creativity and giving her carpal tunnel. But her employer seemed to be obsessed with them."

Miranda's brows shot up in surprise. "Really? Our Elvis impersonator thought Suzie and Ambrosia got along fine."

"Not according to the maid. They fought constantly. Ambrosia wanted everything just so. She was very demanding."

Miranda sat back in the passenger seat. Could Cameron Forest not have known there was tension between his wife and her personal chef? He did seem out of it.

"Both Derrick and the maid confirmed Suzie was planning to leave Tuesday night to visit her sister in Santa Monica, though no one else was home when she left the house."

"Forest mentioned she was going to Santa Monica. And I-15 would be the route she'd take."

Parker nodded. "It would. Ambrosia Dawn seems to have been a creature of habit. The maid said she had a ritual of drinking tea every night. She had Suzie prepare a special blend of mint and ginger and raspberry leaf."

"And Tuesday night, the abrin."

"Tuesday night Suzie left her employer a pot of tea on the warmer before she went to California. The maid found it the next morning."

Miranda's breath caught. "Did she save it?"

Parker shook his head. "She poured it out and washed the pot by hand."

"Crap." Miranda was wondering if they could find something in the pipes when a thought hit her. "Wait a minute. The ME said the abrin would induce vomiting. Sounded like severe vomiting. Did you see the kitchen?"

He nodded. "Derrick showed me that room last."

"Did you see—or smell any trace of—" She waved a hand. "You know?"

"Not a whiff. The kitchen looked spotless. There was a downstairs bathroom nearby."

"Which means—"

"Exactly. Someone cleaned up. And rather thoroughly."

Just what a chef who was trying to cover the evidence would do. "Tell me more about the kitchen."

"It was well done. Spacious, modern equipment, well lit. My father would have loved it." Parker's father was a wealthy real estate developer in Atlanta.

She drummed her fingers on her lap. "Get to the point."

"Despite the good design, it seems the owners wanted more. You know how the wealthy are." He shot her a wry grin.

"Out with it."

"They're building a space onto the kitchen for additional dining. A side room with a bay window overlooking the golf course."

Miranda could feel her pulse in her neck. "Nice."

"Yes, it will be. Construction is about half done. There was a large opening in a wall at the far end of the kitchen. It's going to be an open archway to the dining area."

Her heart started to race. She couldn't take any more. She was about to give Parker a punch when he stopped the car at a light and turned to her.

"For two weeks the opening was covered with polyethylene."

"And now?"

"Neither Derrick nor the maids know what happened, but the plastic is gone."

CHAPTER FIFTEEN

On West Flamingo, they headed east toward the city. Deep in thought, Miranda stared out the window at the now moderate traffic and the more moderate homes.

A tan young woman in shorts and tank top was walking a white miniature bulldog in front of a house painted all pink. The building was too small for a star. Must be a local eccentric.

By now it was after one and Parker decided it was time to eat. Miranda was glad when he turned into a fast food place and ordered hamburgers. The meal would be quick.

He pulled into a vacant spot and they watched the traffic as they munched.

Miranda swallowed a sip of her soda and decided to state the obvious. "Suzie Chan didn't leave for Santa Monica before the rehearsal."

Parker peeled back the wrapper of his burger with the same classy air he displayed in a five-star restaurant. He shook his head. "No, it doesn't appear she did."

Miranda ate some burger and talked while she chewed. "She made the tea and waited around for her employer to get back. According to Cameron Forest, that would have been shortly after eleven. Ambrosia wasn't there when he got home after one a.m."

"That would give Chan just enough time." Parker took a bite of his burger.

"She stayed out of sight, or maybe she told Ambrosia she'd changed her mind about the trip and poured the tea for her."

"To make sure she drank it."

Miranda reached for a napkin and wiped her mouth. "And Ambrosia drank it, all right. A nice big dose. Enough to act fast."

"Within an hour."

"And in that time the victim would have started barfing, having seizures. Then she'd pass out."

Parker's face was granite. "Chan would have to clean up the mess, take down the plastic enclosure and wrap the body in it."

"Then carry it out to her car—which would already be packed with luggage and a wheelbarrow—put Ambrosia in the trunk, and head for I-15. Half an hour later, Chan dumps her on the side of the highway and heads for Santa Monica."

"Hmm." Parker was thinking the same thing she was.

"Timing is awfully tight. And how did Chan carry out the body and lift it into the car?"

Parker reached for his soda. "Perhaps she had help. I don't think the maids or Derrick Dane were involved. It would be unlikely for several members of the staff to murder their employer together."

"Yeah, if they all hated working for her, they'd just get other jobs."

He sipped thoughtfully. "Dane seems very loyal to the family."

"Maybe Forest got home earlier than he said." She shook her head. "No, he couldn't be involved. He was too pathetic."

No way they could figure out what happened without more evidence. Miranda let out a long breath. What did they do now?

She took another bite of burger and let her gaze run absently over the muted charcoal interior of the car. It was a plain sedan. Nothing like Parker's Lamborghini or the speedy red Corvette ZR1 he'd given her on their wedding day, or even the BMW convertible he'd rented on their honeymoon. It was more like the working vehicles the Agency owned.

Cool air was pouring out of the AC vents. She glanced up at the mirror where the direction and temperature were display. Ninety-nine degrees. "How come it's so darn hot here?"

"We are in the Mojave Desert. At the hottest time of the year."

"Hell of a place to build a town."

Chuckling he gave her a tender look. "Artesian wells that support green areas were discovered here in the early eighteen-hundreds. Las Vegas means 'the meadows' after all."

Misnamed, in her opinion. "Except for the golf course, I haven't seen many of those." And that had to be watered with an underground irrigation system.

"True. Then came the Mormons, the railroad, and the pioneers."

"And then good old Bugsy Siegel."

"Yes."

"And the gamblers and the shows and the famous."

Parker nodded.

"Which, speeding things along, brings us up to today and the murder of our celebrity singer."

"Exactly."

She thought of their missing-in-action police sergeant. "Was O'Toole this bad when he was at the Agency?"

"He was one of our first trainees. The program was only a year old. We mostly did one-on-one then."

Like the training she'd had from Parker.

46

"We had three new employees that year. I took two of them and put Judd in charge of O'Toole. It wasn't long before Judd was complaining to me about the young man's performance."

"Such as?"

"Slacking off, not listening to instructions, acting as if the training were a joke."

Miranda shifted in her seat. She'd had a similar attitude when she'd started at the Agency. But that was before she discovered investigating was what she was meant to do.

"Judd thought it was lack of confidence, so we attempted to build some in him."

"How did that work out?"

Parker shrugged. "Fairly well up to a point. But after a year, Sid got the offer with Las Vegas Metro and left." He let out a slow breath. "He was my first disappointment. I always thought he had more potential."

And now they were stuck with him, bringing up not-so-nice memories for Parker. Well, at least she could show him her training wasn't a waste.

She swallowed her last bite and took a final sip of her drink. "Okay, how are we supposed to proceed here, Parker? We're not the police. Can we bring Suzie Chan in for questioning?"

She watched his face turn to calculating as he slipped back into work mode. "Chan might not be at her sister's any longer."

Good point. Miranda's heart sank. "She might never have gone there if she planned to kill her employer and run. Hell, she could be in Mexico for all we know."

"True. We'll have to contact Sid." He dialed his cell phone, waited. After a minute, he hung up with a growl. "He's not answering."

Shaking her head with disgust she balled up her hamburger wrapper and tossed it in the paper bag Parker had set between the seats. "He's working normal hours when he's got a case like this?"

"He handed it off to us."

"We don't have police authority."

Parker wiped his mouth and put his napkin in the bag. "Or jurisdiction. Neither does he in California."

That was all they needed. They couldn't get stalled now. They were onto something. "Wait. There's another detective who was involved. Forest gave me her card." She pulled it out of her pocket. "Kim Ralston. Let's go talk to her."

"Excellent idea." Parker started the car, tossed their trash into the receptacle and turned right, heading for Sierra Vista.

CHAPTER SIXTEEN

They found Detective Kim Ralston in her office. She sat at her desk, her back straight, her gaze focused on her computer.

"What can I do for you?" she asked without looking up.

Parker took a casual step toward the desk. "We're from the Parker Investigative Agency. We've been working with Sergeant O'Toole on the Ambrosia Dawn case."

Ralston stopped typing and looked up at Parker. Miranda watched her eyes go wide when she saw how good-looking he was—a reaction she'd seen many times in women.

Then Ralston gave Miranda a glance and sat back in her chair with a smirk. "So you're the two hot shots from the east O'Toole hired?"

"Something like that," Miranda said as she took in O'Toole sidekick.

Plain dark blond hair pulled back into a ponytail with a simple band. A tan, short-sleeved cotton shirt and matching slacks were divided at the waist by a simple brown belt. Ralston wore no jewelry, no lipstick, no makeup. Miranda liked her instantly.

"Have a seat." Ralston pointed to a couple of chairs—she had two in her office. "The whole department's talking about you."

Parker waited for Miranda to sit then settled himself. "Are they?"

"Nobody wants to touch this case. Too hot. Too much publicity. The Lieutenant, the Commander, all the casino owners, even the mayor is watching our every move. Plus there's the national news coverage."

Miranda cocked her head at the woman. "We're not afraid of publicity. Parker's pretty used to it." And she'd had to deal with some in the past year herself.

"Well, we tend to avoid it around here. But you can't on this case. Ambrosia Dawn's publicist is calling every hour for developments. What a pain in the ass."

Miranda liked her even more. "Does O'Toole have you dealing with that?"

"No, he's just avoiding her phone calls."

Miranda couldn't help shaking her head. Ralston caught the gesture and gave her a cautious half-smile.

Parker leaned forward with his most businesslike demeanor. "Detective Ralston, we've discovered some information on the case and we need some assistance."

"I'll do what I can, but my authority is limited."

"We understand. However, I believe we've uncovered a person of interest."

Miranda knew that understated Parker tone so well. Plus, it was best not to be overconfident with the police or they'd just pooh-pooh your findings.

Ralston's thin brows rose in a mixture of surprise and skepticism. "Already?"

"We think so," Miranda said, continuing the cautious tone. "We just came from Ambrosia Dawn's residence. I spoke to her husband."

"The Elvis impersonator?" She suppressed an eye roll. "Not that that's unusual out here."

"Yeah. But he's a retired Elvis impersonator. He's Ms. Dawn's business manager now. Or he was."

"So I understand."

Miranda went over what Forest had told her about the rehearsal party Tuesday night, their personal chef and the melon balls, and that he said the chef had left town before the party. She explained Parker had learned from the house staff that Ambrosia had an obsession with melon balls and they fought all the time. She also told her about the tea and the missing building plastic.

"You have found a person of interest." Ralston tapped her fingernails on her desk. "Cameron Forest mentioned the personal chef when I saw him last night to tell him about his wife and asked if anyone in the house might have access to a melon baller."

Miranda frowned. "Forest mentioned Suzie Chan last night?"

"Yes. Why?"

"When I spoke to him today, he hadn't seemed to make the connection between the melon baller and his wife's personal chef."

Ralston considered that a moment. "I'm not sure he even heard much of what I said last night, he was so broken up."

"He was that way when I saw him, too," Miranda said. "He probably wasn't thinking clearly." He was in a serious case of denial.

"I wrote those details up in the report I sent to Sergeant O'Toole'" Ralston said. "I don't know why he didn't say anything to you."

That report wasn't in the file.

Miranda looked at Parker. He gave her a let's-not-discuss-the-sluggard-here look.

She nodded and turned back to Ralston. "Since Suzie Chan is supposed to be in California, we're wondering how to bring her in for questioning."

Her brow creased as she thought a moment. "I'll have to talk to Sergeant O'Toole on how he wants to proceed on that." She blew out a breath. "But I can see if I can get a search warrant for Suzie Chan's place."

"You're thinking we might find evidence there?"

"If we're lucky."

Miranda lifted her hands. "Well, this is the place for luck, isn't it?"

Ralston turned to her computer, did a quick check of Suzie Chan in the system and found no priors. Then she picked up the phone, ran through paperwork with someone on the other end, and hung up again.

She turned back to them, her eyes bright. "We are in luck. The affidavit is signed and on its way to the judge. If this goes smoothly—and it probably will for this case—we could have the search warrant in about an hour. When it gets here, I'll pull a couple officers and CSIs and get them over to Chan's place pronto." She got to her feet and stretched. "In the meantime I need some coffee. Either of you want anything?"

"No, thanks," Miranda said.

"When the judge calls, you two want to come evidence hunting with me?"

It was tempting, but Miranda didn't want to sit around here twiddling her thumbs for an hour. Better to keep interviewing people on their list. Just in case the Suzie Chan angle didn't pan out.

Miranda glanced at Parker. He nodded to her, indicating it was her decision.

She shook her head. "I think it would be better if we talked to Ambrosia's sister."

Which would mean heading straight back to the country club, according to the address in the case file.

"All right. I'll be in touch with our findings."

"Likewise."

CHAPTER SEVENTEEN

The hot, early afternoon sun was just starting to cast eastward shadows onto the neighborhood lawns when they arrived at Blythe Star's coral-colored stucco house. The sprawling place was a two-story palace, maybe only half the size of her sister's down the street. Still huge.

And wasn't it nice for family to be so close? Miranda thought as she headed up the winding gray slate walkway in the blinding heat to the elaborate arched door. This one was barricaded with an intricate filigree design over thick blue opaque glass. Owner must like her privacy.

At her side, Parker took in the size of the place. "I'm sure Ms. Star has a bevy of servants, just as her sister did. Should we split the duties as before?"

She shook her head. "This time I'd like you with me to observe. I don't want to miss anything."

He gave her a tender look. "I don't think you've missed anything so far."

That was a nice compliment from a man with Parker's investigative experience, but she thought it was probably the encouraging husband talking. She didn't feel unsure of herself. She just didn't want to take anything for granted.

She shifted her weight and studied Parker's face.

The lines between his handsome brows made her wonder if he was secretly second-guessing her. "I thought we'd see the sister for another angle on things."

"Exactly what I would have done."

"Really?"

"Really."

"Why are you frowning?"

He lifted a hand. "Sun's in my eyes."

"I see."

Parker studied the intent crease between his wife's deep blue eyes. The shape of her dark untamed hair, the sheen on her skin from the hot desert sun. He could see she was anxious about failing on this case. But she needn't be.

She was doing well and it was only their first official venture. He was proud of her. Still, he knew that anxiety would make her work herself to the bone if he didn't look out for her, making sure she ate and slept and was satisfied in...other ways.

And until they had solid proof Suzie Chan was the killer they were looking for, she'd worry about whether she was on the right track. But then, he'd do the same himself.

He'd never dropped a case no matter how perplexing or frustrating it was. He was driven to bring killers to justice. Just as Miranda was. One of the reasons he loved her so much. He knew she would never drop this one. But he hoped they could wrap it up soon so she could feel a sense of accomplishment. And he could feel a relief from his own anxiety over her.

Miranda gave Parker another look, then turned to ring the bell.

This one ding-donged a more normal chime than Ambrosia's. As she waited for someone to answer, she tapped her foot on the rough stone of the porch.

Soon she heard footsteps and the door opened. "May I help you?" said a woman who appeared to be in her mid-forties.

She was on the gaunt side of thin, and her dark, iron gray hair was pulled back from her head so tight, her eyelids were stretched. Her clothes were dark and austere. Obviously she took being a gatekeeper seriously. Miranda wondered if she had been a nun in a previous life.

"We're sorry to bother you at this time," Miranda said, handing her a card. "But we're here from the Parker Investigative Agency on behalf of the local police. We'd like to speak to Ms. Star."

The woman took the card and scowled down at it. "I've never heard of the Parker Investigative Agency."

"We're from the east," Parker said in that easy way of his. He could charm the support hose off even this cold fish, or at least that was what Miranda expected.

Instead the woman handed the card back and gave Miranda a cold, narrow glare. "I'm sorry, I'll have to verify your identities."

Parker opened his mouth in a second attempt to charm, but before he could speak a gentle, feminine voice floated through a speaker on the wall. "Who is it, Hildie?"

The gatekeeper gave a little huff then pressed a button on the box. "People who say they're with the police, ma'am. I think they're autograph hounds."

"Oh, for heaven's sake. If they're with the police, let them in. Show them to the terrace."

The woman stared at the box as if thinking, "I wouldn't do that if I were you." But she was the employee here and evidently she knew her place.

"As you wish, ma'am," she said stiffly.

She opened the door and let them in.

Without another word, the woman led them through an elegant oversized foyer with apricot marble floors and a gurgling fountain with goldfish swimming in it, then down an arched corridor to the back of the house, and onto a wide circular area that was the terrace. The marble floor here was white as angel wings and matched columns that opened to a view of a lush rolling golf course with the pale gray-blue mountains yawning against the horizon in the distance. Soothing and serene.

Blythe Star was stretched out on a white wicker sofa, looking like a Greek goddess surveying her domain. She was dressed in a layered brown-and-blue leather-and-denim outfit with enough fringe to suggest a Southwestern look. Stacked-heel sandals sat on the floor at the end of the sofa, while she rested her bare feet on a cushion. Her toes were painted in a blue-and-pink design that matched her fingernails. Her thick blond hair was styled and fell past her shoulders.

Miranda noted she wore it just the way Ambrosia had. In fact Blythe looked a lot like her sister. Her nose was a little longer. Her cheekbones not as high. Her eyes set a little wider apart. Not quite as good-looking, but with much of the same charismatic beauty. She could probably pass for her in a pinch.

A box of tissue sat on her lap. Used ones were scattered all over the glass-top coffee table and a few on the floor. She stared blankly into the distance.

Hildie touched her on the shoulder, her voice turning gentle. "Ma'am? The detectives?"

Blythe started and blinked up at her as if coming out of a trance. "Oh, yes. I'm so sorry."

"No problem at all," Parker said, extending a hand as Hildie quietly left the space. "I'm Wade Parker, CEO of the Parker Investigative Agency in Atlanta. This is my associate, Miranda Steele."

The woman took Miranda's hand and gave it a weak, fishlike shake. "And you're helping the police?"

"Sergeant Sid O'Toole asked us to consult," Miranda said.

"I see." She waved the tissue she was holding in her hand. "Please sit down. Both of you. Would you like something to drink?" Her voice had the rich, sonorous tone of her sister's when she sang, but with a sweeter edge, Miranda noticed.

"No, thank you." Miranda glanced at Parker. He shook his head.

Miranda settled herself into a wicker chair near the woman's head. Parker took the one on the opposite side. Both were angled outward for the view and she had to twist in it to face her.

When she did, she caught her dabbing her cheeks. Miranda noticed her makeup hadn't run. Maybe it was the waterproof kind.

She took a breath and began. "Ms. Star, we're very sorry for your loss."

The woman pressed the tissue to her nose and nodded. "Thank you. Thank you so much." She gazed off at the mountains. "I couldn't believe it last night when Cameron called me with the news."

"That's a normal reaction," Parker said in a low, soothing tone.

"I still can't believe it. Not even after I saw her."

Miranda sat up. "You identified the body?"

She nodded. "Early yesterday morning. I had to. I had to see for myself that it was her. Oh, the condition that killer left her in." She put her hands over her face.

Miranda gave Parker another glance. Cameron Forest had given her the impression no one from the family had identified the body yet. Maybe he didn't know Blythe had been there. "Did you tell anyone when you went to the police station?"

"Just Hildie. Why?"

So Forest didn't know.

Miranda didn't reply. She decided to ease into the questions. "You're younger than your sister, correct?"

She nodded. "By two years."

"What sort of relationship did you have with her?"

She opened her mouth, shut it again, taking a moment to gather her thoughts. "Right now? I help arrange her music, the background vocals. I do some of the choreography as well."

"You're a performer?"

"I used to sing professionally. Small shows. Small clubs." She smiled modestly, almost as if she didn't like to admit it. "I never had the success Ambrosia had."

Interesting point.

Blythe leaned toward the coffee table and reached for a glass of something cold and pink and probably alcoholic. She took a dainty sip and turned to Miranda. "Are you sure I can't get you something?"

"No, thanks. Ms. Star—were you and Ambrosia close?"

"In the last few years, yes. And of course we were when we were growing up together. We lived outside Minneapolis with our parents."

Miranda had read that in the case file and imagined a small, tightly-knit family, struggling to keep it together.

"Rags to riches?"

Blythe laughed softly. "Our publicist says that, but it was really more like riches to more riches. Our father is a top criminal defense attorney. He ran for governor once. The result was close. I think it must have been the stress of that life that led to his heart attack. Mother didn't last long after he passed."

"I'm sorry to hear that." The woman had suffered some serious losses. But she seemed to be telling the truth. A publicist's spin sounded reasonable. Marketing with the underdog angle. But maybe there was more to dig up in the past. "What was it like growing up with Ambrosia Dawn?"

Blythe's rosy pink lips turned up in a sad smile. "Now you sound like an interviewer." She must have been asked that a million times, but she didn't give the canned reply. "In the first place she wasn't Ambrosia Dawn back then. She was Abbey Johnson. I was Roberta. Abbey and Bobby everyone called us."

Changed their names to sound more glamorous, no doubt. "You were close then?"

"Oh, yes. I worshipped my sister. Like everyone did. Abbey always got all the attention. She was the outgoing one. She was in everything. High school plays. The band. Musicals. That's when she discovered she could sing. I still remember the first night she played in *Les Misérables*. When she sang 'I Dreamed a Dream,' it was incredible. What a voice. What stage presence. At only sixteen. When she finished, the entire auditorium was quiet for five minutes. Then everyone broke out in cheers and applause." Her lip began to quiver and she reached for another tissue. "Oh, my God. How can all that be over? She was only forty-one. She had her whole life ahead of her."

Miranda waited patiently for the poor woman to settle down, wrestling with the anger brewing in her own gut. If killers knew the kind of pain they caused, would it stop them from committing such monstrous acts? Probably not. But she was going to find this killer if it was the last thing she did.

"Ms. Star, were you at the rehearsal Tuesday night?"

Her forehead creased. "Tuesday night? Of course. Everyone was there."

"Everyone?"

She raised her hands in explanation. "The dancers, the background singers, the stage hands, the lighting crew. Everyone."

"I see. What about the personal staff?"

"Some of Abbey's staff was there, as usual. That's what the family calls my sister. Abbey."

"Yes, her husband mentioned that."

She blinked. "You've spoken to Cameron?"

"Earlier today."

She sat up and pulled her bare feet under her as if she had to think about that. "Is he doing all right?"

"He seemed to be holding up." Miranda wondered at the question. Evidently Blythe hadn't been in touch with her brother-in-law. Filing that tidbit away, she continued. "Which members of the staff were at the rehearsal?"

"Which ones? Oh, Giselle. She's one of the maids who's been with Abbey for years. Always accompanies her. Let me think." She put her fingers to her lips in a delicate gesture. "Suzie? No, that's right. Suzie wasn't there. She usually is."

Miranda played dumb. "Suzie?"

"Suzie Chan. Abbey's personal chef. Abbey insists on having food for the staff after rehearsals. She says it keeps them loyal. I think someone said Suzie was away for a few days and couldn't be there. It was a good thing."

"Oh, why?"

Blythe seemed embarrassed for a moment. She shook her head and looked down at her hands. "Because of the melon balls."

"The melon balls?"

Her long eyelashes fluttered close as she drew in a breath. "Abbey had something of an obsession with them. She claimed eye-sized melon balls brought her luck with her biggest hit, 'All Eyes on Me.' She served them the night she won the Grammy. She said they made her a winner, and she started serving them every time she fed the staff. It's almost a joke now."

"Ms. Star, I'm not following you. You said it was a good thing Suzie Chan wasn't there."

She rolled her eyes and made an exasperated gesture with her hands. "Because my sister was having a fit over the melon balls."

"A fit?"

"Some were too small. Some were too big. The symmetry wasn't right."

Blythe sounded angry now. She'd been irritated with Ambrosia.

Then she waved a dismissive hand in the air. "Oh, she was in a bad mood, anyway. She didn't think the rehearsal had gone well. She thought the timing was off on several of her numbers. She would have taken it out on Suzie if she'd been there."

Or maybe she took it out on Blythe. "Was she often upset at rehearsals?"

Miranda watched her cheeks go pink and her long lashes flutter down over them. She looked downright ashamed. "My sister was rather temperamental. She had a hair-trigger temper. I was glad Cameron was there. Sometimes he's the only one who can calm her down."

The same guy who'd told Miranda Ambrosia was happy about the show and rehearsals were going well. "Was that why your sister came here after the rehearsal?"

Blythe cocked her head as if she were confused. "Here? To my home?"

"Yes."

"She didn't come here Tuesday night. Why do you think that?"

"Her husband thought she had." Was Forest wrong about that, too?

She stared at the floor a moment, then reached for her drink and took another sip as if to steady her nerves. "That's right. Abbey went on ahead of him in the limo. I thought she went straight home." She pressed a tissue to her nose. "If only she'd taken one of her bodyguards with her."

"She had bodyguards?"

"Most stars here do. She has two. Part time. They're very good. Cameron gets them from Entertainment Security."

Miranda slipped her notepad out of her pocket and jotted down the name. "Do the bodyguards come to the rehearsals?"

"Yes, they often accompany her when she goes out. Oh, wait. Scottie had the night off. He's her primary guard."

So the singer wasn't guarded that night. The hair on the back of Miranda's neck stood up. She stole a glance at Parker. He was watching Blythe Star intently. He knew all about bodyguards. He had a fleet of them working for the Agency.

"It was probably just as well. She almost lost Scottie recently."

"Because of her temper?"

Blythe nodded. "We were on the tour in London. It was one of those nights when Abbey was chewing Suzie out. Even with her connections, Suzie couldn't find melons anywhere in the city and Abbey was furious. Scottie came to Suzie's defense."

"That was big of him." And pretty unreasonable of his employer.

"He had a reason. That was the night it came out he and Suzie had been secretly dating."

Miranda drew in a slow breath. Suzie Chan had a boyfriend? A big, strong one if he was a typical bodyguard. Strong enough to lift a dead body into the truck of a car. Bingo.

Keeping her voice even, she pressed on. "Why secretly?"

"Abbey had a firm policy. No dating among staff members. She threatened to fire both of them on the spot. Oh, it was awful. Simply awful."

"But she didn't fire them."

"She told them they had to break it off right then and there or she would."

Parker leaned forward and broke his silence. "Exactly when did this happen?"

Blythe put her hand to her head to think. "About a month or so ago."

Plenty of time to plan a murder. And they both had reason to.

Again Miranda kept her tone steady. "What did Suzie and this Scottie do about the threat?"

Blythe lifted her palms with a sad look. "They broke up. I suppose they chose their careers over love."

Or they chose to get even. "I assume Scott is his real name?"

She stared at her intently for a long moment before answering. "It's his last name. Scottie's sort of a nickname. Sean is his first name, I think. Why?"

Instead of answering, Miranda got to her feet. "Thank you for your time, Ms. Star. You've been very helpful. We'll leave you in peace now." She turned to go, but Blythe snatched her hand.

"Ms. Steele. You and Mr. Parker have to find my sister's killer."

Miranda held the woman's red-eyed gaze and squeezed her hand. "We will, Ms. Star. We will."

And maybe by tonight.

CHAPTER EIGHTEEN

With Parker at her side, Miranda hurried back down the ritzy home's winding walkway as fast as she could. As they climbed into the rental, she knew they were reading each other's minds. There was no need for words.

While Parker sped off down the drive, Miranda hunted for Entertainment Security on her cell.

"Got it," she said after a minute.

She dialed the number and discovered Sean Scott was indeed an employee. After pulling the police credentials and mentioning O'Toole's name a few times, she managed to wheedle the guy's home address out of the clerk who'd answered the phone.

She hung up. "South Rainbow." She rattled off the street number.

"Not far from here."

"Let's go."

Sean Scott's place was in an apartment complex called The Chateaux, though it was just a collection of beige brick two-story buildings. Nothing like the homes they had just left.

They found a parking lot near Scott's unit on the ground floor. A lot of empty spots, Miranda thought as Parker pulled into one just outside Scott's front door. No way to tell if any of the remaining cars belonged to the bodyguard.

With Parker close behind, she got out of the rental and marched to the front door. She used the knocker then banged on the painted wood when there was no response. After about five minutes of knocking, she let out a low growl.

"It's as we expected," Parker said. "He isn't home."

She'd hoped he was.

"Guess we can't expect murder suspects to wait around until we catch up to them." Miranda walked around to one of the windows and peered inside. The curtains were open, and she could see a darkened room filled with typical living

58

room furniture and a big screen TV on the wall. Not much in the way of décor. "Looks like he prefers simple living. Or maybe this is just a bachelor pad."

"We could speak to the landlord. He might let us in without a warrant."

She shook her head. She'd love to, but it wouldn't be worth it. "If we find something, it would get thrown out in court if we did it that way."

"True." He knew that already. "What do you propose we do now?"

She eyed Parker's face. She felt deflated, but he was looking at her with pride and love. "Thanks for letting me do this."

"Do what?"

"Take the lead on this case." He was used to being the one in charge and she knew it must be killing him to hold back so much.

The sexy lines around his gray eyes creased in a sly grin. "You won the roll of the dice. Next time, will be my turn."

She laughed, knowing he would play that for all it was worth. She glanced at her watch. "Ralston and her team are probably still at Suzie Chan's. Since I'm calling the shots, I say we check out how they're doing."

"Not a bad idea."

CHAPTER NINETEEN

The evil sun was getting lower now, turning the sky to rosy colors and dropping the temperature, oh, maybe a degree. But the brutal rush hour traffic was so heavy, it took them forty-five minutes to drive the three miles to Chan's place.

The fleet of squad cars parked along the street told Miranda the warrant had come through.

Parker pulled up to the curb behind one of them.

Miranda peered out the window at a hacienda style building with the omnipresent clay tile roof and the omnipresent palm trees in the yard. "Nice place."

"And modest for what one would expect on a top chef's salary."

Maybe Suzie Chan was a hard-working woman who saved her money and just wanted to be respected by her boss. Maybe she just lost it with her one night. Crime of passion? No, there was too much planning involved for that theory. And a top chef might be the type of person who would know where to get a lucky bean plant.

Miranda was startled out of her thoughts when Parker opened the door for her.

She gave him a smirk. "You haven't done that on this trip."

His gaze was steady. "I didn't think you wanted me to in front of O'Toole."

She had to laugh. "You know me too well." She got to her feet and let him close the door behind her.

The chivalrous act was nice, but it didn't make up for the loss of cool air. Out of the car she felt herself start to sweat through her dark clothes and just as fast, felt the liquid evaporate into the dry air.

Ignoring the discomfort, she crossed to the sidewalk and eyed the decorative foliage along the house behind a row of scallop-shaped rocks. "Any of those look like lucky bean plants to you?"

Parker squinted in the sun at the plants. "More like Needlepoint Holly and Bush Sage."

60

How did he know that?

As they neared the house, Ralston spotted them from the driveway. Her dark blond hair looked like it might be getting bleached to flaxen under the sunrays, and there was a sheen of perspiration across her forehead, but her back was as straight as it was in her office.

"No *abrus precatorius* out here, unfortunately," she informed them as they reached her.

"So we see," Miranda said. "Anything in the house?"

"The warrant just came through. We're just now getting started." Ralston folded her arms, but she was smiling. "I'm glad you two decided to show up here after all."

"Things went faster than we expected," Miranda said.

"Did you get anything?"

She told the detective about the bodyguard and his possible connection to the case.

"Good work. I'm impressed. Now maybe you can help us find what we're looking for in there." Ralston nodded toward the house.

"We're happy to help," Parker said.

Ralston led them over to the CSI van where she handed them gloves and booties, which they donned on the front step.

They went inside to an ordinary looking, neutral-colored entrance with a narrow carpeted staircase. Off to one side Miranda could see a small living room with a tan velour couch, a recliner, a coffee table. On the walls were a few pictures that looked like family. Not much else.

CSIs, a man and a woman, were already combing the space.

"I've got two technicians in there," Ralston told them. "Another one upstairs and two outside. I'll get the master bedroom up there. How about you two take the kitchen?"

"We're on it." Miranda gave her a nod and followed Parker down the short hall.

They stepped into a well-lit space that was large relative to the size of the house, as you might expect a top-flight chef to prefer.

Suzie Chan's kitchen featured light wood cabinets topped with loud orange-and-green marble countertops. Ruffled curtains on the window picked up the color scheme. In the center of the room stood a big island with a large wooden turntable, atop which sat various-sized pitchers of similar hues filled with cooking utensils.

Everything was neat and tidy. As if she'd cleaned up before a long trip. Which she could have staged on purpose.

Miranda went immediately to the potted plant next to the sink near the window. She pulled the pot toward her with one gloved finger and studied the clusters of short green leaves. "Looks like some sort of herb."

Parker peered over her shoulder. "Oregano, I'd say."

She let out an exasperated huff. "Okay. Let's get started. We're looking for anything that might connect Suzie Chan to the crime." Not that she needed to tell him that.

They went through the cabinets first. Parker on the lower ones, Miranda on the upper ones. They found all sorts of pots and pans and dishes and cups and serving platters. In the drawers were odd-looking spoons and strange stirring tools and knives and all kinds of carving equipment. One drawer held a whole assortment of melon ballers.

While Parker tackled the island, Miranda went across the counter, searching behind cookbooks, a hook of browning bananas, decorative plates, sugar and flour canisters. She found a small notepad with some grease stains and hoped it had some notes on Suzie and her boyfriend's plan for their boss, but it was just recipes.

Miranda stopped to peek inside one of the canisters. It was brimful of flour. "She could have hidden something in here."

Parker rose from where he'd been crouching, interest on his face. "Not where one would normally look."

Was he thinking—? No. That was too gross. But maybe. "You'd better hope you didn't forget about it when you start to bake cookies."

He shot her a pained look at the grisly thought. "All three will need to go to the lab. Too easy to lose trace evidence if we empty them here."

"Right."

"I'll take them to the van. You keep searching. We're almost done." He started across the tile floor.

Almost done and they'd probably found zip. The AC was turned down and Miranda was sweltering. With a groan of irritation, she reached for the handle of the refrigerator, hoping she'd find a cold beer inside.

She gave the door a yank and peeked inside. "Oh, my God."

Suddenly the heat turned to icy sensations. They traveled up and down her arms, her neck, her spine—and it wasn't from the refrigerated air.

"What is it?"

She heard Parker come back in from the hall. Heard him set the canisters down on the island behind her, even though her ears were ringing with shock. She felt him come up behind her and peer over her shoulder.

She heard him murmur, "Good Lord."

But there it was.

Sitting on the top shelf in a jar of what looked like greenish pickle juice, staring straight at her—was Ambrosia Dawn's eyeball.

Her stomach felt like she was on the Ultimate Flight at Six Flags, but she forced a steady tone into her voice. "Guess we can forget about the flour."

CHAPTER TWENTY

Ralston was ecstatic when Miranda showed her the gruesome discovery. She pulled in her whole team to dust the entire kitchen and sent one of the CSIs back to the lab with the eyeball jar.

If Suzie Chan's fingerprints were on that jar, they'd have her. If they could locate her.

Miranda and Parker left the detective and her crew and headed for Sierra Vista to check in with their favorite cop. Assuming he was in by now.

He was.

They found O'Toole in his office, though not with his feet up this time. This time he had a half a watermelon on his desk and a melon baller in his hand. A glass bowl sat beside the melon, its bottom covered with mangled red fruit. The melon itself looked a little mutilated.

O'Toole glanced up at them as they entered, then studied the instrument in his hand. "The average human eye is twenty-four to twenty-six millimeters in diameter. About an inch. To put it another way, about two-thirds of a ping pong ball. Just the size of a standard melon baller."

Tired of the fooling around, Miranda tromped over to the single chair and plopped down into it. "Don't we already know this, Sergeant?"

"You have to do it just right." O'Toole pointed the baller at her then gestured toward his computer screen. "I've been watching some YouTube videos on it. I think I've just about got the technique mastered." He dug the melon baller into the red flesh of the melon. "You have to press down pretty hard. Then turn." He did so and pulled out a scoop. "There. Now it's the right size. See?" He held it up, then popped it into his mouth, chuckling.

Parker wasn't amused. "And your point is?"

O'Toole waved the baller. "If you're going to use this on an eye, you need some skill. And some strength. You have to know what you're doing."

"Or you'd have to watch a video and figure it out," Miranda said.

O'Toole narrowed an eye at her, his Irish complexion growing a tad rosy. "It would be better to have some experience." He scooped out another wad of melon and popped it in his mouth.

Miranda crossed her legs at the knee and bobbed the top leg up and down. She glanced casually around the room and noticed the showgirl calendar was gone and the walls were now bare. "Motive would be nice, too. And evidence. We think we have some."

O'Toole stopped chewing and stared at them. "You found something?" he asked, his mouth still full.

Parker gave Miranda a glance that said he wanted her to do the honors.

She grinned at him then turned triumphantly to the sergeant. "We found the eyeball."

She thought the man was about to choke. "You did? Where?"

"Suzie Chan's place."

He reached for a mug of what must have been hours old coffee and took a big gulp. "Who the hell is Suzie Chan?"

Miranda gave him a smile of disgust. "The victim's personal chef."

O'Toole glared at her. "You searched her house? We don't have a warrant—"

"Detective Kim Ralston got one for us after we spoke to Ambrosia Dawn's husband and sister and got enough evidence to justify one."

"Ralston?" O'Toole's face turned as red as the freckles on his husky arms as the implication of who would get credit on this case sank in.

Miranda put an innocent finger to her chin. "She's one of your detectives, isn't she? Very efficient lady." She couldn't help emphasizing the word "lady" just a tad.

Parker slid a thigh onto O'Toole's desk. "You could have kept up with our progress if you had answered your cell phone, Sid. But I'm sure you can read the details in the report Ralston will be filing."

O'Toole set his jaw and gave Parker a surly look. "Fill me in now, Parker."

Parker did, briefly. But even that had O'Toole's head spinning.

"Wait a minute." He wiped his hands on a napkin and put one to his forehead, trying to take it all in. "You're saying Ambrosia Dawn's personal chef colluded with one of her bodyguards to kill their employer?"

Parker nodded. "It looks like it, though we're not certain about the bodyguard. He seems to be out of town."

Miranda continued. "Ambrosia, pardon my French, was a downright bitch to the woman. Forced her to make dozens of melon balls for the staff at her rehearsals just to fuel her ego. And she was picky and demanding about how they were made. Suzie Chan is a top chef. Used to own a five-star restaurant in Santa Monica with her sister. *Her* ego couldn't take it. So she snapped."

Or at least that was what it looked liked at the moment.

"And you found the eye in this chef's refrigerator? In a pickle jar?"

"Yep. The lab is analyzing it now for prints."

O'Toole sat back, his face white with amazement. "We'll have to bring this chef in for questioning. Where is she?"

"She went to see her sister in Santa Monica. Ralston has been trying to contact her with no luck."

Parker got to his feet and put his hands in his pockets. "That's what we need you for now, Sid. Can you put out a BOLO?"

O'Toole stared blankly at the watermelon on his desk. "Yeah, but if she's in California, we might need to bring in the federal marshals."

For a long moment they all sat in silence, each of them pondering what it might mean to this case to bring in the Feds, until there was a sharp rap on the door.

Miranda jolted upright and turned to see Ralston stride into the room.

O'Toole gave her a scowl. "What are you doing here? Aren't you supposed to be conducting an investigation at a suspect's house?"

She straightened her shoulders and looked him in the eye. "Yes, sir. We're finished there."

"What did you find? Beside the—eyeball?"

"Nothing much." Ralston shot Miranda and Parker a smile, marched over to O'Toole's desk and popped one of the mutilated melon balls in her mouth. "Except that I just brought in Suzie Chan for questioning."

O'Toole jumped to his feet, his voice squeaking away. "You did? She's here? In the station?"

How'd she manage that, Miranda wondered as she caught the look of surprise on Parker's face. Ralston was some detective.

"That's what I said. We impounded her car. The CSIs are checking it for trace." She pretended to leave, then turned back. "Oh, and Chan's waiting for you in interview room C."

CHAPTER TWENTY-ONE

O'Toole's mood went from sullen to celebratory. By the time the four of them were making their way down the long hall to the interview room, he was downright giddy. And jabbering so much, Miranda wanted to kick him.

"Hot damn, Parker," he chuckled as he scurried along at his side. "You and Steele are good. I've had the Lieutenant on my ass since I got in today. All the casino owners are giving him grief. Their star performers are getting antsy. Everyone's afraid this investigation will impact the entire entertainment industry in Las Vegas. The publicists, the news hounds, even the mayor wants this case solved fast. And now we can do it." He made a gleeful, hee-hee sound. "Maybe I can even get out of that press conference Wells wants me to do. Hey, maybe you can do it, Parker."

Say what?

Parker looked really excited about that. "We haven't even spoken to the suspect yet, Sid."

"Sounds like an open and shut case from what you told me. So how about doing that press conference after we wrap up tonight?"

Parker shot him a glance of disgust. "I'd have to add it to our fee."

Sid just chuckled and gave him a good-buddy pat on the shoulder. "Sure, sure."

They reached the interview room and Miranda caught a glimpse of Suzie Chan sitting in there through the two-way mirror. Her own mood turned solemn and determined.

Somehow it was decided she and O'Toole would start the questioning while Parker and Ralston watched through the two-way. Miranda didn't like the arrangement, but she guessed it would give her needed experience.

Sure, she was game. But there were butterflies in her stomach as she followed the cop inside and heard the door click shut behind them.

Chan eyed them with tense irritation.

Avoiding her glare, Miranda took in the cramped space. One table. Three metal chairs. Concrete block walls painted a "friendly" blue. Security cameras.

Big mirror on one wall that was pretty obviously the two-way. Her throat went dry.

In the past, she had always been the one being questioned in tight little rooms like this and she suddenly felt claustrophobic. Could she pull off being on the other side? She had to. This case depended on nailing Chan.

She took a deep breath and settled herself in the chair opposite the woman.

Chan eyed her cautiously with narrow black eyes. She had a petite, small-boned frame, over which she wore jeans and a pink pullover with a Sissie Chan logo. Miranda took that to be her sister's restaurant. Her dark hair was cropped short and styled into spikes on top of her head. Long fingernails painted black. No jewelry except a pair of big, silver teardrop earrings. Her lips were a deep red. Her chin and nose and cheekbones chiseled and sharp. Despite the pink pullover, she gave off the air of a biker chick.

And she looked mad as hell.

O'Toole slipped into the seat beside Miranda. "Thank you for coming down here, Ms. Chan. I'm Sergeant O'Toole of Homicide and this is Ms. Steele, who is consulting on the case."

Chan gave them both a perfunctory nod, but seemed like she'd just as soon flip them off.

"Did the detective read you your rights, Ms. Chan?"

Chan bristled. "The woman who brought me in here?" she asked with a slight Asian accent. "Sure she did. What the fuck is going on?"

"Why don't you tell us?"

"How the hell should I know?" Her hands started waving in the air, her fingernails like falcon's talons. "I get home tonight and there's a bunch of cops crawling all over my house. And then one of them says she wants to bring me into the station. She says I'm a person of interest. What the fuck?"

Miranda could see the words "police brutality" on the tip of the woman's tongue. Words she herself had used a time or two when she'd been guilty as sin.

"You work for the singer, Ambrosia Dawn?" O'Toole asked in classic cop form.

"Of course, I do." She dropped her hands on the table and stared down at them. "Or I guess not any more. I was visiting my sister in Santa Monica when I heard what happened." She swiped at her face, her expression blank with disbelief.

Miranda watched her in silence.

"Sissie took me to have my nails done today, since I never get to." Chan waved a hand to illustrate her talons. "Then we went to a new place on Third Street to try the lamb sausage. We were discussing going back into business together. And just as we're paying the check, I hear on the news my boss is dead. Somebody killed her and left her body in the desert. So I tell Suzie I gotta go. I turn right around and head back." She made a circle in the air with her taloned finger. "I couldn't believe it. I stopped by my place to drop off my bags and was going to head over to the estate to find out what happened. But when

I get home, I find the pigs—I mean, the police—all over my place. And nobody wants to tell me why. Am I going to have to sue somebody or something?" She brought a fist down on the table.

Miranda shot O'Toole a warning look and turned to the suspect. "Calm down, Ms. Chan. We just want to ask a few questions to clarify things."

"Clarify what things?" Her black eyes flashed with emotion. "How can I calm down with police in my house? How can I calm down when I'm in the police station? You people are acting like I had something to do with it."

Again Miranda was silent and so was O'Toole.

Her eyes went wide. "Is that why I'm here? You think I had something to do with Abbey's death?"

"Nobody thinks anything," Miranda assured her. "Did Detective Ralston offer you anything to drink?" She could barely believe the words coming out of her own mouth. How did she wind up being the good cop here?

Chan bared her teeth like a caged animal. "No, I don't want any fucking thing to fucking drink. I want to know why I'm here."

Miranda took a deep breath. O'Toole wasn't saying anything so she guessed it was still her turn. "What sort of relationship did you have with your employer, Ms. Chan?"

She squinted her face cautiously. "It was okay."

"Just okay?"

Chan glared at Miranda. "What has that got to do with anything?"

O'Toole scooted his chair a little closer to the suspect and finally spoke. "Why don't you tell us how you feel about melon balls, Ms. Chan?" He was playing the bad cop, all right.

Her mouth opened, then shut. Then she leaned back, arms folded. "Are you going to tell me why I'm here or am I gonna have to call a lawyer?"

Miranda knew better than to reply to that. Technically Chan hadn't asked for counsel. Before she did, Miranda took a purposely noisy breath and then gave the woman what she hoped was a motherly smile. "Like I said, Ms. Chan. You're only here because we want to clarify a few things."

"Like what?"

"For example, we understand you prepared a special tea for your employer every night."

Chan sat back and folded her arms. Her face went a little pale as she realized the cops had been digging into the details of her life with Ambrosia Dawn. Her brows twisted with confusion. "Yeah. Special blend. I make it myself. So what?"

"What's in it?"

"Raspberry leaf. Mint. A little ginger. Why?"

"Sounds good." Miranda put her elbow on the table and leaned closer. "Now, when did you leave for your sister's?"

The woman tensed. Her gaze darted from Miranda to O'Toole and back again. "Tuesday night. Around nine, nine-thirty."

"So you didn't make the tea that night?"

Chan glanced at O'Toole then looked Miranda straight in the eye. "Yeah, I made it. She was at rehearsal so I left her the pot on a warmer. Why?"

Suzie Chan didn't look like a liar. No unnatural movements, no picking at her clothes or shifting of her eyes the way people do when they're making stuff up on the fly. Maybe she had her story all planned. Maybe she was better at this than most. Miranda remembered Ralston had found no priors when she did a background check on her. Something didn't feel right.

"Are you sure you left by nine-thirty?" she asked.

Chan's jaw went tight, her look even more cautious. "It might have been a little later. I was running behind."

"And what route did you take out of town?"

Her eyes flashed with temper. "The only route," she snapped. "I-15."

O'Toole pushed his chair back with a squeak and stood up. Time for the bad cop to go into action. "Ms. Chan, what made you decide to dump the body on the side of the road just south of the Last Chance casino?"

Miranda kept her face still, surprised the sergeant had suddenly come to life. It was a bold move. Bold enough that he just might get a confession.

But Suzie Chan glared at O'Toole, looking more shocked than if he had pulled out his service weapon and shot her. "Was that where Abbey was found? I hadn't heard that." She put her head in her hands. "Oh, my God."

"You were with your boyfriend Tuesday night, weren't you, Ms. Chan?"

Open-mouthed, Chan stared at O'Toole. "What boyfriend?"

"Did he leave town with you or did he just help you load the body into your car?"

"What?" Her face went wild. Her eyes began to fill. The tears were real.

Miranda cleared her throat. "You had a relationship with one of your employer's bodyguards, didn't you? Sean Scott?"

"Scottie? He was just a fuck buddy."

O'Toole glanced over at Miranda, as if to tell her he was going in for the kill. "Was he the one who carved out her eye with a melon baller? Did you show him how to do it?"

"What? What the fuck are you talking about?" Her hands balled into fists.

"A melon baller was found beside the body. Ambrosia Dawn's left eye was scooped out with it. The melon baller was just like the ones you used for your employer. But the eye wasn't at the crime scene. Guess where it was?"

Chan blinked at him in what looked like utter shock. "I have no idea." Her voice was a low croak.

"In your refrigerator."

Chan grabbed the sides of the table. She was reeling as hard as if the San Andreas Fault had just split a few states off the map. Her chest heaved once, twice. Then she steadied her shoulders and said. "I think I'll take that drink now. Got any vodka?"

Miranda got up. "Will coffee do?"

She gave her a quick nod without looking at her. "Black."

CHAPTER TWENTY-TWO

Back in the side room with the two-way, Miranda stood beside Parker and watched Suzie Chan pace back and forth, fingernails digging into her head.

"She's upset."

"Trying to come up with a story," Ralston commented.

O'Toole shook a finger at the window. "She won't be able to explain why the eye was in her fridge. Did the prints come back on that jar, yet?"

The corner of Ralston's lip turned up in a smirk. "You know they aren't that fast. Probably won't be until tomorrow."

O'Toole put his hands on his hips and sniffed. "What's the deal with the boyfriend?"

Ralston shrugged. "The victim forced him and Chan to break up a few weeks ago. That might be motive. Chan couldn't have gotten the body in the car without muscle. Would have brought him in, too, but right now he's AWOL."

O'Toole nodded.

Miranda folded her arms and caught Parker's eye. His expression told her he was thinking the same thing she was. She'd prefer to discuss it with him alone but she didn't have a choice right now.

"Are you wondering—?"

He nodded. "If things aren't a little too pat?"

O'Toole turned around and glared at both of them. "What do you mean? This is an open and shut case."

"Are you sure?" Miranda said.

"We've got ninety-nine percent of the evidence we need for a solid conviction. The DA is going to do the Happy Dance on the top of the Stratosphere once he sees it."

Parker's chest expanded as he took in a breath and fought back frustration. "We do want the right killer, don't we, Sid?"

Or did we just want to wrap up this case? Miranda thought, watching O'Toole's eyes flash hotter than Suzie Chan's.

"We've got the right killer, Parker. And I'm going to prove it." He stomped out of the room and down the hall to the men's room.

"I'll go get that coffee," Ralston said, following him out the door.

Miranda watched Suzie Chan sink back into her chair. The woman looked bewildered, lost. She knew that feeling. She thought about the melon baller, the building plastic, the tea, the eye in the refrigerator. "You know what, Parker?"

"What?"

"I smell a setup."

His jaw tight, that hard gunmetal look in his gray eyes, he nodded. "I do, too."

CHAPTER TWENTY-THREE

Five minutes later Miranda was sitting across from Suzie Chan again while O'Toole paced back and forth in the small space.

Finally he stopped. "Tell me again about Sean Scott?"

Chan looked up at him as if coming out of a stupor. "Scottie? What about him?"

"Ambrosia Dawn forced you to break up with him, didn't she?" He put his hand to his chest and made a face like he was appalled.

Chan lifted a shoulder like she didn't care. "Yeah. So what?"

"That must have really made you mad. Him too. Was it his idea to kill her?"

Those black eyes simmered like coal. "I didn't kill her."

O'Toole's chair squeaked across the linoleum as he pulled it out and sat. He put both arms on the table and leaned in. "How do you explain that eyeball, Ms. Chan? The one in the pickle jar in your refrigerator?"

"Pickle jar?" The poor woman looked like she was going to puke. "I can't explain it. It wasn't there when I left. I have no idea how it got there."

"That jar is in the lab right now. It's going to come back with your fingerprints on it. What are you going to say then?"

"It can't come back with my fingerprints. I never touched it. I never saw it."

O'Toole didn't say anything. He just waited. And while he did, he slipped Miranda a glance that said, "We've almost got her." Miranda wasn't so sure.

Then the dam broke.

"Okay," Suzie cried in a voice like a child. "I hated Ambrosia Dawn. She was a goddamn bitch and everyone knows I thought so. I couldn't stand working for her. And maybe I would have liked to kill her at times, but I didn't. That's why I went to my sister's. I wanted to quit my job and go back into business with her."

O'Toole's face fell. So much for that confession he knew was coming. "You know, Ms. Chan," he said, summoning up all the patience in his being, "all this would be easier on you if you just tell us the truth."

Eyes glaring, Chan looked like she was about to spit in his face. "I am telling you the truth."

"The DA might be willing to make a deal. It could mean a lighter sentence."

Miranda bristled. She hated that bullshit when cops used to shovel it at her. "Ms. Chan. Do you have anything that would prove your innocence? Anything at all?"

Suzie Chan looked around the room, as if searching for an answer that wasn't there. She began to blink. Tears formed in her eyes. Again they were real tears, not fake.

"I didn't kill her," she said again. "I didn't kill anybody. I couldn't do that."

O'Toole slid his chair back and rose. "We're going to have to book you, Ms. Chan."

Panic flashed across her face. She put a hand to her head. "Wait. Wait. Maybe I do have something. I stopped in Primm for gas."

"So?"

"I have the receipt. It's got the date and time I was there. I keep it for taxes."

"Where?"

"My wallet. It's in my purse. Your detective has it."

"A gas station receipt?"

"Yeah, yeah. Lucky Dog Gas. Right off Exit One. Get my purse. I'll show it to you."

O'Toole drummed his fingers on the table. "How do we even know the receipt is yours?"

"It's got my credit card on it. You can run it." She was sounding desperate now.

O'Toole lifted a brow. "The last four digits?"

Once again Suzie Chan looked like a lost and frightened little girl. Then her face brightened. "Security cameras."

"What?"

"Security cameras," she repeated. "Lucky Dog has to have them. I went inside for a Snickers bar. I should be on the video at the cash register."

Evidently Chan watched crime shows.

Miranda waited for O'Toole's expression to change.

It did, right on cue, his cheeks glowing almost fuchsia with frustration. But if he didn't check it out, the DA would skewer him. And no doubt Chan would sue the department.

He got to his feet. "We'll be right back."

Maybe, maybe not.

"Sergeant?" Chan said as O'Toole reached the door.

He turned back. "What is it, Ms. Chan?"

"In the meantime, I want a lawyer."

CHAPTER TWENTY-FOUR

Ralston had already gone to get Chan's purse by the time Miranda and O'Toole were back in the two-way room. Parker was wearing a granite look that Miranda couldn't read, but she assumed he was angry at the sergeant for not listening to them.

Miranda didn't think that mattered much. They would have had to go through the motions anyway.

A minute later Ralston appeared, the receipt in question in her hand. "Chan's right. Look." She handed the paper to O'Toole. He read it while Miranda and Parker peered over his shoulder.

"Tuesday's date," Parker said. "Time 10:34 p.m."

"How far away is Primm?"

O'Toole shook his head, looking dazed. "A little over forty miles. It's right on the border."

"In decent traffic, it takes forty-five minutes to get there." Ralston folded her arms and looked at Chan. She was sitting calmly, her hands folded. She knew she had won. "Even if she was zooming no way she could get there at ten-thirty. Earliest TOD estimate was eleven."

Miranda couldn't look at the woman any more. "Dr. Eaton told us it was probably closer to one."

With a groan, O'Toole handed the receipt back to Ralston. "Don't tell me you hot shot detectives are buying this?"

Miranda lifted her palms. "It's an alibi, O'Toole."

"Bullshit. This has got to be fake. Maybe doctored with Wite-Out or something. Hell, maybe she Photoshopped it and printed it on her sister's printer."

Ralston rubbed her face. It was getting late and she'd put in a lot of hours. "Why bother? Why not leave the country? Why come back on her own?"

"Maybe because she believed she had a rock solid alibi."

Miranda had had enough. "She did tell you to check out the videos. Would be pretty hard to doctor those."

"Probably thinks we won't bother. We'll see about that. I know someone in the sheriff's office down in Primm who owes me a favor." O'Toole headed out the door and down the hall.

Miranda followed with Parker at her side.

Ralston shook her head and turned in the other direction. "I've got paperwork to file. You'll have to excuse me."

She was probably going to find something to kick.

CHAPTER TWENTY-FIVE

Back they went to O'Toole's crappy little office.

Parker got an extra chair, and he and Miranda made themselves semi-comfortable while they listened to the sergeant dial his buddy and call in his marker.

O'Toole hung up and said his buddy had a buddy at the gas station, and they might have video results in about an hour since they knew the time in question. He looked down at the watermelon going warm on his desk. "Either of you want any of this?"

Parker suppressed a grimace. "No, thank you, Sid."

Miranda just scowled at him.

He got some paper towels, picked up the mess and carried it down the hall. Probably was going to leave it in the break room for his coworkers. Real thoughtful.

She turned to Parker and spoke in a low voice. "I hate that Chan has to sit in the interview room while we do this."

"The alternative is for Sid to book her."

"Yeah."

"What's your feeling about Chan?" Parker asked after O'Toole was well out of earshot.

Miranda got up and took a few steps. It was hard to pace in the small area. She scratched at her hair. "I didn't see any subtle signs of lying. Her story is plausible."

"And so?"

Might as well just say it. "I think she's innocent, Parker."

"She seemed to be telling the truth."

"Which means we're back to square one."

O'Toole came back, and they waited around and paced the floor and drank coffee for over an hour. It was getting pretty late by then and Miranda wondered if the officer with the gas station buddy had over promised. He could have gotten another call. Maybe his friend wasn't at the store or he couldn't get hold of him. Maybe the clerk on duty was uncooperative.

Maybe they weren't finding anything.

She was wondering if Suzie Chan was going to have to spend the night in the pokey when O'Toole's phone rang.

He picked it up and put it to his ear. "O'Toole. Yeah?…Yeah?…Is that so?" His expression was as flat as a dusty desert plain. "Can you shoot a screenshot or something over to me?" Pause. "That'll do. Thanks."

He hung up and stared at his cell.

"Bad news?" Miranda asked.

"We'll see in about ten minutes." With a jerky motion he got up from his desk and left.

Miranda gave Parker a shrug. "Guess he needs some fresh air."

Parker rose and put his hands in his pockets. He stood staring at the blank wall, since there was no showgirl calendar now. Miranda couldn't tell if he was pondering the case or whether to punch Sid in the nose when he returned.

Must have been the former. Parker didn't move when O'Toole returned with a cup of coffee in his hand. He settled himself into his chair and turned to the computer. He did a few clicks, stared at the screen and gave a low grunt.

"What is it, Sid?" Parker's voice was that smooth magnolia that right now was camouflaging a powder keg of irritation.

O'Toole wagged his fingers over his shoulder. "Come over here and see." He sounded like a little boy who'd just struck out in his first little league game.

Miranda was tired of the testosterone match. A woman who might be innocent was sitting alone in a room wondering what her fate would be. She got up, marched up behind the sergeant and peered at the screen.

"Wow. That's a good shot."

"Good resolution. Maybe too good."

Parker's voice was heavy behind her. "That's her all right."

"Sure is."

Suzie Chan stood at the gas station counter, making her purchase and looking like she was in a hurry. But it couldn't have been because she wanted to escape a crime scene. The time on the photo read 10:42 p.m. Eight minutes after she'd purchased the gas.

Miranda blew out a breath. "She's innocent."

O'Toole stiffened. "This doesn't prove it."

"It gives her a solid alibi, Sid. You can't hold her."

"Yeah, I guess not."

Miranda waited for O'Toole to go tell Suzie Chan she was free to go, but he didn't move. She was about to tell him to move his butt when Ralston knocked on the door and walked in without waiting for an answer.

Her eyes looked a little wild. "I've got Cameron Forest on the phone, sir. The media hounds were arriving in a TV van just as I left Chan's place. The story must be all over the news."

"I'll talk to him. Wait. Put him on speaker."

She nodded and pressed a button. "Mr. Forest? I've got you on speaker. My sergeant and the Parker Agency investigators are here."

The Elvis-like voice scratched through the air. "They are? Good. I just want to know what's going on. I heard someone was arrested regarding my wife's case."

"We've brought someone in for questioning yes, but—"

"Suzie Chan? Our personal chef?"

Ralston rolled her eyes, obviously irritated at how much detail the press had already spread. A sentiment Miranda could relate to. "Yes, sir. But it's an ongoing investigation, as you're well aware. There's nothing we can say about it now. I'm sorry but—"

"Can you at least confirm that she's been charged?"

"Mr. Forest, I'm not at liberty to—"

"What are you saying? Are you going to let her go free?" There was panic in his voice.

"That's undetermined as of this time, Mr. Forest." True for Ralston. She hadn't seen the screenshot.

"But what if she isn't safe? What if she wants to come back here? She must be insane. Can you guarantee my safety? My son's safety? My staff?"

"Sir, we're doing ev—"

"Oh, my God. I'm meeting with everyone involved in the show tomorrow afternoon at the casino to make a statement. What do I tell them?"

Forest was going berserk and Miranda couldn't blame him.

She watched the muscles of Ralston's neck strain with tension. "Please, sir. Calm down. We're being as thorough as we possibly can. I assure you—"

"How can I calm down? My wife is dead. You think you found her killer. What am I supposed to do?"

O'Toole snatched the phone out of the detective's hand. "Mr. Forest. This is Sergeant Sid O'Toole. I'm in charge of the case. Let me assure you that we will do everything in our power to find your wife's killer. I'll see to it myself personally."

Oh, yeah?

There was a long pause, some heavy breathing. At last Forest spoke again. Somehow O'Toole's words had done the trick. "All right, Sergeant. Please work as quickly as you can."

"We will." O'Toole disconnected. He turned and glared at the computer screen as if he were about to smash it in. "Jiminy Cricket on a hot pile of steaming shit. Now I've got the husband on my ass as well as my boss and the publicist and the casino owners and the media."

Ralston snatched her phone back. "Don't forget the mayor."

O'Toole opened his mouth just as Ralston caught sight of his computer screen. "That's Suzie Chan, all right."

"Yep," Miranda said.

Ralston looked rattled. "We've got the wrong person."

The sergeant raised a finger as if he were about to chew her out for that.

Before he could, Miranda pointed to the folder on his desk. "There are plenty of people left to talk to in that file. Didn't Elvis say they were meeting tomorrow?"

"A perfect time to set up interviews," Parker said. "They'll all be together, probably backstage at the casino."

"The killer could be one of them," Miranda agreed. "Just hiding in plain sight. If we surprise them, maybe they won't have time to make up much of a story." At least they'd be bound to pick up some more clues.

His normal color returning, O'Toole rubbed his chin. "You could be right. If Forest was talking about the whole crew, there will probably be fifty or more people there. It will take a while to talk to them all."

"I'm sure Lieutenant Wells will be happy to spare some personnel, sir," Ralston offered.

"Okay." O'Toole pointed at his detective. "Talk to him. Get those extra officers pulled in for tomorrow. And find out exactly when that meeting is."

"Yes, sir." Ralston turned and marched out of the room.

"You and Ms. Steele up for this, Parker?"

"Of course."

"Good. Go home and get some sleep. I'll call you tomorrow and let you know the details."

Miranda stared at the sergeant and could almost feel Parker's shock. Rude as he was being, O'Toole was finally taking some initiative on this case. Instead of commenting, they simply nodded and left the room.

As they made their way down the hall, she muttered to Parker under her breath. "Guess I'm not in charge anymore."

"High time Sid took some responsibility."

They went back to the hotel room, hit the showers and sank into bed. It had been such a long, discouraging day, it was all Miranda could do to wrap her arms around her husband and fall into a deep sleep.

CHAPTER TWENTY-SIX

The next morning, Miranda woke up and blinked at the clock.

"That can't be right," she mumbled, her mouth feeling gummy. The stupid thing said nine-thirty.

Parker turned over beside her. "We didn't get to bed until past one."

She groaned, remembering they hadn't found Ambrosia Dawn's killer last night. And they were no closer to finding the culprit than when they'd arrived. A depressing thought to wake up to.

"I need coffee before I can comment on that."

"Not yet." He reached for her, traced a finger over her lips.

She had to grin. "I know what you want."

"Do you?" He drew her to him in a long, lazy kiss.

It was nice. Classic Parker seduction and she longed to give into it, but she pulled away.

He pulled her back. "Are you sure?"

Oh, she was tempted. Just the lure of those sexy gray eyes were enough to draw her in, not to mention the strength of his arms, the warmth of his body. But she managed to resist. "Too much to do. We're so far behind."

He gave her a look of mock disappointment, then chuckled. "Agreed."

But he lay there and watched her greedily as she pulled on some jeans and a T-shirt and raked her fingers through her unruly hair.

She came over and sank down on the bed to pull on sneakers. "You know who I've been thinking about?"

"Who?" He ran his fingers over her arm, making her a little dizzy.

She reached for his hand, waited a bit then said it cautiously. "Delta Langford."

His hand dropped to the mattress. She watched the lines furrow in his brow. Delta Langford had been mixed up with one of the most painful episodes in Parker's life. The brutal murder of his first love when he was only eighteen.

But he shook off the unspoken emotion she'd aroused, rose, and pulled on a pair of jeans. He always wore the designer type, and Miranda loved the way they hugged his thigh muscles and backside.

"Sisters?" he asked as if the former case had had no effect on him as he crossed to her and extended an arm.

She let him pull her up, eyed his bare muscled chest and reconsidered his lovemaking idea for a moment as sort of a makeup for bringing back a past she knew he'd rather forget. Later, she promised herself, as she had promised him already.

"Yeah. A jealous sister. Didn't it sound like Blythe had a lot to be envious of? Ever since she and 'Abbey' were kids together?"

Parker was touched to watch his wife approach the subject of Delta Langford so delicately. Delta had crossed his mind earlier and as usual, he had ignored his buried feelings. He had pushed the death of his first love out of his mind long ago, but still carried the pain deep in his heart. Miranda understood that. She carried her own scars and knew what it was like to bear them for years. It was another bond they shared.

He had also enjoyed watching her drink him in with her eyes. He wanted to make love to her now, to express that deep bond between them. But she was right about getting to work. He wouldn't tempt her any longer.

He went to the closet to pull on a knit shirt. "Ms. Star's narrative struck me that way when we spoke to her. An older sibling everyone 'worshipped,' as she put it." He moved into the living room area, picked up a phone and dialed room service. Eggs Benedict this morning. And strong coffee. That would bolster his wife's strength and perhaps soothe her wounded ego after last night's defeat.

Miranda sank down onto the thick couch, hoping the breakfast Parker had just ordered would get here soon. She wanted to move. "Ambrosia was popular and into everything. Blythe didn't say so, but I got the impression she wasn't."

Parker nodded and pulled the curtains back to reveal another hot, bright sunny day. Vaguely Miranda wondered if it would get to a million degrees today.

"And she was a singer, too. Small time. She couldn't get her career off the ground while Ambrosia went on to outrageous fame and fortune. And then she ends up having to work for her."

Parker sat and rubbed the back of his neck. "You could be onto something. On the other hand, many others could have been jealous enough of Ambrosia Dawn to kill her."

He was right. "Or just angry at her. She sounds like a real bitch. People like that don't pick on just one staff person. They pick on several of them."

"Unfortunately." Parker blew out a breath. "Delta Langford had some serious emotional problems. Blythe struck me as more self-possessed."

"Yeah, but maybe she's just a good actress."

"Could be."

There was a knock at the door and Parker opened it to a waiter pushing a white-clothed table laden with delicious smelling food. And coffee.

As soon as he'd gotten things settled and tipped the guy, she rushed for a cup.

He snatched it out of her hand and poured from the silver chalice. "Sit."

She shook her head at him. "You're such a Southern gentleman."

He handed her the cup. "It's in my blood, if you recall."

"I do." She slurped it greedily.

Before Parker could pour himself one, his cell rang. It was O'Toole. After they exchanged a look of surprise, Parker answered.

He spoke to the sergeant a moment, then hung up and put the phone in his pocket. "The meeting is at three at the casino's big stage."

"Long time to wait."

He nodded. "We have research we can do. But why don't we go down to the gaming area a little before the meeting and see what we can see."

"Snooping around in a casino? Sounds like fun." They could spend a few hours digging up what they could on the names in the case file, then head downstairs.

Just what she thought they should do. Once again, they were in sync.

CHAPTER TWENTY-SEVEN

After an unproductive morning of research and a light lunch, Miranda headed out with Parker. As the glass elevator whooshed past floor after floor on its way down to the lobby, she could feel the knots in her stomach tighten.

But it wasn't from the rush.

Their first solid suspect had turned out to be innocent. Now they had dozens of other folks to interview and little information on any of them. And the super efficient Sergeant O'Toole had taken over the investigation. Even though she agreed with Parker it was something O'Toole should have done to start with, she couldn't help wondering if they were ever going to solve their first case.

And if they couldn't find a viable suspect, if the case went cold, what would that mean for this enterprise? If Ambrosia Dawn's killer wasn't found soon, there would be outrage in the media. Nationwide. Would the Parker Agency get blamed? They'd probably have a hard time getting another client. Would Parker cut his losses and call it quits before their reputation had been damaged too much?

Well, that just wasn't going to happen. Miranda wouldn't let it. This was her life. Her destiny. What she was meant to do. Besides, she couldn't stand the idea of the famous singer's murder going unsolved. Even if the woman had been a total bitch.

She stole a glance at Parker and wondered if he was thinking the same thing. With the alteration of their plans, he'd changed from his casual breakfast attire, his fine form now clad in a deep charcoal suit, a white tailored shirt, and a red silk tie embossed in a classy pattern. His skin was tan from being outside yesterday, and with his salt-and-pepper hair and the distinguished lines in his gorgeous face, he was hotter than the desert sun.

But though they had been completely in sync a few moments ago, she couldn't read his thoughts.

Miranda had changed, too. Selecting dark slacks, black alligator belt, and a gray silk sleeveless blouse with lots of buttons and fake pockets Coco had picked out for her. Plus she had her thick dark hair pulled back in a roll at the nape of her neck, a style Mackenzie and Wendy had tried on her over the holidays.

Since everyone else would be casually attired, they were going to look pretty intimidating at the interviews this afternoon. She hoped that would get them some answers.

She thought again of what she'd found in that refrigerator yesterday. "Ambrosia Dawn's killer would have to have known about Suzie Chan and the melon balls to set her up. Everyone at the rehearsal would fit that bill."

"He'd have to have access to Chan's house, too."

"Or a way to break in and cover it up. There was no sign of forced entry at the house, was there?"

"No." Parker grew silent, perhaps calculating the odds of finding a killer among fifty plus people.

Before they reached the ground floor, her cell buzzed in her pocket. She pulled it out, hoping it was a text from Mackenzie or Wendy. It wasn't.

"Well, look at that."

"What is it?"

Miranda grinned. "Ralston managed to dig up a photo of Sean Scott."

"The bodyguard who was dating Suzie Chan?"

"Uh huh."

Parker leaned over to view the screen she angled toward him and they both took a look.

Must have been a resume photo from the polished look of it. The guy had a lady-killer smile, with dimpled cheeks and bright white teeth. Blond crew cut. Deep tan. Tight baby blue knit shirt over acres of muscles. The shirt matched a pair of eyes gleaming with self-confidence.

"Looks like a bodybuilder."

Parker stroked his chin. "I wonder if he'll come back to town."

She stared at him. "Are you still thinking he's involved?"

"You never know."

"True, but if they were just casual sex partners, like Suzie Chan said, he probably thought it was more of a joke when Ambrosia Dawn threatened to fire them if they didn't break up."

Parker nodded. "Perhaps. Or perhaps he didn't like being told what to do with his personal life."

"Still, murder someone because of that? Awfully risky."

"Some people thrive on risk." He eyed her closely. Was he talking about her? "If he was close to Chan, he might know about the tea she prepared for the singer."

Good point. "He'd know about how Chan felt about the melon balls, too. Maybe we should check out Scott's place again."

"If he's back, he should be at Cameron Forest's meeting this afternoon."

"True." And it would be better to surprise him there, Miranda decided, feeling the pull in her stomach as the elevator reached the lobby and began to slow.

"I suggest we get our bearings down here and see what we can see."

"As good a plan as any at this point," she agreed.

The doors opened and they stepped out and strolled—at tourist pace—past the sparkling waterfall, the golden stairways, the modern art shapes. They bypassed the halls leading to the spas and restaurants and headed for the gaming area.

As soon as they stepped into the massive space, Miranda's jaw dropped. She had been in small bars with a poker machine or two before and places where there was under-the-table gambling, but she'd never seen a whole floor of them.

They strolled over a gaudy carpet through a huge, dimly lit space that rang out with the happy electronic tunes of a multitude of slot machines. Row upon row of them, five-deep. In fact, it was the machines that provided most of the illumination. Their bright panels and flashing wheels could probably light up a small town in Nebraska.

The air hinted at a flowery scent, something piped through the air ducts to camouflage the smoke, no doubt.

To one side were flashing billboards advertising Keno and Poker. Against another wall was a block of maybe a dozen big screen TVs, playing every sports station in the world. Rows of lighted numbers were displayed and cashiers were on hand to take your bets.

Miranda leaned toward Parker and whispered. "A person could lose an entire trust fund in one afternoon here."

"And some of them do."

She eyed him cautiously. "I know your taste for risk."

He chuckled. "It's you I'm worried about. Shall I give you an allowance?"

There was a time when a remark like that would have her throwing the man flat on his back, sexy ace investigator or not. Since she left her abusive husband over thirteen years ago, it was a point of pride that she had earned her own keep and she'd never take money from any man. Least of all gambling money. But she'd gotten used to the way Parker would spoil her on occasion.

So now she just gave him a cynical laugh. "If you recall, I know how to pinch pennies."

He returned a knowing smile. "I do."

They passed by a wide block of windows revealing a long hall plastered with artwork. Across from them were blackjack tables. Dozens of them.

It wasn't quite noon, so there hadn't been many players at the slot machines, though some diehards were on their stools, attention focused on the flashing images before their faces. There were only a few folks at the blackjack tables as well. About three tables had a decent amount of players.

They strolled toward them casually. Suddenly Parker stopped and nodded toward a column.

Miranda stepped over to it and he followed. He rested a hand against it as if he were about to kiss her.

"Are you getting frisky again?" she grinned.

He bent his head and brushed his mouth against her cheeks. Then his lips were at her ear. "Very slowly, look over at the second table on your left."

She waited for him to pull back, then smiling coyly as if she were seducing him, she cast a nonchalant glance in the direction he described. She almost dropped the flirting ruse when she spotted him.

Sitting at the far end of the third blackjack table from where they stood was a good-looking young man in a tight black knit top and jeans. He had a winning smile, a muscular build, and a blond crew cut.

Sean Scott.

Miranda turned back to Parker and slipped her arms around his neck. She pulled him to her and whispered. "He looks just like the photo Ralston sent."

"He does indeed."

"Maybe we've got a lucky streak going."

"Perhaps."

"We need to watch him," she whispered, her senses coming alive.

"Do you know how to play blackjack?"

She shook her head. "I only bet on games I know I can win. You?"

"My father taught me when I was a boy. I haven't played in years, but I'm sure it's just like riding a bike."

"For you, probably."

"I'll go over to his table. Why don't you find another spot to observe from."

She looked around and located a slot machine not far away.

"I'll be over there." She gave him a kiss on the cheek. "Good luck. And don't lose this nice shirt."

"I don't intend to."

Miranda watched Parker head for the table and take a seat. The dealer, a big man who reminded her of a bouncer she'd once befriended in Sheboygan, acknowledged Parker's presence with a nod. When the bouncer-dealer finished his hand, she watched Parker exchange some cash with the man. Bouncer slid a stack of chips over to him.

Scott stayed put.

Bouncer began to deal the cards. Miranda would have loved to sneak a peek over Parker's shoulder, but they weren't here to play.

She strolled around to one of the nearby banks of slot machines and pretended to shop for a lucky one. She sat down at the one on the end and peeked around it. Perfect view.

Scott was still playing. So was Parker.

She studied the machine's display. It wanted money up front, the greedy thing. Suppressing a groan, she stuffed her hand into her pocket and drew out a buck. She slipped it into the machine.

It greeted her with a friendly little ditty.

She tensed. Did Scott hear that? She peeked around the machine's side again. Scott and Parker were studying their cards intently. Whew.

She turned back to the machine. What now? A large square button flashed madly at her. "Spin," it demanded. She guessed that was it. Here goes a dollar, she thought.

The lights began to flash and, well, spin. Round they went for a while then they stopped. Nothing. "Play Again?" another flashing button suggested.

Not much choice. She hit it.

Once more there was flashing and spinning and some more carnival music. After what seemed like five minutes it stopped. Wishing the machine would be quiet, again she peeked around its side.

Still at the table. How much was Parker going to risk?

Pursing her lips, she hit the "Play Again?" button once more. Once again, the images flashed and spun. Once again, the video game tune played.

And then the numbers stopped, aligned. Seven. Seven. Seven.

Huh?

The whole machine started flashing and beeping and playing more music—much louder music than before.

"Shhh!" Miranda said to it. But the thing just kept on.

Then a mechanical voice said "Winner! Winner! Winner!"

Miranda got to her feet. "Shut up!" she told the thing.

Ignoring her, it spat out a slip of paper. Miranda snatched it up and stared at it. Fifteen hundred dollars.

Suddenly she felt a tap on her shoulder. She jumped—almost up to the rafters above—and spun around. "What?"

A short, wrinkled lady with copper-colored hair teased into a bouffant stood hands on hips, glaring at her. She looked at least seventy. "That's my machine, missy."

"What?" Miranda said again.

"That's my machine. I've been playing it all morning. I just got up to go to the john." She had a shocking pink T-shirt with three aces on the front on her skinny body and matching slacks. She shook her head and her pink hoop earrings bobbed against her face.

This had to be a joke, right? "Look, lady. All I did was—"

The woman reached out a bony finger and poked Miranda in the shoulder. "Sweetie, that's my machine and my money. I primed the pump." Her words were slurred. She'd had a little too much to drink.

Miranda gritted her teeth. "I didn't see your name on it."

The woman's hollow cheeks puffed out and turned from pale to a blush red. "Do you want me to get a manager, honey?"

Miranda wanted to smack the woman, most of all for causing such a commotion. She stole another glance over at the blackjack table. Uh, oh. Scott was gone and Parker was getting up from his seat. She couldn't stand here jawing with this crazy lady.

The woman poked her again. "That's my machine," she said again, almost shouting. She looked like she was about to scream.

Miranda glanced back at the blackjack table. Parker was on the move. Crap.

She turned to the lady and shoved the ticket into her hand with a grunt. "Here."

The woman looked down at her hand, then up at her, suddenly contrite. "Are you sure?"

"Don't spend it all in one place." And Miranda spun on her heels and hurried away. Sheesh, what a sore loser some people are.

CHAPTER TWENTY-EIGHT

Miranda caught sight of Parker heading for a row of glass doors along the far wall, away from the noisy slots. Sean Scott was about fifty feet in front of him.

She hustled in that direction.

Up ahead she saw Scott duck down a yawning opening between a spa and a lounge. Parker followed. As he turned in, she saw him spot her.

He gave her an almost imperceptible nod.

She nodded back and hurried to catch up. At last she reached the opening.

It was marked "Old World Charm Alley," and as she stepped into it, she saw it was done up like a street in a medieval European village. Underfoot were fake cobblestones. Overhead were lanterns that looked like they were lit by real flames, though Miranda was sure that was an illusion.

Shops that appeared centuries old lined the streets with quaint window displays and signs over their doors written in script. The Town Tavern. The Village Boutique. Ye Old Nail Salon. No need to give up modern comforts just because you were pretending to live in the long ago past.

A mid-size throng roamed about, groups of tourists meandering in and out of the shops, others pausing to study the window displays.

The air was cooler here and less smoky, and as she followed the curve of the "road," she caught the scent of baked goods coming from a place marked "La Patisserie." Laughing to each other, a group of teens ambled through the entrance. Trying to appear casual, Miranda strolled alongside a perfume shop across the way, where a middle-aged couple looked like they'd just had a fight. Maybe he'd gambled the rent money. A man in a suit hurried past her in the opposite direction.

Late for a business meeting? Or rushing for another spin at the roulette table?

Craning her neck, at last she spotted Parker. He was standing before a haberdashery window, hands in his pockets, looking like he was just here to browse.

She stepped up beside him and he smiled at her as if she'd surprised him.

"There you are, darling. What do you think of that one?" He pointed to one of the hats.

"Not your style." She gave him a kiss on the cheek, took his hand and leaned in.

"Scott's a few stores ahead. He seems to be shopping."

"Hmm," Miranda said. "Seems pretty free and easy with his money."

Parker nodded. "He lost a good bit at the table."

She wasn't going to ask what Parker lost. "He can't earn that much as a bodyguard. Makes me wonder if he doesn't have a sugar mama."

"Or if he's in debt up to his ears."

She had a thought. "Maybe he was trying to get money out of Ambrosia."

"Perhaps." Parker turned his head to glance at the reflection of the opposite shop in the window just as Scott emerged from its doorway and turned down the hall. He was carrying a single red rose.

What was he doing with that? Miranda wondered.

"There he goes."

"On him."

"Let's stroll together." He squeezed her hand, holding her back.

She tossed him a strained smile over her shoulder. Okay, he was right. It wouldn't do to tackle the guy like a linebacker.

She swung his hand between them and strolled like a giddy teenager in love as they passed another bakery and a beauty salon.

A young couple stood before the window of a candy shop, arms around each other, giggling and pointing at a big chocolate heart on display. Newlyweds, Miranda assumed.

She and Parker kept going. The crowd began to thin. After a few more yards, they rounded another curve.

They were nearing the stage area now. Up ahead large double doors formed a circular entrance with a boldly lit marquee spelling out, "The Diva Theater." Colorful posters on the walls announced who would be onstage.

Apparently they also offered magic acts, comedians, and a variety of performers. But the headliner was Ambrosia Dawn. Her sign was still up. Apparently the casino hadn't decided what to do to fill her spot yet.

Ahead of them Scott slowed.

They slowed.

He turned back and glanced at the bakery as if he were considering picking up a pastry. Miranda caught her breath. With a firm tug that gave the illusion of an invitation, Parker led her over to the jewelry shop window.

Breathing in and out she stared at the display of necklaces, not seeing anything. Had Scott made the tail? That was all they needed.

As nonchalantly as she could, she smiled and pretended to straightened Parker's collar. "I did tell you diamonds are my birthstone, didn't I?"

She risked a quick glance over his shoulder.

Good thing she did. At that moment, Scott ducked into a little side room that looked like a ticket booth.

"What is it?" Parker murmured.

"He—"

Just then one of the theater doors opened and a figure appeared. Tall, long blond hair, dressed in tight jeans and a black knit top with a pink sweater thrown over it.

Instantly Miranda recognized her. Her brows shot up.

"Miranda, what is it?"

The woman glanced around the area with quick, tentative motions, like a deer stepping into a clearing where hunters might lurk.

Miranda hid her head behind Parker. If she recognized them, they were done for. She spoke as softly as she could. "Scott just ducked into a side room. And Blythe Star just came out of the theater."

"Did she see us?"

"I don't think so. Not yet."

Miranda risked another quick peek and caught Star crossing the floor with long, graceful strides. She stepped into the side room Scott had disappeared a moment ago.

Blackjack.

"She just scampered into the room where Scott is."

Instinct taking over, she released Parker's hand and tiptoed across the hall to the door. Her blood surging with anticipation, she shot Parker a glance.

He scowled at her. He thought it was too risky.

She frowned back at him. Wasn't she supposed to be in charge? Turning away from Parker, she inched as close as she dared to the opening and listened hard. Soft moaning met her ears. Then kissy noises.

"Oh, baby—"

"I missed you—"

"Me, too. Oh. Oh!"

Then came stand-up bump-and-grind noises, accented with an occasional mumble.

"Mmm."

"Yes."

"Not there. Here."

"Here?"

"Yes. Oh, yes!" That one was a muffled shout.

Miranda blinked in shock. First Suzie Chan, then Blythe Star? This guy really got around.

An older couple passed by and strolled over to the theater to study the signs. Miranda glanced back at Parker. He was caught in front of the jewelry store, unable to leave without looking suspicious. He pointed to his ear.

Miranda lifted her hands and shook her head, indicating she couldn't hear much. Not words, anyway.

He gave her another scowl, this one sterner.

He had a point. It was getting really dicey to stand here. And she wasn't going to get any more information.

He nodded down the hall in the opposite direction.

She nodded back and while the couple was absorbed in the posters, they made a break for it.

They met in the middle of the hall, locked hands again, and as if they were about to collect on a winning lottery ticket, hurried back down the rustic fake medieval street to the entrance.

Back in the main area, they ducked into the first spot they found, a coffee shop.

CHAPTER TWENTY-NINE

At a plush booth overlooking the walkway, Miranda and Parker sipped cold lemonades and mulled over what they'd discovered.

"I think we found ole Scottie's sugar mama," Miranda muttered under her breath.

"Perhaps." Parker swirled the Styrofoam cup in his hand, a thoughtful look on his face.

"What do you mean, 'perhaps'? Jealous sister. Ladies man. Makes sense." She was fired up now. They could be close. Real close.

"That they're having an affair is plain."

She raised her forefinger. "Not long after Scott broke up with Suzie Chan."

"Which Chan insisted was a casual relationship."

Miranda narrowed an eye at him. "Are you saying that's what this is, too?"

He took a swallow of lemonade. "It seems likely."

With someone as emotional as Blythe Star? Miranda didn't think so. But it really didn't make much difference. "Blythe says she and Ambrosia were close. She had to know about her nightly tea ritual."

"Scott might have learned about that from Chan."

"So maybe he mentions it to Blythe during one of their secrets meetings."

"Assuming this afternoon wasn't their first rendezvous."

Miranda pursed her lips. "Didn't sound like it from what I heard."

Parker watched the people strolling by the window. "Ms. Star undoubtedly had access to Ambrosia's home."

"Probably has her own key. And if she didn't go straight home the night of the last rehearsal, like she told us, she could have gone over to her sister's. Heck, they live down the street from each other. Maybe the diva's hissy fit wasn't just about the melon balls. Blythe said the rehearsal hadn't gone well. Maybe ole Abbey blamed Blythe and lashed out at her. Maybe she found out about Blythe and Scott."

"The murder was premeditated. Not an act of passion."

Had to be with a hard-to-get poison like abrin. "Maybe Abbey had a habit of picking on little sis. Maybe little sis has been planning to get back at big sis for a long time."

Slowly Parker nodded. "That is a plausible explanation."

"Or maybe it was Scott who came up with the idea. Maybe he sweet-talked Blythe into it. If he was involved, he had to provide the muscle."

"True. Hopefully we'll find more to substantiate your theory when we question the people Ambrosia worked with."

Or they might disprove it altogether and be even farther behind. She looked at her watch. Two-thirty.

"Wasn't Sid supposed to call by now?"

Parker uttered a low groan. "You would think so if we're to be at the theater by three."

Miranda put her chin in her hand and stared out the window. "And here I thought he'd turned around last night."

Parker wondered if his former trainee was capable of turning around. He hadn't put as much hope into the man's behavior last night as Miranda had. The man had personal problems. Sid had told him about them after he'd been at the Agency a few months. Parker had tried to help the young man, but Sid had rejected Parker's advice. Evidently, he hadn't done anything about his problems since he'd left, either.

His gaze went to Miranda, staring out the window, and he drank in her profile. Those angular lines were lovelier than the finest sculpture. He watched the concentration on her face. She was absorbed in this case, just as he knew she'd be. If she hadn't been so insistent last night, Sid might have put away an innocent woman. Though her lawyer would have no doubt gotten any charges dropped.

Still, he had hoped for better for their first case. Working with Sid O'Toole could end up in disaster. Or worse yet, the case could go cold. Sid had enough pressure from his boss to ensure he'd keep working the case for a while, though. It was possible to leave it in his hands.

He thought of that moment in the hospital eight months ago when Miranda told him her work was her destiny. That destiny had to be more than finding a shallow, self-centered entertainer's killer. Especially if the case went cold because a slothful sergeant let clues slip out of his hands by not acting immediately. There would be other cases. Cases more worthy of her.

He wrestled with his thoughts.

The more they dug, the closer they'd come to the real killer. And the more nervous that killer would become. If they had no real idea who he or she was, they'd be vulnerable. Miranda would be vulnerable. Especially if the killer sensed how intent she was on discovering his or her identity.

He flashed back to the hospital room where he'd waited for her to come out of a coma, unsure if she ever would. He would never risk her life again.

He felt an odd, sinking sensation in his gut as he realized he was starting to second guess this consulting idea.

Miranda startled out of her thoughts when she felt Parker's hand slip around hers. He had a funny expression on his face. "What?"

"I was just wondering. Have you heard from the girls?"

Frowning at him, she pulled out her phone and checked her messages. Nada. She'd be whooping out loud if Mackenzie and Wendy had contacted her. He knew that. What was he up to?

She shook her head. "Nope."

"I'm so sorry. Children at that age can be so fickle."

"Tell me about it."

"Miranda."

"What?"

"If you'd like—if you feel—if at any point in this investigation—"

She tensed. "What are you trying to say, Parker?"

His grip on her hand tightened. "If at some point in this investigation you feel there's no need to pursue it any longer. For any reason—"

She pulled her hand out of his. "That will be when we have the killer in jail. The real killer."

He nodded. He knew she felt that way. What had he expected her to say? "If at any time, you should change your mind—"

"What?"

"Don't hesitate to say so. There's no shame in cutting one's losses."

Miranda couldn't believe the words coming out of his mouth. Wasn't he always the one who said her passion for crime-solving matched his? This wasn't like him at all. It was O'Toole, wasn't it? The fact that someone who came from the Agency had turned out to be such a dud must be hard on his ego. She could understand that. But that was all the more reason for not giving up.

She reached across the table and patted his hand. "Don't hold your breath."

They sipped their drinks in silence, got refills, and waited for O'Toole to call. Three o'clock came and went.

Miranda drummed her fingers on the table, nerves eating her stomach lining. The meeting had already started. They had fresh clues they needed to go over with the sergeant. They needed a game plan. There'd be over fifty people to interview. Did O'Toole expect her and Parker to do it all themselves?

She gritted her teeth and hissed. "Where the hell is he?"

"Late. He never was a model of punctuality at the Agency." Just as the words came out of Parker's mouth, his cell rang. He answered. It was O'Toole. Finally.

The sergeant and his team were waiting for them at the theater entrance.

"Let's go, then."

Miranda shot to her feet, tossed her empty cup in the trash. As she headed out the door with Parker, she stole a glance at his face and felt a wave of relief.

That hard look of determination she knew so well was back.

CHAPTER THIRTY

They found O'Toole, Ralston, and nine armed uniforms in front of The Diva Theater, just across from where Sean Scott and Blythe Star had had their love fest an hour earlier.

Parker stepped up to the sergeant and didn't bother to lower his voice. "You're late, Sid. That meeting started twenty minutes ago."

O'Toole scowled and waved a hand in the air. "Things don't start on time in this town. Especially when performers are involved. Besides I wanted them to get started. It will be more of a surprise if we catch them in the middle of the meeting."

"You might have informed us of your plans."

O'Toole raised his palms. "You're here, aren't you?"

Parker looked like he might sock the guy, but Miranda had had enough. "Are we going to get started? Or are we going to jaw out here until everyone's gone."

O'Toole narrowed his eyes at her and pulled up his belt. "Nobody's going anywhere." He turned to his officers. "Williams, Young, Green. You enter at the door on the left. King, Hill, Adams, Ralston, you on the right. Mr. Parker, Ms. Steele, and I will head down the middle. The rest of you stand guard and make sure nobody leaves. Got it?"

"Yes, sir," they said almost in unison.

For a minute Miranda thought they were going to salute.

But there was no time to think about the organizational politics of the police. The three guards opened the doors, and she and Parker followed O'Toole inside and down the center aisle.

The place was huge, which she should have expected given the hugeness of everything in the casino. The floors were carpeted in baby blue. Red teardrop shaped panels lined the walls for acoustics. A golden dome stretched overhead and an immense golden curtain had been pulled across a circular stage.

Only a top performer could fill this place night after night.

This afternoon, the members of Ambrosia Dawn's big staff took up only the front rows. As they advanced, Miranda hunted for Sean Scott in the crowd but didn't see him.

Elvis Cameron Forest stood center stage, a microphone in hand. He was dressed all in black with lots of gold chains around his neck and a big gold belt buckle around his waist. The collar of his tight, tailored shirt was pulled up, and with his pompadour and sideburns, he looked like any minute now he might be ready to break into a rendition of "Burnin' Love."

But he wasn't singing. He was speaking to his employees. And there was an ocean of pain on his face.

"So that's our plan going forward. Are there any—" He stopped short and peered down the center aisle. Then he looked toward the right aisle, then the left aisle. Alarm peppered his face. "What is this?"

"Sorry to disturb your meeting, Mr. Forest," O'Toole said in a loud cop voice. "But we have some police business to conduct."

The color drained from Forest's face. "What sort of business?"

O'Toole came to a halt at the foot of the stage.

Miranda watched the sergeant look up at the man. Forest seemed huge, mostly because he was elevated five feet in the air. Or maybe she hadn't realized how tall he was. She'd only seen him sitting down.

"We need to question your staff concerning the matter of your wife's death."

Forest blinked. "Now? We're having a meeting."

"Right now," O'Toole said.

Forest tensed a moment, his expression defensive, as if he was about to argue. Then he seemed to think better of it.

His shoulders slumping, he nodded his consent. "Whatever we can do for you, Detective."

"It's Sergeant. Sergeant O'Toole."

"Well then, Sergeant O'Toole." Forest made a grand gesture toward the group gathered below, who were all looking a bit nervous. "Which members of my staff do you need to speak to?"

"All of them."

Forest's eyes flashed with surprise, but he recovered quickly. Once more, his head bobbed up and down, slowly, thoughtfully, as if he were coming up with how to soothe the ruffled feathers this would cause on the spot.

"Very well," he said and lifted his microphone. "People, this is Sergeant O'Toole of the Las Vegas Metro Police. As you just heard, he's investigating my wife's—what happened to Abbey." His voice broke and he put his hand to his lips.

Once again Miranda's heart went out to him. He was going through such an ordeal. She almost wished she wasn't here to witness it. She glanced over at Parker. He was watching her. That was why he wanted to let O'Toole take over the case and go home. He was concerned for her emotional health, just as he'd been for her physical health. Overly concerned.

He was the first man who'd ever cared about what she felt or what condition her body was in. The first and only man who'd ever truly loved her. It had taken her a long time to get used to that, but she had. And it was nice. And she loved him, too. After all, what was not to love about a man like Wade Parker?

Still, he could be overprotective at times. She decided she'd let it go and turned back to Forest.

"I trust," he said to his audience with the earnestness of a dying man, "I trust for the love we all had for my Abbey, you'll give the sergeant and his men your complete cooperation." Then he set the mic down and left the stage.

CHAPTER THIRTY-ONE

Ralston and O'Toole divided up the staff while two of the officers scoped out the backstage. They discovered several dressing rooms and a few areas they could block off for privacy.

Each of them would get five people to interview, unless some took longer than others. Everyone would wait where they were seated until they were called.

Miranda jotted down the names of her five on her notepad. She had to suppress a smile when Sean Scott was assigned to her. She'd make him wait until last. Let him sweat a little.

Miranda was lucky. She got one of the private dressing rooms with a door.

The first interviewee she called was Giselle DuChamp, who, according to Blythe Star, had been one of Ambrosia Dawn's maids.

"Have a seat, Ms. DuChamp." Miranda gestured toward an armchair she'd pulled up near the corner.

The petite woman nodded shyly and carefully settled herself into it. Miranda took a seat on a stool at the dressing table with the large mirror and rows and rows of lotions and makeup.

Her interviewee sat very straight, feet together, hands clasped in her lap, waiting. Her features were delicate. Her dark hair was fine and she wore it cut to just under her chin. Her eyes were large and doe-like. She had on a dark blouse, dark skirt, dark hose and shoes. Mourning clothes, Miranda thought, turning a page in her notepad.

"How long have you worked for Ambrosia Dawn, Ms. DuChamp?"

"How long?" the woman repeated, pushing her hair behind an ear. Nervously, she glanced around at the rack of costumes, the lights along the mirror, the ceiling. "Oh, a long time. Fifteen years." She had a slight French accent. Miranda wondered if it was fake.

"That is a long time. Tell me about when you were hired."

She frowned as if thinking back. "Miss Abbey was touring Europe. In Paris, her hairdresser fell ill so I was called in at the last minute to replace her. She liked my work and kept me on."

Miss Abbey, huh? "As a hairdresser?"

"As a lady's maid. I assisted her in dressing and getting ready for her appearances or whenever she went out."

"Was that all?"

"I sometimes served light meals when she ate in her room."

Miranda's ears perked up. "You live on Ambrosia's estate."

She gave her an efficient, professional nod. "Yes."

Miranda almost thought she was going to say "*Oui.*"

"And I accompanied Miss Abbey on all her tours. Her life was so exciting. I love to travel." She took out a hanky and held it to her nose. "I don't know what I'm going to do now."

"Were you close?"

She blinked as if the question was improper. "As close as an employee can be to her employer."

Miranda sat back, waited a beat, and wondered how often old Abbey chewed this lady out. Then she pounced. Casually. "Did you know about the tea?"

The woman's thin brows drew together. "The tea?"

"Didn't Ambrosia Dawn drink tea every night?"

Her lips formed an O. "Oh, yes. The tea Miss Chan made for her. Yes, of course I knew about it. Why?"

Miranda shifted her weight on the uncomfortable stool. "Ms. DuChamp, were you with Ambrosia Dawn Tuesday night? The night of the last rehearsal?"

"You mean was I at the rehearsal?"

"Uh huh."

She brushed at her skirt as if to straighten it and frowned again, her expression confused. "Yes, of course. I always accompany her to rehearsals."

"Did you accompany her home?"

Another profession nod. "Yes. I always do."

"Did she go straight home?"

"Yes. We were alone in the limo. Mr. Cameron stayed behind. I wondered about that because the bodyguard was off that night. I suppose she thought she was safe. But—" She put the hanky to her mouth and stared into space.

"What happened when you got home?"

DuChamp took a steadying breath and gathered her thoughts. "Miss Abbey went to her room. She said she was going to take a shower and go to bed."

"You didn't serve her anything to eat or drink?"

"No. She dismissed me. That was—that was the last time I saw her." Her voice broke and she dabbed her eyes again which were filling with tears. Whether real or fake, Miranda couldn't tell.

She decided to go in another direction. "At the rehearsal, did anything happen?"

100

"What do you mean?"

"Was Ambrosia upset or anything?"

Her expression turned to one of disapproval. "She was fighting with her sister. And then she was upset about Miss Chan's work on the food. Miss Abbey always had Miss Chan supply the cast and crew with refreshments."

"I heard Ambrosia had a temper."

The maid brushed at her skirt again. "Oh, she fussed about little things, but she was always good to me."

"She never fussed at you?"

"Not really."

"She wasn't upset with you that night? She didn't think your work wasn't up to par?"

The woman squeezed the arm of her chair and stared at Miranda, eyes wide with shock and a bit of insult. "No. She was always happy with my work."

And the woman was lying. If the singer was pitching a temper tantrum and this little thing got in the way, she'd be run over just like everybody else. So was Giselle DuChamp yet another person who might have a motive to off old Abbey? She certainly had the opportunity to give her employer the abrin-laced tea.

CHAPTER THIRTY-TWO

Next in line was a dancer who went by the name Silver.

She seemed to be in her early twenties. Tall and lean, she wore her long, rich black hair pulled back in a ponytail. Her chiseled features were sharp and distinctive, her sculpted brows and lashes dark against her creamy complexion. Wearing a full body leotard and black ballet slippers, she stretched out in the armchair as if the theater were her only home.

Miranda introduced herself and consulted her notepad. She didn't know what to call the woman. "You go by Silver?"

"Yes."

"Is that your first or last name?"

"It's my only name." She shrugged and made an acquiescing gesture with her hand.

Miranda gave her a police-like glare.

Silver shifted her weight. "Okay. My real name's Sandra Anderson, but my stage name is Silver. It's what everyone here knows me by."

Miranda nodded, suppressing a grimace. What was it with these fake names? Didn't anybody want to be themselves?

"Silver, then." She forced a smile. "What was it like working with Ambrosia Dawn?"

"You want the truth?"

"Nothing but."

She gave Miranda a knowing grin. "I guess you would. Let's see. Where should I start?" She leaned her chin back and stared up at the lights that hung overhead in the high dark ceiling.

"How about with last Tuesday night?"

"Last Tuesday night?" She smirked and put a hand dramatically to her forehead. "Oh, God. That was awful."

"Awful how?"

She sat up and bared her teeth. "The way every night was awful. That woman was so—so full of herself. Rehearsals were a damn soap opera. Every night it was something. The lighting wasn't spectacular enough. The music was too loud. It upstaged her voice. The dancing was flashier than she was."

Now they were getting somewhere. "Sounds pretty arrogant."

An eye roll. "Arrogant is an understatement. And those melon balls! I really felt for Suzie Chan."

Miranda leaned forward a bit. "How well did you know Suzie Chan?"

The answer came too quick and natural to be contrived. "Not very. She didn't socialize with us dancers. I thought she was arrested."

"She's been released."

"Really? How come?"

"I'm not at liberty to say."

Silver lounged back in the armchair again. "Well, I can't say I'd blame her for offing the bitch. Abbey treated her like dirt."

Miranda smiled. "Did you have a reason?"

Silver frowned. "A reason for what?"

"Offing the bitch?"

"Me?" Silver stared at her with wide, dark-rimmed eyes. Slowly a smile spread across her face. She wagged a finger at Miranda. "You're really good, aren't you?" She laughed and shook her head, making her ponytail sway. "No, Ms. Steele. I didn't kill Ambrosia Dawn even though I might have fantasized about it a little. I don't want to go to jail."

"But you had reason to want to."

"As I just explained, she was difficult to work with." She took a breath. "Okay, Abbey and I had words a couple of times. After a few of our encounters, I thought she was going to fire me. But I didn't care. I can always get another job. Anyway she didn't fire me. I assumed Cameron smoothed things over with her like he always does—I mean, did—when she threatened the staff."

Miranda sat up straight at that revelation. "Mr. Forest handles Abbey's employees?"

"We really aren't Abbey's employees. Technically we work for Cameron. He's the one who hires us, pays us."

That was interesting. Miranda jotted it down.

Silver wagged a finger at her. "You know, if you really want to find out what Abbey's temper was like, you should talk to Blythe."

"Her sister?"

"Yeah," she laughed. "Those two have had some real brawls. Outright cat fights. It would get physical and Cameron would have to pull them apart." She smiled a half-sheepish smile. "We used to take bets on who would slap who first."

Miranda couldn't keep her brows from rising. She made another note in her book, trying not to draw conclusions too fast, though her mind was racing to them like an out of control freight train.

"Do you know the reason for these—altercations?"

Silver lifted her palms as if the reason was obvious. "Blythe is ambitious. She's always been jealous of Abbey. Before Abbey took her on about eight years ago, Blythe was a two-bit singer in a string of dives. She's got a good voice, but for some reason her career never took off. When she came to work for Abbey, she hoped her sister would let her do some numbers in the show. But Abbey wasn't about to share the limelight. She relegated Blythe to offstage jobs and raked her over the coals when things didn't suit her just right. Just like the rest us. Only Blythe fought back. I would have left if I were her. But I guess she couldn't go back to her nothing of a career. I guess she felt kind of trapped."

Miranda tapped her pen on her pad. If Silver realized the implication she'd just made, she didn't show it.

"I know she's grieving over her sister, but part of her has to be happy."

"Because she won't get yelled at anymore?"

"Because she'll have what she wants now."

Miranda felt her pulse quicken. "What do you mean, Silver?"

"I guess you didn't hear. Cameron announced it just before you and the police came in. The show's going on as planned. Blythe is taking over for her sister."

Miranda nodded as if the dancer had just made a comment about the weather. But her mind was racing even faster.

"Thank you, Silver," she said. "You've been very helpful."

CHAPTER THIRTY-THREE

Miranda's next two interviewees were stagehands who worked with props and lighting. They knew about the melon balls and the fights with the staff and the fights between the sisters, but they mostly kept out of the temperamental diva's way. They couldn't add anything Miranda didn't already know.

She stepped out into the hallway to get a drink and let Scott percolate a little bit more. Her mind raced with the things Silver had told her about Blythe Star. Once again she thought of Delta Langford. She was onto something. She just knew it. All she had to do was get lover boy to crack.

After about a five-minute break, she returned for her target.

Forcing back any shark-like expression on her face, Miranda watched the bodyguard settle into the interview chair with a cavalier ease.

The muscles under his knit black top were more defined close up. He was in really good shape. His gelled blond crew cut gleamed under the lights. As did his ultra-white teeth.

He crossed his ankle over one knee and folded his hands in his lap. "What would you like to know, Ms. Steele? I'm more than happy to help in your investigation."

She just bet he was. Start slow, Miranda told herself. "In what capacity were you employed by Ambrosia Dawn, Mr. Scott?"

"I was one of her bodyguards. But I'm employed by Entertainment Security. Mr. Forest contracts us through my company." He shot her a charming lady-killer grin.

Little did he know she was married to the ultimate charmer. She knew all the tricks.

"Us?"

"There are two of us. Tony Harris is the other one. We take turns. Or, we did."

"I see. What exactly did your bodyguard job consist of, Mr. Scott?"

"Please call me Scottie. Everyone does." He tried another smile.

Miranda ignored it. "Please answer the question."

"Sure. I'd pick Ms. Ambrosia up at her home whenever she needed an escort and accompany her to wherever she needed to go. Restaurants, shopping, things like that."

"And rehearsals?"

"Yes, rehearsals as well."

"And in that capacity were you at the rehearsal this Tuesday night?"

He seemed surprised at the question. "No, ma'am. I was out of town."

Miranda acted surprised in turn. "Oh? Where did you go?"

"I'd rather not say." His smile deepened.

He was definitely the God's gift type. All flash and arrogance and me, me, me. The type of guy she used to love taking down in a bar. Just to show him a woman could best him.

Miranda gave him her own version of a smile. One with a little bite in it. "Did you have another job there?"

She watched the muscled chords in his neck strain. "I'd rather not say. It's personal."

"Mr. Scott, this is a murder investigation."

The lady-killer smile disappeared. He stared down at his thumbs, which he was twirling. Biding time while he thought up a good story?

At last he raised his gaze again. "I was in Kingman, Arizona, seeing an old girlfriend of mine."

Another one? Jeez. Miranda decided not to go down that path. "I understand you had a relationship with Suzie Chan."

He seemed surprised that she knew that. "I—yeah, a few months ago."

"She said you were fuck buddies. Is that true?"

His blond brows shot up at the blunt expression, and then he chuckled, putting a finger under his nose. "Oh, that Suzie. She's such a wild one. She can mince an onion, but she never minces words."

Miranda scowled at the bad joke. "I also understand you were in London with the show recently?"

He turned up his palms. "Whatever the contract demands."

"And you were almost fired there because of your relationship with Ms. Chan?"

He shifted his weight and cleared his throat. "Not really. Like I said, I work for Entertainment Security and Mr. Forest handles the contracts. He wouldn't have let me go. Besides, Suzie and I were about to break up anyway."

"Not because of Ambrosia's threat?"

He made a pfft sound. "Of course not. She was just having one of her hissy fits. She never scared me."

"But you came to Ms. Chan's defense. You had words with Ambrosia."

Miranda watched his jaw clench as he studied her carefully. Apparently it had just dawned on him that she knew a lot more than he'd thought.

"I just didn't like the way Suzie was being treated."

"What about the way Ambrosia treated the rest of the employees?"

He locked eyes with her. He had to realize the other employees would have talked by now.

He grunted out a breath. "Okay, Ms. Steele. The woman was a total bitch. Is that what you want me to say?"

"And you were tired of her behavior."

"Everyone was tired of it."

"But you decided to do something about it."

"I—" He stared at her with his watery baby blues, his mouth half open. "What?" he laughed. "Are you saying you think I killed her? You've got to be joking."

"You look pretty fit, Mr. Scott. How much can you bench press?"

He frowned in confusion. "Me? Oh, two-fifty on a good day."

A lot more than the weight of a dead singer. "You had opportunity, motive, and means. You knew where she lived. You knew her personal habits. You were alone with her."

He put both feet on the floor and leaned toward her with a tad of defiance. "No, I wasn't. The driver was always in the limo. I sat up front with him."

"And at her home?"

He raised his hands as his complexion grew red. He was losing it. "There were always servants. Besides like I said, I was out of town Tuesday night."

"Were you really?"

His eyes flashed. A bit of anger, a bit of alarm in them. "Yes, you can talk to my old girlfriend if you want. I'll give you her number." He gestured to her notepad.

Miranda tore off a page, handed him her pen and let him jot it down.

But was it his old girlfriend or someone who would conveniently give Scott an alibi? She'd find out later. "One more thing, Mr. Scott."

"And what's that?" Clearly annoyed, he handed back the pen and paper.

Miranda waited a beat and crossed her legs, taking the casual position now. "What are you doing here tonight?"

He frowned. "I don't understand."

"Ambrosia Dawn doesn't exactly need a bodyguard anymore."

"Oh," He glanced over his shoulder as if he were thinking up a reason on the fly. "Mr. Cameron asked me to come. He wants to speak to me about our arrangement. Maybe he wants me to work for Ms. Star now."

"Seems to me that you're already guarding Ms. Star's body."

"What?"

Miranda shut her notepad with a snap and rose.

She wanted to press, hurl accusations at him, but Scott would only deny them. Better to let him mull things over for a bit. Think about the predicament he'd gotten himself into. She hadn't gotten a confession, but she'd rattled him. She'd get the rest when they brought him in. In an interview at the police station, Scott would spill.

"Thank you for your cooperation, Mr. Scott. If we have any further questions, someone from Metro will be in touch with you." She extended a hand.

Surprised that the interview had ended so suddenly, Scott got to his feet. He shook her hand—it was a pretty limp shake for a bodyguard. Then he recovered and laughed as if he didn't have a care in the world. "Aren't you going to tell me not to leave town?"

"I was just about to say that." She turned and left him standing there.

As she stepped into the theater again and hunted for O'Toole, Miranda wasn't sure whose idea it was, but she was pretty sure it was Scottie boy who had helped Blythe Star out the night Ambrosia Dawn was murdered.

She found the sergeant talking to one of his men in front of the stage. Soon Ralston and Parker joined them. They waited for the officers to finish up, and then O'Toole dismissed everyone involved with the show.

As they headed back up the center aisle, Cameron Forest's crew took their places on stage and began the business they'd originally gathered here for. Another rehearsal.

The band started to play and music filled the air. Miranda stopped in the aisle and turned to watch a moment.

The golden curtain parted to reveal a tall glittering staircase at the center of the stage, dancers in leotards moving all around it. And at the very top Blythe Star appeared.

Wearing the standard rehearsal black, she began to sing and slowly descend the staircase. The dancers moved gracefully around her in time to the music. The background singers provided a chorus behind her. They might have drowned out a lesser singer, but Blythe's voice was almost as powerful as her sister's.

And what was she singing? "All Eyes on Me."

Arms outstretched, she looked deliriously happy. She had wanted to be her sister and now she was.

Pursing her lips, Miranda took in the sight and thought about what Silver had told her. The shame of a failed career, the disgrace of being under her sister's thumb, the humiliation of being regularly abused by her in front of everyone. The arguments, the cat fights. Who would blame her? And there it was, right there on stage. Triumph. And everything the singer's sister had ever wanted.

It sure looked like motive to her.

CHAPTER THIRTY-FOUR

Things are getting too hot. Too damn hot. The police are closing in. And those two detectives. How am I supposed to cope with it all? How am I supposed to deal with this?

My heart races. My stomach is churning. I feel sick.

I reach for the prescription bottle on the table. My hand shakes. I stop.

No. I can't use drugs. They'd only numb my brain and I have to think. I have to figure this out. But I'm crying again. I just can't stop the tears. My heart is breaking.

Oh, Abbey. Why? If only you hadn't been so hotheaded, so mean. If only you hadn't been such a bitch, none of this would have happened.

But you were what you were.

We all accepted you and loved you. We loved you just as you were, so maybe it was all of our faults. Even so, you'll live on in our hearts forever. That's what you really wanted, wasn't it? That was really winning.

I wipe the tears from my cheeks with the back of my trembling hand. I manage to pull myself together. I'm calmer now. I can handle things. I'll figure out something.

I can take care of the police. And I'll take care of those detectives, too. Especially that woman. Even if I have to do something terrible again.

Don't worry, Abbey dear. Don't worry. I can do it. I'll take care of everything.

CHAPTER THIRTY-FIVE

Now there were three guest chairs in Sergeant O'Toole's office, and the tiny space was really getting cramped.

For the next few hours, Miranda, Parker, Ralston, and O'Toole poured over the findings from the interviews, studying and comparing each one, combing through them for clues. The conclusion wasn't exactly earthshaking.

Everyone on the staff had a reason to want Ambrosia Dawn dead.

Ralston had interviewed the woman who had rubbed oil over the vic backstage during costume changes, and another woman who helped dress her. Then she'd talked to a third woman who was in charge of Ambrosia's blush palette. After that a lighting guy and a sound guy.

All of them had witnessed Abbey's temper tantrums. All of them had been on the receiving end of one at one time or another. Everyone knew about Suzie Chan and the melon balls. Two of them knew about Suzie and Scott. Nobody knew Scott was seeing anyone else.

O'Toole had discovered Abbey and Cameron liked to throw parties at their house and invite some of the dancers and singers. Of course, the show's executive producer and art director were also invited.

They'd had one just last week and during that time anyone could have scoped out the house and found a way to disable the alarm and break in.

Miranda told them what she'd learned from her interviews, but by now she was second-guessing her conclusion about Blythe Star. Sure, she had motive. But so did everyone else. They needed to re-examine the facts.

She got to her feet for a stretch. "Only a few people knew about Ambrosia Dawn's nightly tea ritual," she said. "One of them is Giselle DuChamp, her lady's maid."

Parker reached for a coffee cup on O'Toole's desk. "Blythe knew about it as well."

Miranda turned to him, surprised. "You talked to Blythe, again?"

"Yes."

"And you asked her about the tea?" They hadn't mentioned that when they'd gone to see the singer's sister.

He started to take a sip of the stale liquid in his cup, scowled at it and put it back down on the desk. "I managed to get her to admit her knowledge of the tea, yes."

Miranda had to smile. Parker could get a confession out of a turnip. "What else did you find out?"

Parker sighed. "Unfortunately she clammed up after that. And grew decidedly nervous."

"Like she was hiding something?"

O'Toole raised his hands "Hey, now. Let's not go on another wild goose chase."

Miranda watched Parker's jaw tense and waited for him to remind the sergeant he was the one who had jumped the gun on Suzie Chan. But Parker didn't.

Instead he turned to her. "What did you get from Sean Scott?"

"He claims he was in Kingston, Arizona the night of the murder. Seeing an old girlfriend."

Parker's expression was flat, but Miranda was well aware of his opinion of players.

"Did he know about the tea?" O'Toole asked.

Miranda shook her head. "He claims he was never alone with Ambrosia in her home. But he would have had the muscle to wrap a dead body in plastic, pick it up and put it in the trunk of a car. He knew Suzie Chan, who made the tea. And he also knew Blythe Star pretty well."

O'Toole looked at Miranda, then at Parker with a you're-holding-out-on-me expression. "And how do you know how well he knew Blythe Star?"

Miranda blew out a breath. "We saw Star and Scott together just before the rehearsal. They were in a ticket booth making out. Actually a little more than that, from the sound of it."

O'Toole's brows shot up. "You recorded this encounter?"

"No. I overheard it."

The sergeant gave her an accusatory look.

Miranda raised her hands. "We're PIs. We were snooping."

"The DA can't use that in court." O'Toole gave a low grunt. Then he pointed at his detective. "Ralston, get me all the background you can dig up on Blythe Star and this bodyguard."

"I'm on it, sir." Ralston hopped up and left the room.

Eagerly, Miranda thought.

But she caught O'Toole looking after her, eyeballing her backside with what seemed like appreciation. Did he suddenly have the hots for his detective?

The three of them sat in silence for several long moments, mulling over what the next move should be. At last the sergeant opened his mouth, but before he could speak, his cell rang.

Scowling, he picked it up. "O'Toole." His face went rigid. "Yes, sir." His eyes bulged, his color turned that rosy shade that meant he was either angry or embarrassed. "Yes, sir." He sat up so erect, Miranda thought he was going to salute. "Yes, sir." At last, he hung up.

"Who was it, Sid?" Parker asked.

O'Toole curled a lip at his cell. "The Lieutenant. He's gathered the media people here for a press conference. Jiminy Cricket eating a crap sandwich."

Ignoring the man's crudeness, Parker rose from his chair. "I assume you'll have to take care of that. We can pick this up in the morning."

O'Toole's finger shot out. "Not so fast, Parker. You promised you'd handle the press conference."

Parker's face flushed with his own shade of angry crimson. "I did no such thing."

"C'mon, Parker. You said you'd consider it."

"You imagined that, Sid."

The sergeant folded his arms. "Well, I'm not doing it. And you two are just as much a part of this investigation as I am."

"Then you'll have to explain your refusal to the Lieutenant."

Miranda looked at O'Toole. Then at Parker. Then back at O'Toole. She felt like she was between two bulls at a rodeo. They didn't have time for these testosterone games.

With a groan she stood. "Knock it off, you two. I'll do the press conference."

Parker turned to her with a glare.

She folded her arms. "I am still in charge, aren't I?"

His jaw tensed. He wasn't happy at all. He didn't want her exposing herself with a killer on the lose. For the moment, she didn't care.

Ignoring him, she turned to the sergeant. "Where are the news hounds kenneled?"

CHAPTER THIRTY-SIX

O'Toole led them out of the office and they zigzagged down the halls until they reached a door where bright lights and noisy chatter flooded into the corridor. The sergeant herded her and Parker—who was still simmering—inside and they stepped into the crowded space.

Reporters were packed into chairs and standing around the back armed with iPads and cell phones, ready to take down all the dirt. There were even cameras.

Dear Lord, Miranda thought. What had she gotten herself into?

Several grim-looking uniforms stood at the front of the room. Beside them was a large, equally grim-looking man in a dark suit who exuded almost as much power as Parker did back at the Agency. From the daggers he was shooting at O'Toole, she took him to be his boss.

After several tense moments, the big man raised a hand and stepped to a podium in the center of the front area.

The place went dead still.

He began to speak into a microphone in a dark, reverberating voice. "Good evening. I'm Lieutenant Henry Wells of the Homicide Division of Las Vegas Metropolitan Police and I'll be conducting this meeting tonight."

Once more he glanced over at the sergeant with a you'd-better-make-this-good glare.

"We are all sorrowed by the death of a key figure in our community. And I want you all to know that my unit is doing all they can to find the perpetrator. At this time I want to introduce Sergeant Sidney O'Toole who is in charge of the Ambrosia Dawn homicide investigation. Sergeant O'Toole and his team have been working tirelessly to bring closure to the family, friends, and fans of the beloved singer. He will now make a brief statement regarding the current status of the case, and then we'll open the floor for questions."

Miranda leaned over and whispered in O'Toole's ear. "Statement?"

He didn't respond.

Lieutenant Wells stretched a hand in O'Toole's direction. "If you'll come forward, Sergeant."

Miranda felt O'Toole give her a nudge. At the same time, she felt Parker grab her elbow.

"Don't do it, Miranda," he whispered to her. "Let him sink or swim."

She looked over at O'Toole and saw his upper lip was glistening. He was sweating. Actually sweating. He must have a horrendous case of stage fright. And in that moment, she felt sorry for him. Hell, who knew what he might say to the reporters if he was that nervous? He could blow the whole case with a slip of the tongue.

She wasn't about to let that happened. She pulled out of Parker's grasp, ignoring his frustrated exhale and stepped to the podium. She turned and faced the reporters.

Her mouth went dry. Her palms went damp. Her knees felt like rubber. Her heart hammered away in her chest.

There were at least three-dozen pairs of expectant eyes on her, waiting for answers. Waiting for her to deliver up Ambrosia Dawn's killer. She'd expected local radio and TV celebrities. She didn't know the station names, but she recognized one reporter from the newscast she'd seen the other day. And was that—? Yes, there were two big media names. Of course, they'd be here. The story went national days ago.

No wonder O'Toole hadn't wanted to do this.

Behind her, she heard Lieutenant Wells clear his throat. She wondered if he would chew her out instead of the sergeant when this was over. Probably Parker would beat him to it.

Realizing she was standing there giving the cameras a deer-in-headlights look, she shook herself out of it, grabbed the podium and took a breath to steady her nerves. Statement. Statement. What could she say?

"Good evening, ladies and gentlemen," she began. And stopped. *And for my next act, I'm going to make a private investigator disappear before your eyes.*

She was sweating harder than O'Toole now. She looked like an idiot. If the sergeant had any feeling, he'd step up here and rescue her. Wait a minute. Since when did Miranda Steele need to be rescued by a man?

Suddenly words came to her. "My name is Miranda Steele. I'm a private investigator with the Parker Agency in Atlanta, Georgia. Las Vegas Metro has called in Wade Parker, the Agency's president, and myself to help investigate the death of Ambrosia Dawn."

A woman coughed in the front row and Miranda caught a skeptical gleam in her eye. She went on.

"This is a very sad time for the family of the victim. All our thoughts and prayers should be with them. At this time, there's very little I can say about the investigation except that Metro is putting much of its manpower and resources into finding Ambrosia Dawn's killer."

It was all she could come up with. She was about to turn away when the skeptical woman raised a hand. "Ms.—Steele, is it?"

"Yes."

"We've heard certain evidence was discovered missing at the crime scene. Namely, an—eyeball?"

Lead with the gruesome. Miranda forced herself not to growl at the woman. "What is your question?"

"Why wasn't this detail given to the press?"

Because they didn't want the killer to know? They didn't want to gross out the fans? Reporters must not have any common sense, she thought. "We were unable to divulge the information due to the ongoing investigation." Now that was a nice piece of double-talk.

A man from one of the big stations started talking without being acknowledged. "I understand Ambrosia Dawn was found in the desert. Doesn't that indicate the murder was premeditated?"

"I'm not at liberty to say." *As you should know.*

"Have you drawn any conclusion as to why the body was discovered in such an easy-to-find location?"

"Not at this time."

Someone in the back row. "What is the significance of the eye? Does it point to a serial killer?"

That's right. Send the entire Las Vegas area into a panic. The casino owners will love that. "We don't suspect a serial killer at this point."

"We understand you had someone in custody but released her yesterday. Can you tell us why?"

"Not at this time."

On and on they went. How were they dealing with the fans? Why wasn't there enough evidence against Suzie Chan? When would they be ready to charge the killer? Miranda dodged and tap-danced around the queries like she was a finalist on *Dancing with the Stars.*

Just before she was ready to challenge the guy in the front row to a fistfight, she raised a hand. "That's all the questions for tonight. Now if you'll excuse us, we have a job to do."

They were still calling out to her as she spun on her heel and marched out of the room, giving O'Toole a dirty look as she passed him.

CHAPTER THIRTY-SEVEN

By the time they got back to the sergeant's office, Parker was hotter than Miranda had seen him in a long time.

"That was low, Sid. Even for you."

His anger sparked hers. "I handled it, Parker," she snapped at him. "It's over."

Parker gave her a brusque glance but kept his attention on the sergeant. "We were hired to assist with this investigation. Not to run it and certainly not to perform your media duties for you."

O'Toole waved an arm in Miranda's direction. "What are you talking about? She did great. Even the Lieutenant thought so. He told me right after you left."

Lucky for O'Toole.

"See? I did great." Not that she was happy about the sergeant's cop out.

That should have put an end to it. But no.

Parker took an enraged step toward the sergeant. "I will not have you taking advantage of her."

O'Toole's lip curled in an expression halfway between disbelief and disgust. "What is she? Your girlfriend or something?"

Parker's gray eyes flashed dark. His voice became a low growl. "She's my wife."

O'Toole sank into his chair, his chin dropping nearly to the desktop. He stared at Parker. Miranda could see the questions and nepotism accusations forming in his mind.

Fuming, she spun around to her husband. "What the hell, Parker?"

They'd agreed not to tell anyone they were married. For professional reasons.

Before O'Toole even had a chance to ask what had happened to Parker's first wife, his cell rang.

It took him a minute to answer, but at last he picked it up.

"O'Toole," he said into the phone with a faraway voice. Then he blinked and shot straight up. "Wait a minute. Say that again?"

116

He spoke to the caller in a low tone for several more minutes, then hung up, his mood completely altered. Wearing a triumphant grin, he leaned back in his chair and put his hands behind his head. "The boys in the lab just got back to me."

"Yeah?" Miranda's pulse started to quicken.

"Guess whose prints were on that pickle jar in Suzie Chan's refrigerator?"

She held her breath. "Whose?"

He jerked his thumb in the general direction of Costa Rica Hills. "Blythe Star's."

Miranda felt as if the wind had been knocked out of her. She'd been right about the sister.

"Let's go pick her up, then," she snapped.

And without waiting for confirmation from either man, she turned on her heel and stomped out the door.

CHAPTER THIRTY-EIGHT

Miranda was so pissed at Parker for spilling the beans about their marital state to O'Toole, she snubbed him and snagged a ride with Ralston to Blythe Star's mansion instead.

Why had he done that? It had been his idea not to divulge the fact they were married. She thought he wanted to keep their private relationship private. That was the way she wanted it, too. Professional courtesy and all that.

And now he was going all macho on her? Just because she'd done a press conference?

But she didn't have time to think about Parker now. It looked like a real arrest was within their reach and Ralston was talking to her.

With an efficient motion, the detective put on her blinker and made a right onto Flamingo. "Star's prints were in the system due to a string of DUIs about three years ago. Seems she had an alcohol problem."

"No kidding?" Miranda stared out the window, still seething about Parker.

"I also discovered our Blythe Star, whose real name is Roberta Ann Johnson, was married years ago before she hooked up with her sister."

Now Miranda's ears perked up. "Oh yeah?" She knew the name, except for the middle one, but Blythe hadn't mentioned any previous husband.

"An older man. Much older. And much wealthier."

"Really." Miranda watched a stretch limo pass by heading for the freeway. "A sugar daddy?"

Ralston nodded. "Seemed to be. Someone to provide her luxury while she made a pittance trying to get her singing career off the ground."

"Interesting."

"He died under suspicious circumstances."

Miranda's stomach did a flip. "Whoa."

"It was cleared up later, but one of the servants was under investigation for a while."

"You think Blythe could have been responsible? And got away with it?"

"Hard to tell. It happened eight years ago."

Miranda chewed on that a moment. Eight years ago was around the time Blythe Star went to work for her sister, according to Silver.

"Did she get an inheritance?"

Ralston shook her head and made another turn. "There were medical bills and home care bills. There wasn't much left after that. Not for the lifestyle Blythe had become accustomed to."

"And so she turned to her sister for help."

The detective's thin brow rose in admiration. "Right. She joined Ambrosia's company about that time. Now she's part owner of Cameron Forest's corporation."

Miranda let out a low whistle. That was some whopping motive. "So now, she's got everything she wants. Everything she ever dreamed of."

Including taking the place of her sister on stage. She'd known it when she saw the look on the woman's face on stage when she sashayed down that staircase singing her sister's song.

"Could be."

Miranda wondered if Blythe's desire for what Ambrosia had extended to Cameron. Maybe Scott was just a fling on the side. Or she was trying to make Elvis jealous.

Her thoughts racing, Miranda studied the intent expression on Ralston's thin face. She saw a kindred spirit there. The detective was really good. Too bad she had to be under someone like O'Toole. Parker could be aggravating at times, but when it came to work he'd always respected her abilities.

"Can I ask a personal question?"

Ralston gave her a surprised glance. "Shoot."

"How come you stay in the job?"

Ralston's head spun around so fast, it made her ponytail swing. Turning back to the traffic, she lifted a shoulder. "I like the work."

"I mean why work for this police department? Why not transfer somewhere else?"

She gave her a knowing half-smile. "You mean why keep working for a jackass like Sid O'Toole?"

Exactly what she meant. "He doesn't treat you very well. And well, he avoids work and shoves it off onto you whenever he can. Whenever he finds it distasteful or too strenuous." Which seemed to be pretty often. "Why do you think we're here?"

Ralston laughed. "Yeah, he does. But he's had personal problems. His wife left him about six months ago."

"Oh." Miranda suddenly felt a tinge of pity for the guy.

"He was really in love with her and she walked out and left him flat."

"That's too bad." She meant it, even though she usually took the woman's side of a breakup. But it wasn't any of her business.

"Besides, he's kind of a cute jackass."

Miranda's brows shot up. She thought of the way O'Toole had eyed Ralston's backside earlier. Was there something going on here? On the other hand, if there was, she didn't really want to know about it.

"Plus I have family here," Ralston continued. "My parents died when I was little and my grandparents took care of me. They're in assisted living now and I visit them all the time. If it weren't for me, they wouldn't have anyone to look after them."

Miranda was quiet. Ralston was a really good person as well as a good cop. And her tender story brought an old ache to her heart for the normal family life that she'd never had. Her father had abandoned her when she was little. Her mother was a cold shrew, her first husband beat her and stole her child. But things were better now. A lot better. All thanks to Parker.

By the time they pulled past the security guards and into the Costa Rica Hills country club, her anger at Parker had completely evaporated.

CHAPTER THIRTY-NINE

Blythe Star's coral two-story estate had an eerie glow under the outdoor lamps that lit it up under the desert sky. Or maybe it just seemed that way because they were about to arrest a killer.

Miranda got out of Ralston's car and watched O'Toole, Parker, and three officers march up to the door. She wondered if the extra police were overkill. It wasn't as if they needed a swat team or anything.

On the other hand, some women could be pretty vicious. She'd tangled with a few. Didn't matter. The surge of adrenaline she felt at the prospect of wrapping up their first case overshadowed everything, however this went down.

O'Toole pounded on the door. "Metro police," he said loudly.

No answer.

He pounded again. "We need you to open the door. We need to speak to Ms. Star."

After what felt like a half hour, the door opened and the woman named Hildie appeared. "What in the world is going on?"

She had a robe wrapped tightly around her thin body. Instead of being pulled back, now her graying hair hung to her shoulders. Her face looked more drawn and wrinkled than it had yesterday. Her expression said she was outraged at being disturbed so late.

"Ma'am, I'm Sergeant O'Toole of the Las Vegas Police. We need to speak to Ms. Star."

"At this hour?"

"It's regarding the death of her sister."

"Ms. Star has been very distraught over that. Right now, she's getting some much needed sleep. Can't you come back in the morning?"

"I'm afraid this can't wait. May we come in?"

The woman glared at him, then at the other officers. But realizing things would only get worse if she refused, she opened the door. "You can wait in the east room."

Miranda followed the woman as she led everyone across the marble floor, past the fountain with the goldfish, between two marble columns and down a short hall to a room on the left.

"Wait here and I'll see if Ms. Star will receive you." She turned and walked stiffly away.

A bulldog couldn't have been more loyal or protective of her master, though Hildie made a pretty skinny pug.

Miranda took a seat on an overstuffed red velvet couch that faced a huge fireplace built into a square white brick column in the middle of the room. Now what would you need a fireplace in the desert for? Especially when the A/C was set to a temperature that gave her goose bumps, despite the cruel heat outside.

Ralston took a seat on a Queen Anne's chair across the white carpet. All the men stood, pacing or shifting their weight from foot to foot. Ralston's shoe began to bounce up and down. Miranda resisted the urge to tap her foot on the thick carpet.

"Star must be a sound sleeper," she said at last, attempting to break the tension.

No one responded. But Parker gave her a look that said he feared this wasn't going to go well.

She had a feeling he was right.

After an eternity, they heard the plop-plop-plop of Hildie's bedroom slippers approaching from the hall.

She was moving fast.

She rushed into the room. "I don't know what's happened. I can't find Ms. Star anywhere."

Skipped, Miranda thought, wanting to cuss.

"What do you mean?" O'Toole demanded.

"She's not in her room or the terrace or the downstairs kitchen. I—I don't know where she is."

O'Toole pointed at one of the officers, then at Hildie. "Stay with her. The rest of you, search the house."

"You can't do that," the woman protested. "It's an invasion of privacy."

O'Toole's face went hard with more irritation than Miranda had ever seen on it. "I happen to have an arrest warrant for Ms. Star, ma'am, and it appears she's now a fugitive. So yes, we damn well can search the house."

"Oh, my God." Hildie tottered backward and sank onto the couch, a hand to her mouth in horror. But she stopped protesting.

As Miranda hurried out of the room with O'Toole and Parker, she heard the woman mutter, "This can't be happening. This just can't be happening."

CHAPTER FORTY

Back in the wide, marble-floored foyer with the goldfish pond fountain, Miranda took stock of the place.

The officers were going room to room until reinforcements arrived. They'd be needed. There were too many rooms and only three officers right now. And just a little while ago, she had thought they were overkill.

She turned to Parker. "You want to take the west side while I take the east?"

He hesitated a moment, his expression dark and unreadable, and she wondered if he were questioning that she'd taken charge—which she was supposed to do if they were still following the original plan.

But at last he nodded. "Good plan."

While O'Toole headed for the back, Parker studied her another moment again hesitating, as if he were about to say something. Then he simply turned and strode off down the hall.

Feeling a sudden sense of loss, Miranda tromped off toward the opposite corridor.

By the time she reached it, officers were darting in and out of rooms along the arched passageway. Their faces told her they were having no luck finding the suspect and Miranda doubted she would either.

If Blythe Star's trusted assistant couldn't find the woman, she probably wasn't in the house. No doubt Sean Scott had gotten to Blythe after rehearsal and told her the authorities were on to them. The pair might have taken off. They could be in Tucson by now. Hell, if they hopped a plane, they could be on their way to Indonesia.

She was passing the cops who were slowly making their way along the hallway's raised panels to what looked like a kitchen, when she spotted a cherry wood staircase with a crimson runner along the wall. Something told her that was the way to go.

She took it—two stairs at a time—to the second floor.

123

It was quiet up here, more open, with the night sky pouring through massive floor-to-ceiling windows. Like the cops, Miranda went through the rooms one by one. Why did wealthy folk need so many of them? Guest rooms, bathrooms, a kitchenette in rosy marble with a lounging area done in a pastel blue.

Another bathroom, this one lined with tiny mirrors so you could check out every part of yourself and make sure it was up to par. Two exercise and dance rooms filled with all the latest, fanciest equipment, including colorful Pilates balls and a rack of pastel dumbbells. The kind the guys back at the Agency called sissy weights.

These were also lined with mirrors and ballet bars. The air reeked of self-absorption. The lady was definitely a narcissist. But that must have been in her genes.

At last, Miranda came to what must have been the master bedroom. Two words struck her immediately. Big and pink.

The walls were white with pink trim. The large windows were covered with pink curtains decked with little white hearts. The matching furniture was white with pink trim. A white bear skin rug stretched across the cherry wood floor. In the middle of the room sat a huge heart-shaped bed, piled high with pink-and-white throw pillows. A silky pink comforter stretched across the bed, and beneath the silk a white fur dust ruffle encircled the shape. Ermine?

And yet the most striking feature of the room was that the white walls were covered not with mirrors this time, but with photo after photo of Ambrosia Dawn.

Not Abigail Johnson. Not vacation trips or holidays or family time. It was all Ambrosia Dawn, the performer. The diva. The star. Pictures of what must have been that high school performance of *Les Misérables* Blythe had mentioned. The early years of her career. The night she won her Grammy. Photos from her heydays. The few movies she'd been in. Every tour she'd ever been on.

Can you spell—obsession?

But still, there was no sign of Blythe. The bed had been turned down, revealing white satin sheets with pink hearts, but it didn't look like it had been touched.

Miranda stepped over to the closet. The door was ajar. She peeked inside. A huge walk-in, twice as big as the one Parker had given her back home. It was hard to tell with the massive wardrobe, but it didn't look like there had been any hurried packing.

She moved to the bathroom. Another large room with a pink sunken tub and lots of mirrors. There was a towel on the floor. Miranda crouched down to feel it. Still damp. The shower looked like it had been recently used.

Miranda's pulse kicked up. If Blythe had bolted after a bath, she couldn't have gotten far. Time to wrap this search up and start hunting outside. She had only one room left. Procedure compelled her to check it out.

Back in the hall, the faint odor of chlorine caught her attention. She headed for the opaque glass double doors that must have been eight feet tall. She wrapped her hand around her shirttail to preserve any fingerprints, pulled it open, and stepped into the room.

But it wasn't a room. It was an indoor pool.

Nearly Olympic size, as far as she could tell in the dim light. It wasn't square or oval. Not exactly kidney-shaped either. It curved this way and that around muted mosaic tile decked with lounge furniture and potted palms and columns. The surrounding walls were tall windows, stretching into a curved dome, while crystal blue water gurgled under low lights that echoed the twinkling stars overhead. The whole place was silent except for the sound of a maintenance engine humming quietly.

A pink-and-white beach ball floated idly by. Miranda stood watching it for a moment, breathing in the moist air. Then something caught her eye at the far end of the room. She stepped around the chaises and wrought iron tables, making her way to the back.

As she approached, she could make out a long white shelf that ran along the far wall like a mantelpiece without a fireplace. Suspended about five feet from the floor, it held half a dozen antique Chinese vases symmetrically arranged.

But the one that should have been on the end was missing.

She made her way around the last curve of the pool to the shelf. Before she got there she stopped short. At her feet lay shattered porcelain pieces. But what make her skin tingle was the blood spatter on the walls and floor tiles.

And the bloody footprints.

She dared to peek over the edge of the pool. A pumping system was making gentle waves in the blue water under the low light. She was about to turn away.

Then she saw it.

Way down on the bottom. A form. Long, tan limbs. A naked backside. Flowing blond hair. It was her.

Still alive?

Without hesitation, Miranda kicked off her shoes, stripped off her jacket and dove in.

Down she went, butterflying her way as fast as she could to the bottom. When she got there, she tried to slip her hands under the woman's arms, but her skin was slippery and her long silky hair washed over Miranda's face.

She pushed it away and twisted it into a knot as best she could. This was taking too long, but she didn't have much choice. She worked her fingers under the armpits once more. She almost had her when the knot came loose and the fine hair floated over her cheeks and eyes once more.

She wanted to grunt aloud, but she was holding her breath—something she couldn't do much longer. Grasping the hair with both hands, she spun it into a ponytail and put it between her lips. Trying to spit out the water without losing the hair, she gave one more determined shove and got the woman up.

Up, up she swam. God, she was heavy. Up, up. Just a little farther.

When she didn't think she could hold her breath another second, her head broke through the surface. Gasping, she opened her mouth, spat out the hair, and drank in air. Blythe's soaking ponytail was now plastered along her neck and breasts.

Miranda swam as hard as she could. At last she made the short distance to the edge of the pool and dragged both herself and the woman out of the water.

She positioned her body, cleared her airway, pressed hard against her chest, trying to revive her. But she'd already seen the gash along her throat and the glassy stare of her eyes. She knew it was useless.

She was gone.

Miranda got to her feet, not noticing she was shaking from head to foot. She started for the door. "Parker," she shouted. "O'Toole."

They were downstairs. No way they could hear her. She fumbled in her wet pockets and found her cell phone. Thank God it was waterproof.

Parker answered on the first ring. "What is it?"

"I found her. In the pool room. Far end of the second floor. She's dead."

"We're there."

Just as he disconnected she heard a scream in the doorway. She turned to see Hildie, followed by the officer who was supposed to be guarding her. "I couldn't keep her downstairs, Ms. Steele. She insisted on coming up here."

The woman gave Miranda a crazed glare. "What have to you done to her? What have you done?"

Instinctively, Miranda's hands shot up and she went into a defense pose, soaking hair and clothes and all, but the officer grabbed Hildie before the woman could reach her. "Calm down, lady."

"How did you know Blythe was up here?" Miranda demanded of the woman.

Her face went white. "I just had a thought. She often goes for a swim late at night."

"Did you kill her?"

"What? How dare you—"

"What's going on in here?" O'Toole stepped through the door with Parker at his side.

Ralston and the other officers appeared in the doorway behind them.

Immediately Parker rushed to Miranda's side.

For once, she wanted him to hold her, but she knew he wouldn't in front of the men. "I was searching room to room on this floor," she explained. "I came in here last. I found her on the bottom of the pool. I tried to save her, but it was too late."

O'Toole stepped around the body and peered down at the lifeless form.

As the officers got busy, Parker slipped his arm around Miranda's wet frame. Man, that felt good.

"Are you all right?" he whispered in her ear.

She nodded and touched his hand. It felt warm and reassuring.

126

"Dammit." O'Toole made a sound like a cat in heat. He shot a finger at his detective. "Ralston, go pick up that bodyguard."

"Yes, sir."

CHAPTER FORTY-ONE

O'Toole called in the ME and the CSIs. An hour later, the whole area around the pool was swarming with technicians. Outside officers were checking the yard and talking to neighbors. But Miranda remained at the pool with Parker at her side.

Feeling numb, she watched Dr. Eaton as he crouched beside the body and performed his preliminary examination.

After what seemed like an eternity, with a weary movement, he rose. But he couldn't quite tear his eyes from her.

"Well?" O'Toole asked.

"She was dead when she got into the pool," Eaton said. "There was no water in her lungs."

"Pretty clear the killer would have had to slash her first."

The doctor nodded. "There are no defense wounds, but she was attacked from the front. The killer hit both the jugular vein and the carotid artery. She would have been dead within sixty seconds."

No wonder there was so much blood spatter. "So the killer was quick," Miranda said. "Took her by surprise."

The doctor nodded. "The laceration to the throat was jagged enough to suggest a piece of the broken pottery might have been used."

"You mean as a weapon?" Miranda asked.

"Yes."

Carefully, Parker stepped to the spot where the shards of the vase had lain before the CSIs bagged and tagged them. He studied the empty spot on the shelf. "This particular weapon indicates it was a spontaneous act. Perhaps an act of passion."

Miranda's gaze followed his and she nodded. "Like maybe they had a fight?"

"Yes," he said.

O'Toole put a hand on his hip. "You think Blythe fought with Scott?"

128

Miranda considered that. "Maybe he came to see her after the rehearsal. To tell her what I'd said to him when I interviewed him."

O'Toole's mouth went back and forth. "The housekeeper didn't let anyone in. She claims the vic told her to go to bed as soon as she came home."

"And she says she did." Parker had spoken to Hildie briefly before the others arrived and had calmed her down. He was good at that.

Miranda took a step toward the pool, envisioning the scene. "So maybe Scott says, 'baby, the jig is up. We've got to leave town.'"

Parker moved closer to the shelf, as if he were putting himself in the killer's position. "Or perhaps he told her he was leaving town."

"And so she gets upset, yells at him. He yells back, flies into a blinding rage." Miranda stepped between Parker and the shelf. "But he takes a slug at her or just gestures and his hand hits the vase." She mimicked the move.

"Or he grabs the vase in anger and hurls it to the floor." Parker acted out his version.

"Either way, the vase falls and shatters. Scott stares down at the shards and gets an idea. He's still in a frenzy, so he picks up a piece and slashes out at her."

O'Toole scratched his chin. "Could have played like that."

"Blythe falls to the ground," Miranda continued, pointing to the area where it might have happened. "Scott rolls her over into the water, hoping it'll wash away some of the evidence."

"Or she falls into the pool from the force of the attack." Parker frowned. "What about the pottery shard? We didn't find a bloody piece."

O'Toole crouched down and studied the tiles. "The murder weapon would be nice to have."

Miranda thought a minute. "Maybe he puts it in his pocket and leaves."

With a frustrated grunt, O'Toole straightened. "We'll know more once we process those bloody footprints. If we can get a match."

Miranda scratched at her hair. "Yeah, and the killer's clothes would be bloody, too."

The three of them fell silent, pondering the scene.

O'Toole's phone rang. He took the call, and after a minute or two hung up with a grin of triumph. "Ralston's got Scott back at the station. You two up for some late night interrogation?"

Miranda felt a surge of hope that they might have their killer at last. Suddenly, she was wide-awake.

"My favorite kind."

CHAPTER FORTY-TWO

This time it was Miranda's turn to watch through the two-way mirror.

The sergeant ushered her and Parker into the small space, then huffed out that his officers just reported no neighbors had seen anyone entering Blythe Star's house that night. That meant little if nobody was paying attention. Miranda was about to say so when the sergeant asked for her notepad to go over her interview with the suspect.

She handed it to him and watched him rush off to consult with Ralston before they took a turn at Sean Scott.

"He thinks we've got him," she murmured to Parker.

"Mmm." Parker's wise gray eyes were objective lasers as he moved to the window.

There still was room for reservation, Miranda thought as she turned her attention to the young man who'd been waiting in the interrogation room for over an hour.

But she hoped O'Toole was right and they had their man.

His arms crossed, his sandaled foot tapping a mile a minute against the linoleum floor, Scott sat at the little table, his gaze darting this way and that, as if he were looking for a hole in the wall he could escape through. He was dressed in a wrinkled plaid shirt and an old pair of jeans. Clothes he must have thrown on in a hurry. He wasn't flashing the lady-killer smile tonight.

Right now, he looked lost and afraid.

She heard Parker's low murmur beside her. "I apologize for earlier," he said simply.

Keeping her focus on the suspect, she decided to play dumb. "What for?"

From the corner of her eye, she watched his gaze narrow on her. But she wanted to hear it.

"For letting it slip to Sid that we're married. I realize it upset you."

"You were pretty steamed yourself." She turned to face him.

Hands behind his back, he inhaled stiffly and gave her a curt nod. "I apologize for breaking our agreement. And for losing my temper, as well. As you know by now, Sid has a special knack for irking me."

She almost let herself grin. "He does seem to get on your last nerve."

Parker ignored the observation. "We'll have to come up with a policy for public appearances."

Now he was getting down to the heart of the matter. The press conference. She still didn't see what the big deal about her doing it was, but for now she just nodded. "And about when to tell people about our personal relationship."

"Yes."

She rocked back on her heels and decided to go all the way. "And about exactly what being 'in charge' means."

She felt his chest expand and his body tense. But now it was his turn to nod. "Agreed. We'll discuss it when we get home."

Whenever that might be. But there was no time to talk now. O'Toole and Ralston had entered the interview room and the detective was reading Scott his rights.

They both turned their focus to the two-way.

The guy looked so pale with shock, Miranda almost felt sorry for him.

Ralston slid into her chair, her back board-straight, her plain face cold. She opened a folder and consulted it. "Mr. Scott, you've been an employee of Entertainment Security for three years, is that correct?"

"Yes, about that long." He tried to smile at her, but she didn't even notice.

"And that's why you were at the rehearsal Cameron Forest called this afternoon? The one where you were questioned in regard to the death of Ambrosia Dawn?"

Scott's smile fell away and he folded his hands on the table like an adult. "Yes. I—I was one of her bodyguards. Mr. Forest wanted to speak to me about my future employment."

"And did he?"

Miranda saw a flash of caution in the bodyguard's baby blues. *That's right. Be careful how you construct your story.*

"Yes, he did. After the rehearsal, we went out for a drink. He said he wanted me to perform the same duties for Ms. Star."

Ralston's eyes narrowed. "Have those duties begun?"

"Not yet. I'm supposed to start in two days. I've got vacation coming to me."

"I see." Ralston drummed her fingers on the table and studied her folder with a frown.

Like a well-timed dance move, O'Toole leaned over the table close to Scott, his face flushed. "Are you telling us that you didn't accompany Ms. Star home tonight?"

Scott looked over at the sergeant, eyes wide with shock. "No. Like I said, I went to have a drink with Mr. Forest, then I went straight home."

"Right away?"

"Of course, right away."

O'Toole leaned a little closer. "You didn't stop anywhere else?"

Backing away, Scott seemed confused. "No."

"What is the nature of your relationship with Ms. Star?"

Scott's eyes bugged out. "We're—friends. We talk and joke around during rehearsals."

Miranda noted the present tense. *Nice touch. Act as if you don't know she's dead.* And O'Toole didn't give it away, either. He could show some savvy once in a while.

"That's all?"

"Pretty much."

O'Toole pursed his lips, stared down at the notepad and tapped the desk with the end of his pen. "Someone on our staff saw you and Ms. Star just before the rehearsal. You were in a side room near the entrance. You were doing more than talking and joking."

Scott's mouth opened. He glared at O'Toole. Then at Ralston. He looked like he was about to cry. He pressed his palms to his temples and groaned. "Okay. I was trying to get close to her. She has inside connections."

"Inside connections?" O'Toole echoed.

"Music connections."

Ralston's eyes turned hard. "You were using her?"

Scott rubbed his muscled arm, then his crew cut. "I want to be in the stage band. I play rhythm guitar and I'm good, but it's so hard to find a break in this town." His voice sounded shaky and desperate. "Okay, I admit it. I've been playing Blythe, hoping she could get me in the band. She's so easy."

Miranda shook her head. A woman desperate for attention and needing love. And this guy takes advantage for his own gain.

Ralston chewed on the side of her cheek. "But she didn't come through for you."

"Huh?"

"Mr. Forest wanted you to continue on as a bodyguard, not as a guitar player."

He pressed his lips together in frustration. "I mentioned it to him tonight. He didn't say anything."

"And so you were angry with Blythe, the woman you'd been stringing along."

"No. Okay, I decided to step things up with her."

"And you went to see her tonight after you left the bar?"

His eyes took on a glazed expression. "Tonight? No, I was beat. I went home to get some shuteye. I was going to pick up with her tomorrow."

O'Toole and Ralston looked at each other.

At last O'Toole rose and folded his arms. He glared down at the suspect with all his cop authority. "Mr. Scott. Blythe Star is dead."

Scott shook his head as if he were hearing things. "What? That's a lie."

"Her body was found in her home a few hours ago. It's been taken to the morgue."

There was a long moment of silence. Scott worked his mouth open and shut, but no sound came out. At last, he whispered. "No, that can't be." He ran both hands over his head. "It can't be. It just can't be."

Miranda thought she saw tears forming in his eyes. This guy was good.

O'Toole strolled around the table and parked his butt next to Scott. "So let's try this again. When did you get to Blythe Star's house tonight?"

"I didn't go there tonight. I've never been to her house."

"But you know where it is."

"Down the street from Abbey's place I passed it when I picked her up. That doesn't mean anything."

"Come on now, Mr. Scott." Now it was Ralston's turn to get to her feet and come around the table to crowd the bodyguard. "You planned Ambrosia Dawn's murder with Blythe Star, didn't you? You planted evidence to incriminate your former girlfriend, Suzie Chan."

Scott stared at Ralston. Then at O'Toole. Then at Ralston again. "You two are crazy. I was in Kingman, Arizona when Ambrosia was killed. I was with my old girlfriend, Jessica Martin. You can call her. I'll give you her number." He reached into his pocket, but they must have already taken his cell. "Get my phone. The number's in there."

"We'll do that," O'Toole said, getting to his feet. "In the meantime, Mr. Scott, you're under arrest."

Miranda turned to Parker. "The DA's going to throw that out. There's isn't enough evidence yet."

"If Scott is guilty, those footprints at the scene should match his."

She hoped so. But it could take days for those results. "He'll lawyer up soon. Before he's confessed to squat."

"No doubt." Parker let out a weary sigh and glanced at his watch. "It's late, Miranda. Let's go back to the hotel."

It had just hit her how tired she was. And how deflated. "Good idea."

CHAPTER FORTY-THREE

By the time they got back to the hotel suite, Miranda could barely keep her eyes open. She stumbled into the shower and jolted when she turned and discovered Parker had followed her in there.

As his wet arms slid around her in a comforting embrace, she pulled his mouth to hers and drank in the scent and touch of his moist skin as she devoured his lips. She needed this after the night she'd had. She wanted to wash away the image of Blythe Star, of swimming down in that pool, of struggling to pull out her lifeless body.

She threw her head back and let Parker take her with all the passion the man could muster. She knew he was taking her out of her troubling thoughts, soothing her the way only he could right now. With his hard muscled body, firm against hers, he engulfed her whole being in pleasure.

Once upon a time, she'd resisted him with all she had. Now she gave into him and his power, gave herself over to it and completely let go.

He had so mesmerized her, she didn't even notice what time it was when she fell into bed.

But she fell asleep instantly.

CHAPTER FORTY-FOUR

An hour later Parker stared through the open curtains at the view below of the city's gaudy nightlife, a Bacardi on ice going warm on the silver end table beside him.

After twenty years in this business, he knew the mind of a criminal. Once cornered, a killer feels threatened. He gets desperate, takes more risks, makes mistakes. He will do anything to save himself. Murder anyone who gets in his way.

The thought of his wife desperately giving that woman CPR beside the pool tonight played over and over in his mind. If things had gone differently, if she'd come across the killer before he left the scene, that could have been Miranda lying there dead.

In his mind he heard her telling him she could handle herself.

He was well aware of that. She had gotten both of them out of several dire situations. Thanks, for the most part, to her intelligence and strength and skill and indomitable spirit. But in this business there was always an element of luck.

And if Miranda's luck ever ran out?

Irritation at his own chagrin rippled through him. He had wanted this consulting service. To share the thrill of investigation with her. He had wanted to give her the excitement she craved. To give her an extensive range of experience. Opportunities to grow into the best investigator she could be. But now that they were actually on a job?

All he could think about was the hours he'd spent in that hospital eight months ago, waiting for her to wake up from a coma, fearing he'd never hold her in his arms again, never hear her laughter, never taste her lips, never delight in her bold spirit.

That he'd lost her for good.

He ran a hand over his face, hating the decision he'd made.

He wouldn't tell her directly. That would only provoke her. Instead, he would explain the idea of consulting was just that. To aid law enforcement, not put themselves in the middle of danger. They'd done enough. The police had a viable suspect in custody. Sid could handle wrapping things up from here.

The idea nagged at him. And he knew it wouldn't be enough for her.

He'd remind her he was only too familiar with the frustrations of police procedure. If Sean Scott wasn't the killer or if Sid couldn't build a strong enough case against him, this investigation could go on for years. It would be a waste of time for them to linger here. Would those facts convince his persistent wife to end this first assignment?

He sighed aloud. Probably not.

Perhaps he could distract her with other cases. Her appearance at the press conference, as much as it had annoyed him, had attracted attention. He had already received three emails inquiring about their consulting service.

That might not work, either.

But somehow he would persuade her they should wrap things up with Sid and go home. Perhaps take a respite before the next case. And when they were home, he'd have a chance to think through whether to continue this enterprise.

Disappointed with himself but as satisfied as he could be with his new plan, Parker swallowed the rest of his drink and went back to bed.

CHAPTER FORTY-FIVE

The ground beneath her feet was sandy and almost too hot to tread. But she kept going. Something drove her on, though she couldn't tell what it was. Gulls cried overhead and the air had a strange, musty smell. The sun beat down on her, stirring the air surrounding her to a bubbling temperature. Sweat ran down her back, her forehead, her arms. Still she kept going.

What was she looking for? If only she knew.

All at once, the sand grew soft, like a beach. She began to sink into it up to her ankles. It became hard to walk. She pulled her feet up, step by step. The effort took her breath.

She looked down.

The earth was mud now, caking along her feet, her shins. The air had turned cold and dank and dark. The sky overhead threatened a storm. The birds flew away.

She pressed on and on until she came to a dark pool. She stared down into the murky water. Was what she was looking for there?

She blinked. What was that?

Beneath the water were two bare arms, moving in a swimming motion. And hair. Long blond hair swirling around the arms, shimmering somehow under the mud. The figure turned and a face appeared. A woman's face. Lovely. Familiar, but she couldn't say who it was.

The lips began to move as if calling out to her. She heard a faint voice. "I'm innocent. Innocent."

The voice grew louder, repeating the words again, as if afraid she hadn't heard. "I'm innocent."

The arms, the face swam up to her. Closer. Closer.

Suddenly the limbs shot out of the water. Two waterlogged hands reached for her, slipped around her neck. She couldn't breathe.

"I'm innocent. I'm innocent." But the voice wasn't the woman's any longer. It belonged to a man.

She looked up into the crazed blue eyes of Sean Scott. And then the eyes turned black. The cold black slits she knew so well.

Leon.

Miranda shot up with a start, her heart banging in her chest. She gasped for air. She looked down and saw her hands were tight around her pillow in a death grip. She let go of the pillow and sank back onto the bed, relief washing over her.

A dream. A nightmare.

She hadn't had one of those in a long time. She thought she was done with them.

She ran her hands over her face and thought about Suzie Chan. Her mind raced with data. She'd thought the woman had killed Ambrosia Dawn. All the evidence they had at first pointed to it. But she'd been wrong. Now she thought Blythe Star had killed her sister with the help of Sean Scott, the bodyguard. And Scott had killed Blythe when he thought the police were getting close to the truth.

She stared up at the ceiling. That's what she'd been missing so far, wasn't it? In the past she'd always had some kind of premonition, for lack of a better word. An eerie sensation, a gut feeling she couldn't explain. And dreams.

And now she'd had one of those. What did it mean?

Was the real killer leading them down the wrong path again? Was this—another set up?

She had nothing to base it on, but something deep in her gut said she was onto something.

Realizing it was daylight, she sat up again and yanked the covers back just as Parker came into the room.

Holding a large mug of coffee, he smiled at her tenderly. "You slept past noon."

"Did I?" she craned her neck to glance at the clock. "Why did you let me?"

He handed her the cup and sat down next to her on the bed. "You were exhausted. We didn't get to bed until past two."

She took the cup in both hands and guzzled a sip of the delicious dark liquid, ignoring its temperature. "We're turning into night owls like the late night gamblers in this town."

"Perhaps we are." He chuckled softly.

Then she noticed a look in his gray eyes. One she knew only too well.

"What is it?"

He reached for her hand. "I called Sid while you were sleeping. He's closing the case."

Her stomach sank. She set the mug down on the silver nightstand. "And leaving things unfinished?"

"They are finished, Miranda. Our job here is done."

Shock raced through her at his words. And a flash of rage. But she managed to control both. "Parker, we both know there isn't enough evidence to convict Scott."

"Sid seems to be taking ownership of the case now. He and Ralston have the manpower to find the remaining evidence they need."

She squeezed his hand and bobbed it up and down for emphasis. "What if we're wrong?"

"What do you mean?"

"What if Scott is telling the truth? What if he had nothing to do with either murder?"

He gave her a dark look. "Do you really believe that?"

She didn't want to tell him about her dream. It made her feel like she needed a crutch. As if she couldn't solve a case on her own.

"Don't you want to see the girls?" he said gently.

How dare he bring them up? She pulled her hand out of his with a scowl. "You know damn well I haven't seen Wendy or Mackenzie for months."

She watched his jaw tighten as he pressed his lips together. "But you ought to think of them, Miranda. They're your children."

"Neither of them is really my child."

Not in the sense of Miranda being a day-to-day mom. They both knew what she meant and what the situation was.

"Nonetheless, you have to consider the implications of the risks you take."

Her temper spiked. "What are you saying? That finishing this case is too risky because of Mackenzie and Wendy?"

"I weigh risk every time I take on a case." He was referring to his long and successful career as a PI.

Parker had had two children. One by his first wife, one he'd taken into his home out of the goodness of his heart. And yet he took a hell of a lot of risks. And now he was throwing Mackenzie and Wendy in her face? Implying she was being reckless because she wasn't thinking of them?

"That's a low blow, Parker."

"I'm sorry you feel that way." His voice was calm and patient.

She ground her teeth and glared at him. She knew perfectly well what he was doing. Protecting her, the way he always had. If it were months ago, she'd tell him to go to hell and walk straight out the door.

But now?

She took a deep breath and gave herself a minute to calm down. And to come up with an idea. Two could play this sneaky detective game. She twisted her lips into a pout she hoped didn't look too unnatural and took his hand. "I don't know—"

"What is it?"

"We're in Las Vegas. I didn't want to go home until we took in some of the sights." She smiled her best wifely smile.

He eyed her suspiciously. "What would you like to do?"

He had to know she was up to something, but he couldn't resist giving into her whims. Besides, he probably thought he could talk her out of any plan she might come up with.

Problem was, she didn't have a plan. If Blythe Star and Sean Scott weren't the killers, she had no idea who was. She'd just have to keep Parker busy until she did.

She scooted out of bed, sashayed over to the window and pointed at the needle-shaped building, the tallest one in the skyline. "I'd like to see what's at the top of that casino."

"The Stratosphere?"

"Uh huh."

"That's the second tallest in the Western Hemisphere."

"Uh huh." She turned around and gave him a flirtatious grin. "And they have rides up there, don't they?"

With a defeated groan Parker got to his feet. "Get dressed."

CHAPTER FORTY-SIX

He let her go on all the rides.

One called Insanity, that dangled and spun her more than a thousand feet over the city. The Big Shot Ride that made her giggle and shriek as it yanked her up a hundred and sixty feet atop the tall casino tower. The X-Scream that felt like a cross between a teeter-totter and a roller coaster. And her absolute favorite, the Sky Jump, a bungee jump off the top of the Stratosphere.

What a rush.

Parker opted to watch but afterwards, he took her to the revolving restaurant and marveled as she wolfed down a filet and a Canadian lobster with the works. Maybe it was because they'd skipped breakfast, but the adrenaline rush and yelling her head off had given her a monstrous appetite.

Chewing a tender piece of meat, she gazed out the huge beveled window toward the west and Costa Rica Hills and concentrated on what she was really after.

What was she missing?

Sean Scott was a womanizer, boinking three different women either in short succession or at the same time. If Blythe Star killed her sister and Scott helped, and he thought the police were zeroing in on her, he'd realize it would only be a matter of time before she gave him up. If she told him that's what she was going to do, it would stand to reason he'd be mad as hell at her. Especially if he'd only been using her all along and found out he was the one who'd really been used.

But why would a self-centered ladies' man let himself get into that position in the first place? Blythe invites him over and says, "Hey, baby. I want to knock off my bitchy sister, but I need someone to hoist her body into the trunk of my car. Can you help me out?"

Even if Scott had been really pissed about the way Ambrosia treated Suzie Chan, he wouldn't risk going to jail. Not for someone who was just a casual sex partner. Not for a rebound from his old girlfriend.

Last night it had made so much sense, but today with the bright sun in her eyes, it all rang hollow. So what was she missing? She asked herself again. Who else knew about the tea? That Ambrosia would be alone in the kitchen? And where to get abrin? Who else was pissed off enough at her to risk everything?

"Penny for your thoughts?" She turned to see Parker's cold stare.

He'd read her mind, as he so often did.

But she dismissed it and lifted a shoulder. "Just taking in the sights."

"They are seductive, aren't they?" He tossed down his napkin and studied her.

She could tell he knew her mind was still on the case. But where did he expect it to be? He was the one who'd made her a professional, after all.

She just smiled and swallowed the last bite of her steak. "Are you sure you don't want to try the X-Scream?"

"I'll pass. We need to get going."

Darn. She needed more time.

Back in the car, she managed to talk him into taking her to see the white tigers and after that going on a monorail ride halfway around the city. That ate up several hours. On their way out of the station, she was about to suggest Madame Tussauds when Parker insisted on calling it quits and she caved.

But it was okay. Suddenly she'd remembered something.

By the time the sun was getting low on the horizon and they were back in the hotel suite, Miranda knew who her next suspect was.

CHAPTER FORTY-SEVEN

Miranda watched Parker pull out their suitcases from the closet and lay them on the bed. A hard knot formed in her stomach.

She couldn't let him get her on that plane. Not yet. Think. Tapping her fingers against her crossed arms, she eyed a brochure sitting on one of the nightstands.

"Hey," she said, picking it up. "There's a UFC fight tonight at the MGM."

He reached for a suit. "We have a plane to catch."

She stuck out her lower lip and gave him her best imitation of a baby doll look.

He tossed the suit on the bed in disgust. "Miranda. You don't pout."

Had her there. "I do want to see it."

"And what else do you want?"

She sank down on the mattress next to the suitcases and dropped the cutie-pie act. "I want to check something out. It shouldn't take more than an hour."

His expression turned dark. "About the case?"

"Yeah. I just want to make sure we've tied up some loose ends."

He studied her with a measured look, the lines in his handsome face growing deeper. His jaw was tight. His sexy salt-and-pepper hair seemed grayer in the moonlight from the window. He seemed wiser than ever. He was probably right. They probably had the killer in custody.

But she just couldn't let it go.

"And it will only take one hour?" he said at last.

Her heart soared, but she forced herself to sound casual. "It shouldn't. I just want to cross some t's, dot some i's, you know?" And if she found something, she was sure he'd change his mind and stay to pursue it. "So why don't you get our boarding passes while I run this little errand?"

"Very well. I'll see you back here in an hour." He turned back to his packing.

"Okay."

Miranda picked up the car keys from the dresser and decided the jeans and light shirt she'd worn on the rides would do. She gave Parker a peck on the cheek and headed out the door, surprised he hadn't even asked where she was going. He probably assumed she was heading back to the police station. She would get there, but she had a little detour to make first.

As the glass elevator doors opened in the hall, she realized Parker hadn't needed to ask where she was headed. He would be tracking her whereabouts on her phone.

That sneaky bastard. No wonder she loved him so much.

CHAPTER FORTY-EIGHT

She found the Blue Palm Lounge on East Desert Inn near the Wynn Resort. As soon as Miranda stepped into the place, she was plunged into the dark, smoky twenty-four-seven party atmosphere that made you forget if it was noon or night outside.

Not that she was surprised by that. She wasn't a stranger to bars. She knew their vibes, their typical décor, their often seedy clientele. Even in Las Vegas, they were about the same, she expected. And as bars went, this one wasn't a dive, but it wasn't ultra-chic either.

Polished tables, fairly clean. Decorative red and blue neon lights streaming around the perimeter. A row of slot machines along one wall. Behind the bar backlit glass shelves holding multi-shaped bottles gave off a subtle, muted quality that made you feel like you were in another world.

Ah, the allure of booze. Stay up all night and drink your troubles away. If only life were so easy.

The patrons seemed on the sparse side for a Saturday night, but it was still early and she guessed there was a lot of competition in this town.

Miranda slid onto a stool near a bar-top video poker machine that advertised free drinks if you won.

A burly bartender in a black button-down shirt with the sleeves rolled up to his bulky biceps was wiping the bar's polished surface. He shot her a toothy grin. "What'll you have?"

Miranda smiled back. No reason not to be friendly. "I'm wondering if there's a Reedy Max here?"

The smile faded and he studied his polishing job instead. "What do you want with her?"

Her? Reedy Max was a woman? Interesting. "A mutual friend told me to look her up if I was ever in town."

No need to show your hand too early.

The bartender stopped wiping and cocked his head at her. But instead of giving her a hard time, he turned and headed for the back.

Miranda was afraid he'd return with a shotgun and run her off. Instead a woman emerged from the door he'd disappeared into. An average-sized, busty woman clad in low-cut black leather.

She sauntered over. "Are you the one asking for me?"

Miranda gave her a bland look. "Are you Reedy Max?"

She echoed Miranda's expression. "None other. Welcome to my place."

Her voice was low and husky, like someone who'd smoked way too many cigarettes in her lifetime. She owned the bar? Must have done well as Cameron Forest's business associate.

Reedy Max moved in close to study Miranda. Her bare arms were tattooed and looked in pretty good shape. Lots of makeup. Glittery blue shadow. Thick black mascara. Lots of studs on the leather. A narrow ring through her lower lip. Long, spiky earrings dangling from under a too teased 'do. Her hair was either platinum blond with black streaks or jet-black with platinum blond streaks. Miranda wasn't sure, but she looked to be in her late-fifties. What some men might call a tough old broad.

Miranda noted a dark mole on her left cheek and wondered if the woman had been a Marilyn Monroe impersonator in her heyday.

She leaned a strong-looking arm on the bar. "What's your pleasure?"

Miranda met her hard gaze. "I'll take a root beer."

"You want a little Jack Daniels in that?"

"No, thanks. I'm working."

Instead of getting the drink, she eyed her up and down, probably thinking "working" meant she was a prostitute. Miranda took a card out of her pocket and slid it across the bar.

The woman picked it up, pursed her lips back and forth as she examined it. "Oh, yeah. I saw you on the news last night."

The infamous press conference.

"You're looking into Ambrosia Dawn's murder." She handed the card back.

Miranda put it back in her pocket. "I am. I understand you used to work with Cameron Forest. Ambrosia Dawn's husband?"

"Maybe."

"That's what he told me."

"So what of it?"

"I just want to ask a few questions about his family life."

Reedy Max studied her a long while with her street-wise gaze then turned to grab a glass. She filled it with ice and root beer and set it down in front of Miranda.

"What do you want to know? I'm always happy to help the police."

Yeah, right. But at least she had gotten to first base. She'd see if she could get a little farther. "How long have you known Cameron Forest?"

Reedy Max gave a disinterested shrug. "We go way back. He tell you I used to be his manager?"

"That's what he said."

146

Studying her again, the woman played absently with an earring, sizing up her interrogator, deciding how much she ought to say. "He used to do Elvis," she said at last. "I got him jobs all up and down the Strip. He was better than most and believe me, I've seen them all come and go."

She sounded fond of her protégé.

Miranda stirred the root beer with her swizzle stick. "But he couldn't make a go of it?"

"He could have if he'd stuck with it and listened to me. But no, he had to go after the big fish." She blinked and looked away, as if she knew she'd said too much.

Miranda pounced. "You didn't care for Ambrosia Dawn?"

"In my opinion—" She stopped herself and slid her gaze over to the burly dude, who was serving someone at the other end of the bar.

Her expression said she was wrestling with her thoughts. Wouldn't do for a bar owner in this town to get in trouble for not cooperating with the authorities. And maybe her opinion of Ambrosia Dawn wasn't so secret. Maybe she didn't keep her opinions to herself, though she probably wished she had at the moment. But if those opinions could be easily confirmed by her employees, it wouldn't do to fudge the truth. Not when the police were involved.

The woman eyed her cautiously then raised a long, black-painted fingernail. "I'm sorry she's gone. Really. No one deserves to bite the big one that young. And especially the way she went." She paused for a breath. "But I can't say she lived a good life or anything like that. Anyone who knew her knew she was a hotheaded, self-centered prima donna. If you're investigating the case you've got to know that already."

Smart lady. Miranda sipped her drink and let Reedy go on.

Shaking her head the woman picked up the rag Burly Dude had left on the counter and began wiping. "I warned Cameron not to hook up with that woman when he met her. 'She's trouble,' I said to him. That boy deserved better."

"He didn't listen."

She uttered a husky smirk. "Hell, no. They met at a party one night, she started coming to his shows and three months later, they were hitched."

Miranda stirred her drink some more. "He was with her for eight years. They must have had a decent relationship."

"He loved her all right," she snarled. "No matter how much of a bitch she was. But I think she only stayed with him because of the work Cameron did for her. He has a good head for business. Thank God he had enough sense to become her manager so she wouldn't take him for a ride. I hope he got a good chunk of change from her estate."

Was Cameron Forest after his wife's inheritance? That didn't seem to play. She had to be careful how she phrased herself now. "I think you're right. He seemed pretty broken up about losing Ambrosia when I spoke to him. Guess he was the only one who got along with her."

She tossed the rag into a sink and smirked. "He bitched about that woman all the time. Oh, the fights they had. He told me he didn't think he could stay with her much longer, but I knew he'd never leave her."

"He wanted to leave because of her temper?"

"Because of his son."

Son? Miranda remembered Cameron mentioning the kid was from a former marriage. She'd wondered whether he was still pining after his first wife. "What did his son have to do with it?"

"He's a sixteen-year-old kid. Been tossed around ever since Cameron's first wife left him. They've had nannies and tutors when they went on tour, put him in public school when they were here. Now he's starting to get into trouble, hanging with the wrong crowd, you know?"

Miranda nodded. Oh, yeah, she knew. "The boy didn't have a good relationship with his stepmother?"

"From what Cameron said, Abbey wasn't very nice to the kid."

Miranda stiffened. "What did she do to him?"

"Cameron never would say, but it wasn't good from what I could guess."

That certainly would be motive. Knock off your wife to save your son. Get her inheritance as a nice bonus. She took another sip of the root beer and prepared herself to change tactics. If Cameron Forest was responsible for his wife's death, she had to have more than the idle talk of a middle-aged barmaid.

She cleared her throat and tried to sound like a friend instead of an investigator looking for a killer. "This past Tuesday night Cameron told me he came to see you after the rehearsal."

Reedy straightened. She knew this was getting serious. "Yeah, he stopped by here for a drink."

"What kind of mood was he in?"

She looked around for her rag, but it was already in the sink. For a moment she looked as if she wanted to toss Miranda out, then thought better of it. "He was upset. That woman had pitched another fit. She was furious at her poor sister."

"Blythe Star?"

"Right. I met her a couple of times when she came in here. She's a sweet thing. And she had to put up with absolute shit from that woman. How could she treat her own flesh and blood like that, I'll never understand."

In Miranda's experience, flesh and blood often treated each other like shit.

Obviously, Reedy hadn't heard about Blythe's death. Forest and his publicist might be scrambling to keep it out of the media or the bar owner might have been too busy to catch the news. Probably not unusual to avoid daily reports of tragedy when you lived in a town built on escape.

"By any chance, do you know if Cameron went straight home after seeing you that night?"

Reedy tapped her fingernails on the glossy bar and glanced around as if trying to find a good answer. Apparently she failed. "I don't know for sure," she said at last. "But he was too upset to face the bitch. He probably went to one of his parties."

"Parties?" Forest had failed to mention that during her interview.

Reedy waved her hands in the air as if in surrender. "What he couldn't get at home, he managed to find elsewhere. You know. Men have their needs."

"Yeah, I know." Except for more bitching about Ambrosia Dawn, she wasn't going to get much else here. She slid off the stool and reached into her pocket for some cash.

Reedy held up a hand. "No charge."

"Oh?"

She smiled, showing off the mole on her cheek. "I'm always happy to support the police department."

And keep herself out of trouble. But she'd take it.

"Thanks," Miranda said and smiled back with extra sugar on top.

Reedy Max's smile faded. She'd said too much.

Miranda turned to go.

"Wait a minute."

She turned back.

The woman wagged a finger at her, her face turning hard. "If you're thinking Cameron had anything to do with his wife's death," she barked in her husky voice, "you're wrong. He was too drunk to think straight when he left here."

Something that would be hard to verify. "He shouldn't have been driving in that condition."

"He wasn't driving. Andersen was. Just like usual."

"Andersen?"

"His limo driver."

CHAPTER FORTY-NINE

Back in Parker's rented sedan, Miranda's head was spinning. When she'd gone to see him, Cameron Forest had lied to her like one of his fancy Persian rugs.

He didn't go straight home the night his wife was killed as he claimed. He knew about the bad rehearsal and the temper tantrum Ambrosia Dawn had pitched in front of the entire crew. And their relationship hadn't been as peachy as he'd led her to believe.

No, he was worried about the way his second wife treated his son. Maybe he was afraid of her. So he turned to "other sources" for comfort. Maybe he'd planned it all from the beginning. Pinning his wife's death first on his cook and then her bodyguard. Maybe the former Elvis impersonator was a whole lot smarter than he looked.

But why was he so upset about her death, then?

She thought of the tears he'd shed in front of her, his anguished cries, his open display of grief both during her first interview and at the rehearsal yesterday.

She'd been so sure that grief was real. She was still sure.

But you could love and hate someone at the same time, couldn't you? Maybe he loved what she once was or what he thought she was. Could you love someone and cheat on them? Maybe in the minds of some men. Men who were married to celebrities.

She let out a long, frustrated sigh.

None of this proved Cameron Forest killed Ambrosia Dawn. None of it proved anything about Sean Scott. Or how Blythe Star came into it or why her fingerprints were on that jar in Suzie Chan's refrigerator. Or why she was now dead.

She needed more. Tapping her hands on the steering wheel as she waited for a light, she forced her thoughts to focus. And then she got it.

The limo driver. He was at the rehearsal yesterday. Someone had to have interviewed him. She glanced at the time on the dash. Her hour was almost up.

150

"Just a little longer, Parker," she murmured as the light went green. Hope burning in her chest, she turned onto the Strip and headed for the police station and Detective Ralston.

Parker, she thought on another sigh as she hit the brake for the heavy traffic. She couldn't figure him out, either. Why did he want to up and leave before they were certain who the killer was?

Was he just trying to protect her? Hell, he was always trying to protect her. By now she knew he'd never overcome that chivalrous, knight-in-shining-armor, Southern gentlemen syndrome he had. He was born with it. It came along with the silver spoon in his mouth. It was bone deep.

And she knew he'd gone through hell in that hospital last October. If their roles had been reversed, she'd have been a basket case. And she'd be just as jittery about him on a dangerous assignment. This one hadn't been so dangerous yet, but you never knew when you were chasing down a murderer. And what were they supposed to do? Shut down their lives? What was she supposed to do? Put on an apron, stay in the house and play Suzy Homemaker? They both knew that wasn't gonna happen. She had a life to live. And as corny as it sounded, she was still convinced she had a destiny to fulfill.

She'd do that with or without Parker, but she'd really prefer to have him by her side. She was determined to make that happen tonight.

If Ralston had the information they needed, she'd have some evidence to show her husband that would make him stay and see this case to the end.

She'd call him, he'd rush over to the station, and they'd be off and running again. Everything would be just fine.

CHAPTER FIFTY

Miranda marched down the hall to Ralston's office, exhilaration and adrenaline streaming through her veins. They were close. She could feel it. She reached the door and knocked.

Then she peeked inside. It was empty.

She hailed a uniform passing by. "Where's Detective Ralston?"

"Got the day off. Her case is closed."

"Thanks," Miranda murmured, her excitement plummeting like her body on the Insanity ride this afternoon.

She turned on her heel and headed for O'Toole's office, but her spirits didn't rise. If Ralston wasn't in, the slothful sergeant would probably have gone fishing at Lake Mead.

She was shocked when she found him at his desk, typing away on his keyboard.

"You're here," she said, slinking into the room and sinking into the guest chair, which was back to a single.

He turned to her with a smirk. "I gave the team the day off and decided to finish up the paperwork myself. I've almost got it all ready for the DA."

"Parker said you'd closed the case."

"Mm-hmm," he murmured as he kept typing.

Watching him, Miranda was overcome with that familiar ants-crawling-up-your-backside feeling. "You think the DA is going to go with what you have on Scott?"

O'Toole lifted a shoulder without looking at her. "Not much choice. We still haven't been able to reach the alibi."

Miranda wondered vaguely if the young woman in Kingston who was Scott's alibi was dead. But maybe not if her new theory was right.

"We impounded Blythe Star's vehicle. Lab is combing it for evidence. They're still working on the footprints, as well. And we found a wheelbarrow in a shed in the backyard."

Could be a week or more before they had anything conclusive. She cleared her throat. "I've been checking out some loose ends."

"Oh, yeah?" He sounded as interested as a teenager engrossed in a video game.

"I went to see an old friend of Cameron Forest's. His former manager, actually. Her name's Reedy Max."

Now the sergeant stopped typing and turned to her. "Why?"

"Like I said I wanted to check some things out. I discovered some interesting details."

"Such as?"

"Such as Forest and Ambrosia didn't get along so well. She mistreated his son. They fought all the time and he used to complain to his former manager about it."

O'Toole's dark chestnut brow rose in cynicism. "You're suspecting the husband now? We have nothing on him."

"All I'm saying is we all bought his grief act and didn't check him out. Turns out he lied about a bunch of things."

"Such as?" O'Toole asked again.

"Ambrosia's mood during her last rehearsal. Her fights with Suzie Chan and her sister."

"That was probably to avoid bad publicity."

"Maybe, maybe not. The man was cheating on his wife, according to the ex-manager."

O'Toole sat back and put his tongue against his cheek to consider what she'd said a moment. Then he frowned with disapproval. "That's all interesting, but not enough to even bring him in for questioning. Not when we've got someone like Scott on the line."

"I know. That's why I'm here. Forest led me to believe he drove himself to and from the rehearsal this past Tuesday night. But his ex-manager says he had a limo driver."

"Ambrosia's?"

Miranda shook her head. "A second one. If that's how Forest normally travels, and according to the ex-manager it is, that driver must have been at the rehearsal last night. One of your men would have questioned him."

"And you want to see his report?"

"I thought that would be a good place to start."

O'Toole paused a moment to consider the request, then turned back to his keyboard and began to type.

Feeling triumphant, Miranda got up and came around the desk to peep over his shoulder.

"Wait a minute." He pressed another set of keys. "The report of Blythe Star's phone calls just came in."

He scrolled a bit while Miranda tried to read the text. He was going too fast.

"She called Scott three times last night. No answer."

"Were there any texts?"

The sergeant studied the screen then shook his head. "None. But look here. She called Forest once."

She squinted where he was pointing and saw the time. "That would give Forest enough time to get to her place before she was killed."

If he was the one who killed both his wife and her sister.

"You're right. Let's get back to that interview." O'Toole's enthusiasm seemed to have revived. "Would you happen to have a name for said limo driver?"

"Andersen, according to Max."

He flipped through some more screens. "You'd think that name would be on top, but they're sorted by case number."

Which meant the fifty or so interviews they had would all be lumped together. Which could take forever to sort through. Crap.

Miranda tried not to grind her teeth while she breathed down the sergeant's neck as he worked away.

"Here we go," he said at last.

"Finally."

He gave her a scowl over his shoulder then pointed to the screen. "King interviewed him."

"And?"

"Says he was evasive, seemed a little nervous."

Anybody would be nervous being questioned by the police about a murder. "Anything else?"

"After the rehearsal Tuesday night, Andersen says he took Forest to the Blue Palm Lounge on East Desert Inn."

"That's where I went to see Reedy Max just now. She confirmed Forest was there Tuesday."

"Said he went inside with Forest and had a coke at a table by himself while he waited. Said his boss was generous that way."

"Then what?"

"Forest didn't stay long. After about half an hour, they left the bar. Now Andersen gets really evasive. Doesn't want to say what time Forest got home."

The hair on the back of Miranda's neck stood up. "See what I mean? That doesn't sound too kosher."

"No, it doesn't." He read more. "Good work, King. He gets it out of the driver that he took Forest to a party before they headed home."

"Where?"

"Another country club where local celebs and well-to-dos live. Catalonia Cove."

"Is that close to Costa Rica Hills?"

"Three miles."

"And when did they get home?"

O'Toole read through a lengthy passage that must have been more back and forth. "Andersen says he's not sure of the exact time he pulled into the drive, but he thinks it was at least twenty minutes after one."

"After?"

"He's not sure. TOD was between eleven and one. It could be off a few minutes."

"Not by that much," Miranda scoffed.

"Maybe the limo driver fudged the time."

"TOD isn't public knowledge."

She thought a moment. "But if he wanted to protect his employer, he could have stated the wrong time. Say by half an hour. That would be plenty of time to make sure she drank the tea, stash the body in the trunk of another car, and take it out to I-15."

O'Toole scratched his chin. "What about Blythe Star's fingerprints on the jar with the eye?"

Good question. "I don't have all the answers yet. But I think we've got enough to pay Elvis another visit. Which is what I'm about to do." She got to her feet.

"You're going there now?"

"Yep." She turned to head out the door.

"Hold on, Steele. I'll go with you."

She spun back to him, brows raised. "You sure you don't want your time off?"

He responded with a snort. "Please."

He gave her an after-you gesture and the two of them headed out.

They marched down the corridor side by side. Miranda had no idea what had made the sergeant change his tune about this case.

But whatever it was, she was glad for it.

CHAPTER FIFTY-ONE

The mourning fans who had declared their love forever in front of the Costa Rica Hills country club entrance had dissipated. The guards waved in O'Toole's car, recognizing it by now, and the rest of the drive was the same as before. But under the summer moon, Ambrosia Dawn's apricot mansion was lit up like an octogenarian's birthday cake.

Too bad there wasn't much to celebrate. Despite its luminosity, it looked as hollow and empty as a corpse.

O'Toole drove up to the curb near the circular drive and looked at the place. "Here we are."

"Yep." Miranda gazed at the rows and rows of glowing arched windows in the oddly shaped building blocks that made up the big home. Its design was as capricious as its owner's temper had been. And maybe as her husband's devotion as well.

No way to know for sure until she got some more answers. She reached for the door handle.

"Wait," O'Toole said in a whisper. "Look."

He pointed at the garage. Its door was rising.

A moment later a sleek black limo began to slowly back out. It paused in the drive, reversed, and the garage door slid down again as the car cruised around to the front door of the house. After another moment, a figure emerged.

His blue-black hair and sideburns were neatly trimmed. He had on tight pants, a blazer, an extra shiny shirt with the collar turned up. Lots of chains around the neck. A swagger in his step. He carried a black tote bag in his hand.

The driver got out, held the door open and Cameron Forest slid into the backseat.

"Where's he going?"

Miranda bit the inside of her mouth. "Not to any memorial service, I bet."

The limo took off. O'Toole waited a respectable about of time then followed.

They zigzagged through the residential streets and Miranda had to hand it to the sergeant. His tailing skills were excellent. If the driver or Forest thought they were being followed, they didn't show it. And they didn't seem to alter their path because after a short drive, they pulled into the Catalonia Cove country club.

"This is where the driver took him the night Ambrosia was killed," Miranda said, her skin prickling as they turned a corner, cruising several car lengths behind the limo.

"Yeah, funny coincidence, huh?"

Maybe he celebrates every time he kills a woman, Miranda thought. She'd known men who would.

"Odd time to party. Just after your wife and your sister-in-law have been murdered," O'Toole said, echoing her own thoughts.

"Maybe he's not going to a party. Maybe he's going to see a friend."

"Not so sure about that." O'Toole followed the road as it curved around a center circle decorated with palm trees and bushes planted in a bed of rocks, then he headed down another street until the limo drove through an iron gate.

The sergeant pulled over to the curb and the two of them stared at the structure. What they could see of it, anyway.

It was another sprawling super castle, this time situated on the corner. Its gate opened to a winding drive and a tall entrance tower. But Miranda couldn't see much else. It was dark and the iron bars, the stone security wall that ran around the estate's perimeter, and the palm trees alongside it obscured her view, as was their purpose.

She could tell the place was lit up, just like Forest's own home. But this one wasn't empty. Miranda cracked her window and the sound of 80s pop music and laughter wafted into the sergeant's car, along with a blast of warm desert night air.

Miranda heard a faint splash. "Pool party."

"Guess so. And here comes another guest."

Through the iron bars they watched Forest's driver get out of the limo and come around to open the passenger door for him. Then the two men went inside, the driver carrying the tote bag.

"Nice of him not to make the help wait in the car."

"Unlike us," O'Toole groaned, switching off the ignition.

Miranda let out a sigh of agreement. They couldn't exactly go knock on the door and invite themselves in. There was no choice but to wait for Forest to come back out. Sometime.

Another limo pulled up, this one white, and glided through the gates. After a moment, two chatty couples got out, the men carrying liquor bottles, and hurried noisily inside.

O'Toole rubbed the back of his neck. "Looks like they're just getting started."

"Guess we're in for a long night." Stake-outs were the part of the job she hated most. Especially unplanned ones.

After about five minutes, a red Rolls Royce arrived at the gate. This one held three giggling young girls. Miranda wondered if they were local dancers or call girls hired for the night. Ten minutes passed and three more cars arrived with a variety of guests. The sergeant's car grew hot and stuffy.

After another half hour, it looked like the gang was all here.

O'Toole yawned and tried to stretch. "You got any good games on your phone?"

Miranda gave him a smirk but reached into her pocket. Just as she did, her cell began to vibrate. She took it out and looked at the display. Parker.

She glanced at the time. Uh oh. She was just a tad over an hour. By about three.

He was going to kill her. And she knew what she'd uncovered so far wouldn't be enough to convince him to stay. He'd tell her Sid could handle it.

She turned the phone off and slipped it back into her pocket. "Nope, no games here." Not video ones anyway.

"How come you're on your own tonight?"

Miranda coughed at the unexpected question. "Uh, Parker had some things to do."

The sergeant raised a skeptical brow. "He sounded relieved when I told him I was closing the case this morning."

"He's anxious to get back home and take care of some stuff at the Agency." Like chewing her out. But she'd be damned if she'd leave their first case with the wrong person in jail.

"I still can't believe you two are married."

Miranda felt her shoulders tense. The heat was getting to her. All she needed right now was to be razed by this sergeant. "You got a problem with it?"

He scratched at his ear. "No, no. I just wondered what happened to his first wife?"

"She died of cancer about four years ago. It was before we met." She really didn't want to discuss her personal life. Or Parker's.

"Sorry to hear that." Then his cheeks rounded in a teasing grin and his green eyes sparkled. "And so instead of a socialite, this time he goes for another PI. Interesting."

Miranda gritted her teeth. She wasn't in the mood. "What is it with you and women detectives, O'Toole?" she snapped.

He held up his hands. "Nothing. Really. I mean, I was about to say— working with you—with both of you these past few days has been kind of— inspiring."

Now it was Miranda's turn to look skeptical. "Now you're sucking up?"

"Oh, hell, Steele. Okay. I misjudged you at first. I've had a hard time with women lately." He rubbed at his nose with a sniff.

She softened a little, remembering what Ralston had said to her. "I heard you divorced recently."

He folded his muscular arms over his chest and focused out the window. "Yeah, well."

"I'm sorry."

He shrugged. "What could I expect? She wanted more than I could give her."

"Didn't like being married to a cop?"

"Didn't like being married to a cop who couldn't get promoted."

So that was it. Ouch. She recalled Parker had told her O'Toole had some personal problems. Suddenly, she felt for the guy. "Parker mentioned you had a hard time at the Agency when you were there."

"Did he, now?" O'Toole sneered.

"That didn't come out right. I meant he said he thought you had potential."

His lip was still curled. "What? That I didn't live up to?"

What could she say? She'd never had Parker's tact, especially when it came to talking about personal stuff. And she had to be honest. "Something like that. But I think I've seen you grow on this case. Like being here now."

He snorted. "I didn't expect a performance review from the PIs I hired."

Okay, be that way. She glared out the window and stared at the house. "I was just trying to say something positive." She'd really hit a raw spot.

"Yeah, right. My old man always told me I'd never amount to much. So glad to learn you and Parker agree."

She turned back around. "Your old man?"

"He raised me after my mother left when I was a kid. It was rough."

"Yeah, I know what that's like." He'd touched her own raw spot.

He narrowed his eyes at her. "How would you know?"

She didn't want to talk about it, but she was cornered. "My old man took off when I was five. My mother raised me and she thought I was good for nothing."

They stared at each other for a long moment.

Never in her wildest dreams did Miranda think she'd have a connection with a police sergeant, especially not this police sergeant. But there it was. They had a bond. Somehow in an instant they had gone from being near strangers to colleagues who really got each other.

She spoke softly now. "So I know what you mean about never thinking you'd amount to much. I felt that way for a long time. Until I met Parker."

He nodded slowly, old memories playing over his face. "Yeah. Parker might think I didn't live up to my potential, but if I hadn't had that time at his Agency, I'd probably be a panhandler on Sahara by now."

Feeling awkward and not knowing what to say again, Miranda looked away and stared at the house. No sign of Forest yet. Time to get back to business.

"Is this guy going to stay and party all night?" Maybe she was barking up the wrong tree.

O'Toole reached between the seats under the computer equipment and took out a small pair of binoculars. He handed them to her. "Here. See if you can get anything with these."

She took it and scanned the windows, the doorway, the cars. Nothing. "You know, Ralston's a solid detective," she said eyes still on the front door.

"Now there's somebody who's grown on this case."

Miranda put down the binoculars and stared at O'Toole. She'd been expecting the sergeant to make some snide remark, like "Yeah, when she's not putting on her makeup." But Ralston didn't wear a lot of makeup. Maybe she'd grown on the sergeant.

"And she's kind of cute, too."

Miranda smiled to herself. The same thing Ralston had said about him. "You ought to ask her out sometime."

He lifted his shoulders with a grimace. "Can't date if you're in the same unit. Against regulations."

O'Toole wasn't softened up enough yet. "Too bad. I think she likes you."

He blinked at her in genuine shock. "No shit?"

"Just a hunch." She rolled her window down some more and listened to the music. It was getting rockier.

She looked up at the bright stars then at the lamps along the street. She ran her gaze along the pale stone wall that bordered the house. A couple of decorative palm trees had been planted in a symmetrical line. A little farther down stood another tree. One with more foliage.

The sergeant followed her gaze. "My old man used to run a local nursery," he sighed. "Hated that I didn't take it over for him."

Now she knew what to say. "Me? I'm glad you're a cop."

That made him grin.

She pointed down the block. "You know what that third tree over there is?"

O'Toole craned his neck and squinted. "Looks like a Chilean Mesquite. They're good for shade in the daytime."

And at night for coverage.

"Could a person climb it?"

"If it's mature enough. Looks like that one is."

"You sure?"

"Pretty sure."

Good enough. She was tired of waiting around. She reached for the handle and pushed her door open.

"Steele, where the hell are you going?"

"I'll be right back." She held up the binoculars. "Mind if I keep these?"

Without waiting for a reply, she shut the door as quietly as she could and strolled along the sidewalk like a normal pedestrian. The warm, dry air cooled her body temperature a few degrees and at least there was a breeze now that the fierce sun had set several hours ago. It felt almost good out here.

She reached the mesquite tree and eyed it, nerves building in her stomach. She put her hands around its trunk for a pre-test. Not as sturdy as she would have liked, but better than the palms.

Well, here goes nothing, she thought.

She slung the binoculars around her neck, found a notch in the trunk, put her foot onto it, wrapped her arms around the trunk and pulled herself up. Nothing to it. She felt for another notch with her free foot, steadied her weight on it and lifted again.

She repeated the movement and ascended higher. Exhilaration shot through her.

She hadn't climbed a tree since she was a kid. She remembered the elm in her front yard and getting stuck in it and yelling for her mother, who never came. By nightfall, she'd managed to pull her foot out of her sneaker and clamber down on her own. By some miracle her mother never found out. Good thing. She would have beaten her to a pulp or locked her in a closet, no doubt. So this was nothing.

She was getting higher and the branches were getting thinner. She reached out for one and stuck her palm on a spiky leaf. Ow. O'Toole didn't tell her about that.

Don't look down, she told herself, sucking her flesh. Just relax. After all, this was as good as the Sky Jump ride, right? Except she wasn't strapped in.

She craned her neck. She was up about fifteen feet now. A little farther and she could see clear over that wall. Up she went again. Just a little more.

The laughter and splashing grew louder, the 80s music had turned to rap, and the smell of southwestern-flavored meat sizzling on a grill drifted up and made her mouth water.

The pool was in sight, but she needed her hands. She steadied herself across two branches that formed a V and slowly let go. Her feet held her up, thank God.

She reached for O'Toole's binoculars and peered down over the wall.

The pool was large and shaped like a cloverleaf. Lounge furniture had been placed around the perimeter of it. In the background, tiki torches lit up the area. Everyone was in bathing suits and held beer bottles or wine coolers. A group of young women danced and giggled near the diving board while two horny-looking men watched. Another group at the far end sat in chairs and gossiped. A man nearby manned the grill. No sign of the limo driver.

Frustrated, she swung her view to the side of the pool near the house. There he was.

Cameron Forest lay stretched out on a chaise surrounded by three bikini-clad women sporting a variety of hair colors.

He'd changed into swimwear—must have been in his tote bag. His robe was open, exposing his chest, which the pink-haired girl was licking. The long-haired tawny blond had her fingers in his hair. The one with the metallic blue hair and the Elvis tattoo on her back had her head between his legs. His shorts were around his knees.

He was getting his needs met elsewhere, all right. And he didn't seem too broken up about the deaths of his wife and sister-in-law at the moment. Or maybe he was drowning his sorrow in booze and semen.

Miranda felt like she had swallowed a cactus. It was all she could do not to barf over the wall. But that would give her away.

Then she had a thought.

Had Ambrosia Dawn found out about her husband's fooling around recently? Maybe she had one of her temper tantrums about it. Maybe she told old Forest she was going to divorce him. Can't let that happen. Someone like her had to have a pre-nup. One that would leave Forest back in the dives singing Elvis tunes. Not where you want to be at his age. Not after all he'd done for her. So instead, he knocks her off.

Keeping her balance, Miranda put down the binoculars and reached into her pocket for her cell. She set it for the camera, and holding it steady, focused. Hoping the shots wouldn't come out too grainy, she snapped five of them.

Good thing she had. Just as she got the last one, Forest groaned and tumbled onto the cement to a chorus of giggles from the girls.

He got up, pulled up his pants and stumbled toward the house. He was probably leaving. Had to get back to the car.

She shoved the phone back in her pocket and scrambled down the tree.

When she reached the sidewalk, she found O'Toole waiting for her, hands on hips, a weird look on his face.

"What?" she said, ready to take him on.

"Get something juicy?"

"Did I ever."

He shook his head. "Miranda Steele, you are one amazing woman."

She didn't know what to say to that, so she just pointed at the car. "We have to get back. Forest could come out any minute."

They strolled back to vehicle at a pace she hoped wouldn't attract any attention and slipped inside just as Forest and the limo driver emerged from the house.

CHAPTER FIFTY-TWO

Elvis was heading back home, all right. He'd probably fall into bed in a stupor when he got there and be out for the night.

Miranda pulled at her hair in frustration as once more they glided through the gates of the Costa Rica Hills country club. She had to get more information on him. A late night visit ought to throw him off guard. Let him go inside, get settled.

Then she and O'Toole would ring the bell. The house manager would try to put them off, but she wasn't about to let him.

Grill him, she told herself. Show no mercy. She'd get the truth out of him. But right now, she wasn't exactly sure what the truth was.

Now that she'd had a little time to think it over, the divorce-the-cheater-so-he-killed-her angle wasn't playing. A hothead like Ambrosia would have kicked him out of the house right away. She'd have made noise. Noise that everyone around her could hear. If she and Forest were breaking up, people would have known about it. But no one on the staff had mentioned it in the interviews.

Heck, it would have been in the news.

The only way a break up could have been kept quiet was if Forest had killed her right after she told him she was kicking him out. If Ambrosia had been stabbed with a kitchen knife or her throat had been slashed, like her sister's had, Miranda could believe that scenario. But the singer was poisoned. With abrin.

And that took time. Planning.

"What are they doing now?" O'Toole muttered.

Miranda turned her attention to the road. They were almost to Forest's street now, but the limo was slowing down. After rolling a few feet, it pulled over to the curb.

O'Toole smirked. "What the hell?"

"Maybe the driver forgot to get gas."

"Forest could probably fuel the vehicle with his breath."

Under the streetlamps, Miranda watched the back door of the limo open with no help from the driver this time. Forest got out and began to stroll along the sidewalk.

The limo took off.

"Stretching his legs?" O'Toole smirked.

Miranda stared at the tall man's head as it turned from side to side while he trekked along—like he thought he was being watched.

"He's going to spot us," she whispered.

"He doesn't know this car. We've been going ten miles an hour to keep out of sight."

"But now there's no one else around. Act like you're lost." She waved a hand in the opposite direction of Forest. "Turn down that street. Don't turn on your blinker."

"I know how to tail someone."

But just as the sergeant was about to comply, Forest stepped into a dark spot and ducked between two of the estates.

"Where's he going?" she squeaked. "Pull over."

Rolling his eyes, O'Toole did as she said. She had the passenger door open before he stopped the car.

"What the hell are you doing, Steele?"

"We've got to follow him."

His face went blank. "We can't do that. We don't have a warrant. It's trespassing."

"He's trespassing. Maybe you should arrest him for that."

He scowled. "I can't do that."

"You're a policeman, aren't you? If I were one I'd do it myself."

His face flushed with irritation. "Fine for you to say. Your job's not on the line."

Anger and disgust shot through her. She'd been wrong earlier thinking O'Toole had turned around. All this guy thought about was covering his ass.

"Your job wouldn't be on the line if you had the guts to do it," she snapped and got out of the car. "Stay here, then. If I'm not back in half an hour, call for backup. And then call Parker."

She left the sergeant with his mouth hanging open and hustled down the walk as fast as she could go. At the spot where she'd seen Elvis disappear, she took the same turn and plunged into darkness.

CHAPTER FIFTY-THREE

Miranda picked her way through the narrow passage in the yard that ran between the two huge houses. It was so dark, she veered off and almost bumped into the trunk of a tree. A palm from the feel of it. And from the fresh scratches its bark made on her hands.

She ignored the pain and kept going, favoring the other side of the path now. She discovered she'd overcorrected when she hit a set of spiked plants that fanned out like snake tongues. She pressed her lips together to fight back a curse as they dug into her already cut hands and snagged at even the hardy denim of her jeans. Vicious things.

She skirted around the plants, stumbled back to the path and pressed on.

She heard a dog barking in the distance. And up ahead, the soft sound of steady footfalls. She squinted into the shadows and barely made out Forest's lumbering figure. He wasn't struggling with the landscape. He looked like he knew the area well. He knew just where he was going.

At the end of the house, he made another turn.

She scrambled along, crouching now so he wouldn't see her. When she reached the spot where he'd turned, she peered into the darkness.

It was dead still now, the silence spearing her nerves, the warm air drying her skin, the houses like slumbering giants under the starlight.

Suddenly she spotted Forest's silhouette on a sidewalk that ran along the rear of the mansions.

She was out in the open. He could turn and see her any minute.

To her side, about twenty feet behind her target grew a row of waist-high grassy shrubs. She took cover behind it. Scooting down, she followed the moving shadow, thankful the foliage wasn't thorny.

He moved quickly, passing house after house. Miranda kept up, duck-walking in the bushes, her legs screaming in protest. Just when she thought her thighs would give out, he started to slow.

And came to a stop.

He stood rigid and still, staring at the back of one of the homes.

Her muscles aching as she struggled to keep her breathing silent, Miranda followed his gaze—and felt the blood chill in her veins. She squinted into the dim light and recognized the terrace she'd sat on with Parker a few days ago.

This was Blythe Star's house. The beautiful, ambitious, obsessed woman who was now dead.

She thought of the sickening smell of chlorine. The sight of the woman's body when she'd spotted it under water in the pool. The weight of death as she pulled her out. The flat expression on her lifeless face.

Wait. Her gaze moved to the left.

A jutting space with a lot of windows and reinforcement below it. Wasn't the indoor pool right there? At that end of the house? Recalling the layout, she was almost sure of it.

She watched Forest turn toward the house. He followed a curving walkway that led to a stone stairway she hadn't noticed until now. The stairs led to a door on the second floor that had to open to the indoor pool.

He reached them now and hurried up them.

What was he doing? Returning to the scene of the crime? That was clichéd even for an Elvis impersonator. But no, he didn't go inside. He came to a halt near the top of the stairs.

The undergirding beneath the pool had to be steel and concrete to hold the weight. But decorative rafters had been added on the exterior to make it look as if crisscrossing columns held it up. And in that crisscross design were a lot of little cubbyholes.

Bracing himself on the railing, Forest extended an arm and reached into one of them. He tugged for a moment as if to jiggle loose whatever he was after. If only she hadn't left O'Toole's binoculars in the car. Finally Forest withdrew his arm and tucked something into his pocket.

Glancing around with a fearful motion, he turned and began to descend the steps.

Quickly Miranda ducked behind the bushes again. She listened hard for the sound of his footsteps. After a moment, she heard them. Soft on the walkway, almost too quiet to hear, but growing louder.

He was getting close.

She held her breath as he came near her hiding place. Her heart pounded so loudly in her chest, she wasn't sure she could hear him anymore. Had he stopped? Had he seen her?

She waited. Then the rhythm started up again, remained steady. Step, step, step. After an eternity passed, the footsteps grew faint.

When she couldn't hear them anymore, she counted to ten and dared to raise her head.

He was gone.

She peered down the path where he'd come, assuming he'd go back the same way. Nothing. She turned and looked the other way, squinting hard.

There. Hurrying down the sidewalk past more big homes.

She was a little disoriented in the dark, but that had to be the way back to his house. Now it made sense. His clandestine chore was complete, so he was heading home.

Once more she scooted along behind the bushes. Her muscles were screaming again and her breath was ragged. She could barely keep up. Her target moved faster. He was getting farther and farther away. Just when she thought she'd lost him, she saw him ducked between another set of houses. He couldn't see her now.

She got up, hurried over to the sidewalk and ran the rest of the way.

CHAPTER FIFTY-FOUR

At the end of the walkway she stopped and peered into another murky gangway between two buildings. She'd lost him again.

All she saw before her was more landscaping buried in darkness.

Had he seen her, after all? Was he hiding in there, ready to jump her from one of the bushes? Elvis might be into Kung Fu Fighting, but she could handle him. She hoped.

Gritting her teeth, she plunged into the shadows and plowed her way through the passage. At least she was upright now.

He didn't jump out at her. She reached the front of the houses and found herself staring across two stone-and-cactus covered yards and into the next neighborhood.

Forest was heading that way.

The shadows cast by a trio of palm trees in the middle of the yard hid her from view.

She watched Forest cross the street, head down the walk and up the drive of another house. She made out the form of mishmash shapes under the pale street lamps and recognized the road.

It was his house.

The inside lights were off now and the darkness hid everything but silhouettes.

She squinted at the shadowy figure, expecting him to go straight to the front door. Instead he moved toward the garage. After a minute, he vanished around the far corner.

Back door entrance? He didn't want the neighbors to see him coming home at this time.

One thing was sure. Cameron Forest knew his way around his neighborhood. And he'd gone this route before. Probably just last night.

She took a deep breath and stepped out of the shadows.

Hoping he wouldn't come back around that corner, she walked at a casual, I'm-just-strolling-through-the-neighborhood pace. She crossed the street, went up the drive and took the path he'd taken around the garage.

When she got to the back of the house, Forest had disappeared again.

Then a light on the first floor came on. He'd gone inside. Through the kitchen, if she recalled the layout correctly. She studied the path from the door to the garage. That was where he must have carried his wife's body before he stuffed her in the trunk of his car and headed for I-15 to dump her.

And to carve out her eye.

It was a big garage. There had to be another car in there in addition to the limos. And a wheelbarrow.

Heart pounding Miranda huddled down behind another row of sticky shrubs and stared at the sliding glass doors. The curtains were drawn. She couldn't see anyone inside.

She should go bang on the back door. Confront the bastard. But she couldn't arrest him. If only O'Toole had come with her. If only she had her Beretta on her.

She reached into her pocket.

Making sure her phone was on silent, she turned it back on. Five missed calls from Parker. Last one was an hour ago. He could be on his way here. She'd be glad for him to show up now, even though he'd probably kill her.

Once more, she studied the door. Weigh the risks, Parker had said. If she snuck into that house, Forest might do the job for him before he got to her. But she'd been chasing Elvis through the yards for more than thirty minutes. O'Toole would have called for back-up by now. They would be here soon.

Plus there was nothing like the element of surprise to get a confession.

Deciding the risk was worth it, she stepped out of the bushes and headed for the kitchen door.

CHAPTER FIFTY-FIVE

Four hours late.

Parker paced back and forth in the suite, the fury of Hell flaming in his chest. How could she be so irresponsible? So thoughtless? So reckless?

And why didn't she answer her damn phone?

He knew the reasons. And he had a good idea where she was, though he'd lost her signal after she headed into another subdivision after she'd been to the police station and to Costa Rica Hills. He stomped to the window and stared out at the night sky, fighting back his anger.

He could say she was headstrong, recalcitrant, insubordinate. He could also call her unrelenting and persistent and passionate. The very traits that had made him fall in love with her.

That didn't mean he was any less furious with her.

Tie up some loose ends. He hadn't believed it when she'd said it but he'd indulged her. So it was his own fault she was out there on her own.

He sank into a chair and ran a hand through his hair. Since she'd been gone, he'd had a chance to think through the evidence of the case. The tea, the temper fits at rehearsals, the set up with the melon baller. He'd come to the same conclusion Miranda obviously had.

Sean Scott was a long shot. The only other suspect that made sense was the husband.

Cameron Forest.

He stared at his cell. He'd given up calling when it had gone to voicemail five times and had hounded the police station instead. Ralston was off duty and no one knew where Sid was. Miranda had to be with the sergeant. He had to hope for that. If she had gone after a killer entirely alone—

He dialed Sid's number, which he hadn't answered on the previous three calls.

At last, the man picked up. Thank God.

"Hello, Parker," he said, resignation in his voice.

Parker didn't bother with a greeting. "Where's Miranda, Sid?" he demanded.

"Take it easy, Parker. I think she's okay."

"You *think* she's okay? Where the hell are you?"

"Costa Rica Hills. I'm out front of Ambrosia Dawn's place. We tailed Forest to a party. He came home some time ago but had his driver let him out and walked the rest of the way. Miranda took off after him."

Parker's blood froze in his veins. "What do you mean? Where is she?"

"I'm not sure, but I saw lights go on in his house a few minutes ago."

Rage and worry pounded in his guts. "Sid O'Toole, if anything happens to my wife, I'll have your badge. After I tear off your limbs and stuff them down your throat."

"Take it easy, Parker. I've got back-up coming. They should be here any minute."

Parker ground his teeth. "They had better. I'm on my way."

He snapped off his phone and raced out the door. He'd lost his first love when he was hardly a man. He'd lost his first wife to ovarian cancer. He'd be damned if he'd lose Miranda.

But even as he ran for the elevator, his chest felt as if it were caving under an avalanche of heavy rock. If Miranda were in danger in that house, if she was facing a crazed killer who would do anything to avoid prison, it would take far too long for him to get there.

CHAPTER FIFTY-SIX

As quietly as she could, Miranda tugged on the handle of the glass door at the back of Ambrosia Dawn's house. Relief washed over her when it slid back on its rollers. She stepped onto the terrazzo tile, silently closed the door behind her and looked around.

As she'd expected, she was in the kitchen. The place where Ambrosia Dawn drank her last cup of tea.

She tiptoed past the gleaming appliances, the countertops, the unfinished side room, and into a long hallway.

Here the floor became sleek hardwood and she had to move carefully so that her sneakers wouldn't make a noise. Along one eggshell-painted wall stretched a long row of small photos. Ambrosia Dawn on stage during this tour or that. On the other wall hung a long tangle of some sort of filigree artwork.

No sign of Forest.

She kept going until she reached a cream-colored settee with gold striped pillows. A crystal chandelier glittered overhead to light the space. Here the hall forked in two directions.

To the right she decided, letting instinct take over. More pictures. A side table with a vase of flowers. Landscapes on the walls here. Guess it was too crass to hang your own photo on every space, even for this woman. She took a few more steps and grinned.

Lookie here. A staircase. Different from the one the house manager had led her up.

Miranda stood a long moment staring up it. It had to lead to the bedrooms. Forest probably had gone up to bed. He'd had a busy night. She'd just go tuck him in.

She put her foot on the first step. Sure would be nice to have a weapon in her hand when she surprised him.

A light switched on to her right.

Tensing, she swung her head toward it. A few feet away on the opposite side of a hall stood an archway. Holding her breath, she hesitated on the step and gaped at the opening. As she waited, listening to her heart pound in her chest, a low sob echoed from the room.

She knew that sound.

Carefully she removed her foot and crept across the floor. As she went the sobs grew louder, more heart wrenching.

She took a deep breath and dared to peek into the room.

It was a huge, domed space with another chandelier overhead. A tall fireplace against the far wall, potted ferns scattered about, some sort of Aztec art covering the wall opposite the fireplace. A wide floor-to-ceiling window behind the sitting arrangement completed the décor.

And there on a lime green sofa of soft leather a few feet away from the window sat Cameron Forest, elbows on his knees, ring laden fingers dug into his thick black pompadour, weeping.

He'd draped his blazer over the arm of the couch and his electric blue satin shirt shimmered as his shoulders shook with grief and his gold chains dangled over his lap.

His eyes were open, staring. She followed his gaze. On the polished mahogany coffee table before him lay two objects.

A large piece of broken pottery. And a gun.

The ceramic piece curved in the shape of the vases she'd seen on that shelf near Blythe Star's pool last night. Flecks of gold and blue on the underside. Pure white on the inside. And along its sharp white edge, a deep red bloodstain.

The gun was a revolver, Miranda thought, eyes now fixed on it. Looked like a .357. Loaded? She had to assume so. What was he planning to do with it? Use it on himself? Or had he heard her come in and was waiting for her? Didn't look like it.

Could she get to that gun? Was Forest that distracted? She had to try.

Not daring to breathe, she stepped into the room and glided silently toward him. He didn't move except for his broad, bobbing shoulders. Suddenly her heart broke for him. Those tears were real. Somehow she still believed that. He'd had a weird love-hate relationship with Ambrosia. Maybe he was really sorry for what he'd done. Maybe a good lawyer could use that sorrow to get him less time.

What was she thinking? He was a killer and she had to bring him in. She was almost to the end of the couch now. She took another step and the floor creaked.

Forest lifted his head and spun around, lips parted in shock. He glared at her through moist, long-lashed eyes. "Ms. Steele. How did you get in here?"

She jerked a thumb toward the archway. "You left the back door in the kitchen open. The one you came in after your stroll through the neighborhood tonight?"

His eyes went wide. He glanced down at the pottery shard and shot to his feet, awkwardly trying to block her view of it.

But it was too late.

"I know you went to your sister-in-law's house, Cameron." Miranda gestured at the table. "I saw you get that from the stairs under the indoor pool where she was killed. That's the murder weapon, isn't it?"

He reached down. Wildly, Miranda hoped he was going for the shard, but instead he scooped up the gun and pointed it at her. "Are you the only one who knows?"

She shot up her hands, palms facing him, as if that could protect her from a bullet. "Knows what, Forest?"

His mouth opened and closed again.

"That you killed Blythe?"

"I—I—" He sank back onto the couch and pressed his free hand against his face again. He didn't let go of the gun. Instead he shoved his elbow onto his lap and kept it pointed at her. An awkward position, but still dangerous.

But he started talking. Maybe out of nerves.

"Blythe called me last night after rehearsal and wanted me to come over and talk, so I did. She wanted to go to the police. I tried to tell her that was crazy."

He looked up at Miranda as if he'd just realized he'd implicated himself.

Why was he telling her this? Was he unburdening his conscience before he shot her? And then himself?

He went on. "I tried to reason with her. Really, I did. I begged her, but she just wouldn't listen."

"So you got angry."

Another sob escaped him as he nodded. "I couldn't help it. I was furious. I reached out for something to throw at her and my fingers found that vase. I flung it on the floor instead and watched it smash to pieces."

That must have gotten her attention. She should have run, but that probably wouldn't have saved her.

"What happened next?"

Forest shrugged as if it were obvious. "She turned around and screamed at me to get out. She told me she would call the police, even if I refused. She was going to do it right then. I couldn't let her. I saw that piece on the floor." He gestured to the shard on the table with his free hand then rubbed his forehead. "I don't even remember doing it. Or thinking anything. But I must have picked it up. I must have swung it at her because the next thing I knew, her throat was sliced. Blood was everywhere. I tried to tell her I was sorry. I didn't mean it. I reached out for her, but she fell back into the pool. And then all I could do was get out of there."

"But you covered it up."

He nodded. "I was already in swimming trucks. I thought we were going to swim while we talked. I thought she was going to tell me some ideas she had for the show. I dove into the pool to wash off the blood, swam to the other side, picked up my clothes and left."

"And you took that with you."

"I put it in my teeth when I swam. I was afraid the police would come to my house so I hid it outside where I thought they wouldn't find it."

And they hadn't. Nobody had thought to look in that spot.

"I was panicking. Not thinking clearly. I should have left it in the pool."

"What were you going to do with it tonight?"

His face twisted into a grimace. "Grind it into powder and plant it in the backyard somewhere, I guess. I don't know. I don't know." He began to whimper like a lost puppy.

Miranda dared to take a step toward him. She held out her hand. "Why don't you give me that gun."

He got to his feet again and pointed the weapon at her with both hands. He glared at her. "I can't let you. I can't go to jail."

He was crazy. She could see it in his eyes. But she'd dealt with crazy before.

She kept her voice very steady. "It's all right, Cameron. Everything's going to be fine. I understand why you got rid of your wife. She must have driven you insane with her outbursts." Or maybe his philandering caused her outbursts. Not something to say to a man with a gun in his hand.

His face contorted as if he'd gone hard of hearing. "What are you saying? I didn't kill Abbey. I loved her. I'd never hurt her." His voice broke with emotion and for an instant, Miranda believed him.

She risked another step. "Was it Blythe's idea then? Did she get you involved against your will?"

"No, no. She adored her sister. We all did."

Was he that delusional? And why was he covering up for his sister-in-law now?

"But Abbey was so angry all the time. She was an embarrassment. She made everyone who worked for her miserable. She made your job impossible."

He made an exasperated sound of frustration. "She was a temperamental artist. She was moody. I understood that. Sometimes I think I was the only one who did."

"Cameron," Miranda said softly with the tone of a mother rocking her baby to sleep. "Blythe's fingerprints were on the jar we found in Suzie Chan's refrigerator. That jar had Abbey's eye in it."

If he really loved his wife, that thought should rattle him enough for her to get the gun away from him.

For a second it looked like the trick had worked.

Forest's mouth opened in an agonized cry, but then he turned away and stumbled toward the fireplace. "Pinning it on Suzie was Blythe's idea, yes. She helped me clean up—everything. Oh, God, that was awful. I used her car to take Abbey to the desert. And her wheelbarrow. Oh, God. I hated doing that. She said I had to take out her eye to make it look like Suzie—" He gasped in pain. "Blythe had a key to Suzie's house. She was dating Sean Scott, Suzie's ex-boyfriend. She made him give it to her when he broke up with Suzie. Yes, she put the eye in her refrigerator. When the police release Abbey's body, we can give her the burial she deserves."

Jeez what a mess. But even if Forest had lost his reason, she had to keep hers. She had to get that weapon out of his hand. She had to get him down to the station where all this could be recorded. Where the hell was O'Toole with that back-up?

For all she knew, the sergeant had fallen asleep in his car.

She took a deep breath. "Cameron, people will understand. You have to tell them your story. You can't go on this way. Let me help you."

"Help me?" He swung his arm and pointed the gun at her again. "Get away. Don't come any closer." His eyes took on a wild look of desperation. "Oh, God. I'll have to get rid of you, too. Won't I?"

Fear zigzagged up Miranda's spine. Her heart pounded in her ears. Was this crazy dude going to pull the trigger?

Think, she told herself. Think.

Suddenly there was a youthful voice behind her. "What the hell are you doing, Dad?"

CHAPTER FIFTY-SEVEN

Miranda's head jerked toward the sound. She saw a skinny boy in baggy gray pajamas with dark, shaggy, sleep-tousled hair that hung over his eyes. He wore a look of sheer horror on his too-young face.

"Brandon," Cameron barked. "Go back to bed."

Miranda tried to lunge for the weapon. Forest stepped back and aimed it at her chest. "Get back or I'll shoot."

"Dad, what the fuck?" the boy screeched.

"I told you not to use that language, son."

The boy sputtered out a nervous laugh. "You're holding a gun on some woman and you want me to watch my language?"

"Go back to your room. I'm handling this."

The young man ignored him and padded into the room barefooted. He stared at Miranda. "You're one of those investigators they brought in from out of town on my mother's murder, aren't you?"

"Brandon, I said I'm handling it."

Miranda decided to risk it all. "Brandon," she said to the boy. "There's a cop in a car outside down the street. Go get him for me."

"Don't you dare go, son," Forest barked. "All right," he screamed at Miranda. "I killed her. I killed Abbey. You've got your confession. Let your cop come and arrest me. Are you happy now?"

The boy cried out in pain. "No, Dad! You can't go to jail for me. I won't let you."

"Brandon!"

"You got to stop all this, Dad. It isn't working." He crumbled to the floor near the coffee table and began to cry just like his father had.

With the gun still trained on her, Forest shuffled over to the boy and awkwardly touched his head. "It's all right, son. I told you I'd take care of everything."

"No, Dad. You can't. It's too late. Some things you just can't fix."

Miranda took a closer look at the boy. It looked like he had a dark bruise under one eye. She remembered what Reedy Max told her. His stepmother was mean to him. Now everything was starting to make sense.

"What are you saying, kid?"

He looked at her with the most pitiful round eyes she'd ever seen. "I killed Abbey."

"No," Forest shouted. "He's making that up. He's trying to protect me."

"Give it up, Dad."

"Son, please."

"You have to let me tell her the truth. You have to." He stared at Miranda and took a deep breath. "About a week ago we had a bad fight. Worst one ever. I'm getting my license soon and I wanted to borrow one of the cars. She said no. I argued with her and she lashed out at me. She hit me."

"That's how you got that black eye?"

He nodded. "I was so mad at her. Madder than I'd ever been before. So when I was hanging out with a friend, we started joking around about how to, you know, off someone.

Forest's face went white. "What friend? That boy in the gang? We warned you not to hang around with him."

The boy rolled his eyes. "No, Dad. Not Cody. Trevor. He graduated last year. He works in a medical research center on Rainbow."

Medical research. Just like the ME told her in the morgue. "Trevor gave you the abrin?"

The boy nodded. "I told him I wanted something to make her sick. I didn't really know what it was. I didn't think it would kill her. Honest."

Forest spat out a weak laugh. "Can't you see the boy is lying? Why would a friend risk his job over that?"

"Maybe because he is my friend, Dad," the boy sneered. "I didn't think about his job. I guess I owe him big time."

Lose his job? This Trevor kid was an accomplice to murder. And then it hit her.

Brandon, Cameron, Blythe, Ambrosia. These people lived in a world of fantasy. A universe of glitz and glamour and make-believe. A world of adoring fans and groupies and plastic surgery that made you look ten years younger than you were.

They couldn't process grim reality.

Staring down at the floor, Brandon took another deep breath. "Anyway, I took the stuff home. I didn't really know what I was going to do with it. I had it in my pocket when I came in the back through the kitchen. I saw Abbey's teapot. She always drinks it before she goes to bed. I knew Suzie had made it and left it for her. I remembered she was going out of town. I just stared at the pot for a long time. I had decided not to do it. Then my eye started to throb." His voice grew high-pitched and pitiful as he touched the tender spot on his face. "I got mad again. I just opened the pot and dumped the stuff in."

He put his hands over his face.

The poor kid. Miranda felt for him. How often had she thought about poisoning her abusive ex when she was nursing bruises from his fists?

But no matter how sorry she felt for the boy, she had to finish this. "What happened then?"

He sniffed and pushed his hair back. "I went to bed. I thought she'd get sick and when she was feeling bad, I'd get her to let me have the car. Or maybe I'd tell her what I'd done and say if she hit me again, I'd make her sicker. But that's not what happened." His eyes began to fill with tears.

"Go on."

"I woke up when I heard her yelling down in the kitchen. I ran down the stairs. I found her kneeling on the floor, barfing her guts out. Oh, God. There was puke everywhere. She reached out and grabbed my arm. 'Help me, Brandon,' she said. I tried, but I didn't know what to do. I got a pan from under the sink and told her to barf in there. I told her to just keep barfing. I thought if she got the stuff up, she'd be okay. But she wasn't." Tears streamed down the boy's cheeks now. "She started puking up blood. She couldn't stop. She started to shake all over. She fell on the floor and started gasping for breath. I didn't know what to do. And then she turned blue. And she stopped moving. I called out to her over and over, but she didn't answer. I just sat there staring at her and then I realized my dad was in the room."

Forest stared down at his son as if he still couldn't believe what had happened that night.

The boy sniffed and looked up at his father, helpless shame on his face. "I'm so sorry, Dad. I didn't mean it. I swear I didn't."

"I know, son."

The boy's gaze returned to the floor. He had more to say. "That was when Aunt Blythe came in. She said she wanted to talk to Abbey about a fight they'd had that night. When she saw her there on the floor, she started screaming her head off. Dad calmed her down. He told her what happened. He begged her to help us. She said okay." He started to sob again.

Forest bent down and put a hand on his shoulder. "I told you I'd take care of everything. Didn't I that night?"

Without looking at him. Brandon nodded.

Forest turned to Miranda. "You probably know most of the rest. Or can guess it." But he told her the rest, sounding like a robot with no feeling at all. "The three of us cleaned up the kitchen. We scrubbed down everything with bleach until there wasn't a trace of vomit or blood. I washed her body in a downstairs bathroom and dressed her in a fresh robe. I wrapped her hair in a fresh towel. I tore down the construction plastic from the room we were building and wrapped her body in it. As I did, Blythe came up with the idea of making what happened look like Suzie's fault. It was a horrible thing to do, but we had no choice. I got one of her melon ballers from the drawer, carried my wife's body out to Blythe's car and put her in the trunk. While she stayed with Brandon, I drove out to I-15 and left her there. I found a dumpster on the south side of town and put the clothes and dirty rags in it."

And then he came home and they all acted like they knew nothing about it.

Miranda felt her eyes getting moist. Her heart broke for them. For all of them. The neglected, abused boy. The delusional father. The jealous sister. Even the self-absorbed, temperamental singer. A sick, dysfunctional family with no sense of reality. And even all those worshipping fans who thought they lived charmed lives.

Far from it.

She straightened. "Forest, you have to talk to Sergeant O'Toole. He can work something out for you."

"What? Are you crazy?"

He thought she was the crazy one?

"It's the only way."

He waved the gun at her again. "No, no. They can't have my son. They can't."

"What kind of a life is he going to have now? With all this on his conscience?"

"He's going to have a fine life. He'll be just fine. I'll take care of him. I'll take care of everything." He raised the gun.

Miranda held her breath. He was going to shoot her right there. Her only option was the boy. If she were fast enough, she could reach down and scoop the kid up before his father fired.

Hell, no, she thought. She couldn't risk his safety.

But she didn't have to. With a sudden jerk Forest bent his arm and pointed the gun at his temple.

"Dad!"

"No!" she cried.

"You said it yourself," he screamed at her in sheer agony. "I have no choice."

Miranda rushed for him, hoping to knock the gun out of his hand. But before she could get to him an earsplitting blast exploded the front window. The whole room seemed to shiver. Glass shattered everywhere.

She went deaf from the noise, but she saw Forest's mouth open wide in a cry of pain. She watched him grab his arm. Saw blood spurt out of it. Saw him drop the gun.

Quickly, she scrambled for it, got it in her hand and covered the boy's body with her own.

"Get back, Forest," she cried, trying to hear herself.

But Forest was staring in shock at the broken window.

Miranda turned her head and blinked through the empty frame. In the distance she saw police lights flashing. She saw Parker running up the yard from the street.

And in the window she saw Sergeant O'Toole standing with his service weapon in his hand, still aimed at Cameron Forest.

CHAPTER FIFTY-EIGHT

"The hospital is going to release Forest tomorrow. He'll be taken to the detention center to await trial."

It was the next afternoon and Miranda sat beside Parker in O'Toole's office, on chairs the sergeant had not only fetched but seated them in himself.

In a green checked shirt that set off his Irish complexion, O'Toole leaned back and studied them from behind his desk, a grim sort of satisfaction in his wide-set green eyes.

"Got his full confession last night. Forest admitted Ambrosia Dawn had been physically abusing his son for years. He'd always covered for her, made excuses, turned a blind eye. He says everything was his fault."

"That's putting it mildly," Miranda said, feeling a little empty.

"He copped to killing Blythe Star, too. He'll plead guilty, which might get him a lighter sentence."

Taking that in, Miranda nodded solemnly. "What about Brandon?"

She could still feel the boy clinging to her, sobbing against her chest, as he had all the way to the police station last night.

After they'd left him with O'Toole, she and Parker had decided to back off and had returned to the hotel, leaving the rest in the sergeant's hands.

"By state law, Brandon's been charged as an adult with second-degree murder. But Forest's attorney has worked with the DA. If Brandon agrees to plead guilty to involuntary manslaughter, he'll be transferred to the Juvenile Detention Center. They have good rehabilitation programs for kids. He might be sentenced to a youth camp or a state juvenile facility. Best case scenario, he'd get probation."

She felt some hope for the kid. But the court wouldn't be so lenient with Forest.

"The boy might get out before his dad," Miranda said. "What will happen to him?"

"If he gets probation, he might go to stay with Forest's old manager if she checks out. She called the station and offered to help when she heard what happened."

The story had already hit the news.

"We'll have to look around for other relatives," O'Toole said. "In the meantime like I said, Juvenile Justice has a lot of programs for troubled kids in custody. He'll get education, counseling. In fact, Ralston and I have volunteered to mentor the kid."

Miranda glanced over at Parker and watched his expression soften. He was dressed in a pale blue polo shirt and designer jeans for traveling.

He'd been quiet since last night. Since witnessing what O'Toole had done. Since seeing her in that house with a killer with a gun in his hand. She had no idea what he was thinking.

But just now, he smiled. "That's a wonderful thing to do, Sid. I hope you can help the boy."

"We'll do our best. Oh, I'm doing a press release this evening."

Miranda cocked a brow at him. "All by yourself?"

He chuckled. "Me and the DA and Lieutenant Wells. You're both welcome to stay and watch, but I'll be fielding the questions."

Miranda had to grin at that. "You're going to tell the news hounds that contrary to popular opinion Ambrosia Dawn was an angry bitch who abused her stepson and drove him to kill her?"

"I'll clean it up some, but I'm not backing down on the truth."

The sergeant really had grown a pair of *cojones*.

Parker got to his feet. "I'm afraid we won't be able to stay for the press conference, Sid. Our plane leaves in a few hours."

"Understood." O'Toole rose and walked them to the door.

At Parker's side, Miranda studied the floor. "What you have to tell the media won't help Ambrosia Dawn's postmortem record sales, O'Toole. The estate might sue."

The sergeant opened the door. "Such is life. The department will back me up. Though Forest could use the money for the team of lawyers he's hiring for him and his son. But then, he won't be inheriting the estate once he's convicted."

Miranda stepped into the hall. "How's he going to pay for the lawyers?"

"I understand he had his own bank account. A pretty hefty one."

"I see." Between the sergeant and Parker, she headed down the green-painted corridor. "If he gets paroled, he'll need the cash. I don't see him playing Elvis here again."

"Oh, I'm not so sure. Las Vegas may not be forgiving, but we are forgetful."

"Good point," Parker said as they turned a corner.

They continued past the benches that were mostly empty now, taking in the sound of keyboards from the offices, and conversations mixed with the smell of bad coffee.

"I've been on the phone all morning, wrapping up the details and the paperwork," O'Toole said. "Dame Destinado is closing down the theater for remodeling and looking for a new act. Anything but a singer, I heard. Maybe a juggling team to compete with Cirque du Soleil."

"I imagine the staff will find other jobs," Parker mused.

O'Toole nodded. "Sean Scott's going back to Kingman, Arizona to be with his girlfriend. Turns out she verified he was with her, as he claimed. Speaking of lawsuits, Scott's threatening to sue the department for harassment."

"He won't get very far."

"I don't expect him to. And Suzie Chan is going back into business with her sister."

"Hope she does well with that," Miranda said. And she meant it.

O'Toole stopped in front of the glass entrance doors and rocked back on his heels as if reluctant to say goodbye. He looked at his feet and swiped at his nose.

"The Lieutenant told me he was proud of me for bringing you two in on this case. Said it was the smartest thing I ever did. In fact," his face flushed, "he's giving me a raise."

"Excellent," Parker said.

He held out a hand. "Thanks for coming, Parker. Thanks for the, uh, remedial training."

Parker took his hand. "You're welcome."

O'Toole held up a finger. "One more thing. The Lieutenant was so pleased with Ralston's performance on this case, he's moving her under Sergeant Jones. She'll be training to take his spot when he retires next year."

Miranda had to grin. "That's great news. Tell her congratulations."

"I will." O'Toole gave her a nudge and lowered his voice. "So since we won't be in the same unit now, I asked her out."

"Did you?"

"We're going on a picnic to Red Rock next weekend."

"Good for you."

Parker's gaze went back and forth between the two of them. He seemed genuinely surprised at the odd bond they'd formed.

At the door, he gave O'Toole a fatherly pat on the arm. "I'm proud of you, Sid. You've come a long way."

The sergeant beamed. "Thanks for inspiring me. Especially you, Steele."

"No problem."

He gave her hand a hearty shake and she felt her heart warm. Maybe there was an upside to this case, after all.

CHAPTER FIFTY-NINE

Two hours later, Miranda sat in the window seat of the jet that would take them home, staring out at the tarmac.

Was this really her destiny?

This case had been so different from the others she'd worked. No sense of victory here. She didn't feel like she'd won. There was a sense of accomplishment, sure. But it was bitter. Very bitter.

Beside her Parker murmured softly in that low, tender voice of his. "You were right, Miranda."

She turned around to face him, surprised not that he had read her thoughts, but at his words. "What did you just say?"

"I said you were right. This case couldn't go unresolved. It took your resilience to follow it through. You even inspired our reluctant sergeant."

She blinked at him, stunned. "When I snuck into Forest's house, I thought about what you'd said. About risks and all. I knew you were right. I knew it was too risky. But I still had to do it."

"I know. It's who you are." As if to prove he meant it, he took her hand and pressed the palm to his lips in a kiss of intense sincerity. Then he looked at her with his wise gray eyes. "This is hard for me, Miranda."

Instead of bristling, he made her heart melt. She understood what he meant. What he'd been through. He'd lost a lover when he was eighteen. He'd lost a wife of twenty-two years. And less than a year ago, he'd almost lost her. She got that.

"I know," she whispered to him and reached up to touch his cheek. "But we have to work things out."

"Yes, we will. We'll discuss it when we get home. When we're rested."

And had some distance from this case. She opened her mouth to reply when her cell buzzed. She pulled it out of her pocket and saw a message. As she read it, deciphering the acronyms and teen-speak, she let out a squeal. When she got to the end, her smile was so wide, she thought she might block the aisle with it.

"What is it?" Parker asked.

She bounced a little in her seat with excitement. "A text from Mackenzie. She says she's sorry she hasn't been in touch for so long. They lost track of the time. She's been teaching Wendy to skate for competition. Wendy's going to enter the Atlanta Open next month. They can't wait 'til I get home so they can show me her moves."

Parker's handsome face melted into a loving smile. "They're still your children after all."

"Yeah, I guess so."

She couldn't wait to see Wendy gliding over the ice as gracefully as Mackenzie used to. And that meant Mackenzie was really on the mend now.

The captain came on the intercom and the flight attendants did their thing about masks and flotation devices and such. Miranda watched Parker lean back and close his eyes. He was the best thing that had ever happened to her.

Her phone buzzed again. Excited that it might be Wendy now, she scrolled to the text.

Her smile faded and a bolt of fear shot through her as she read it.

I know who you are.

What in the world did that mean? she thought, her heart pounding.

She read it again. A third time. Who would send her something like that? It was anonymous.

Her mind raced. Her ex was gone. She hadn't made any enemies on this case. Had she? Who was this?

As she sat there staring at the screen, that resilience Parker had mentioned must have kicked in. She felt herself calm down. Her heart rate slowed.

It was a prank. A mistake. Some kid playing a joke on a friend, who'd fat-fingered the number or something.

She stole a glance over at Parker.

His eyes were still closed, thank goodness. Holding the phone at her side, she slid her thumb over the screen and deleted the text. She put her cell back in her pocket and kept her gaze steady on the runway as they took off.

They could discuss the future of the consulting business when they got home, all right. But they weren't going to call it quits. She refused to let that happen.

She'd handle Parker. She took his strong hand in hers, watched him smile with his eyes still closed. She leaned her head back and closed her eyes as well.

And as she snuggled into the headrest, with a flush of excitement she wondered what their next case would be.

THE END

ABOUT THE AUTHOR

Writing fiction for over fifteen years, Linsey Lanier has authored more than two dozen novels and short stories, including the popular Miranda's Rights Mystery series. She writes romance, romantic suspense, mysteries, and thrillers with a dash of sass.

She is a member of Romance Writers of America, the Kiss of Death chapter, Private Eye Writers of America, and International Thriller Writers. Her books have been nominated in several RWA-sponsored contests.

In her spare time, Linsey enjoys watching crime shows with her husband of over two decades and trying to figure out "who-dun-it." But her favorite activity is writing and creating entertaining new stories for her readers.

She's always working on a new book. For alerts on her latest releases join Linsey's mailing list at linseylanier.com.

For more of Linsey's books, visit **www.felicitybooks.com** or check out her website at **www.linseylanier.com**

Edited by

Editing for You

Donna Rich

Gilly Wright
www.gillywright.com